Forever at Midnight

The Cynn Cruor Bloodline ~ Book 2

ISOBELLE CATE

Birmingham UK
July 18th 2015

Dear Laura,
Here is Roarke +
Deamai's story. Hope
you like it too! Love
Isobelle Cate

Birmingham, AL
July 18th 20[illegible]

Dear Laura,

Here is Brooke's
Dream story. Hope
you like it! Love,

[illegible]

ISBN-13: 978-1494213978

ISBN-10: 1494213974

Isobelle Cate

http://isobellecate.beaucoupllc.com

Published by Beau Coup Publishing

http://beaucoupllc.com/beau-coup-publishing.html

Cover and Technical Assistance by Added Touches

http://addedtouches.com

DEDICATION

To everyone that make up Beau Coup LLC – Sable Hunter, Barb Caruso, Ryan O'Leary, Mike Leche, Jess Hunter and Debbie Workman, and to Beau Coup's beta readers and proof readers. Thank you for believing in the Cynn Cruors' story and for making it the best that it can be.

To my family, for your encouragement, your understanding, and for giving me the space and freedom to write. You mean the world to me.

To all who read paranormal romance and
to new readers who are getting to like it.

This is for you.

CONTENTS

Chapter One

Hamel Dun Creag, Loch Awe, Scotland 1557

Roarke entered his bedroom with Deanna in tow; their steps muffled by the fresh thresh on the floor. The fire in the hearth, diagonally across from the bed, gave the room a warm glow. The spark in the air, sensual.

Roarke stopped by the side of the canopied bed. "Are ye sure?" He flung his cloak on the wooden chest which sat at the foot of the bed.

He turned to Deanna, his heart swelled with love; it hurt.

"Seeing my beloved aunt is in her cups in the great hall while my Da is being regaled with feats of valour by The Hamilton?" Walking around nonchalantly, her eyes widened a fraction at the sight of Roarke's bed. She took a deep breath, belying her nervousness and excitement, stopping to look at Roarke before she smiled. Deanna felt weak in the knees. The lone wooden armchair in the room was a temptation, but she forced herself to stand. She placed her hand on the chest of drawers, steadying herself. "Aye."

Roarke stared at her, cherishing each feature. Her copper hair tumbled in curls and waves around her shoulders and down to her waist. Her eyes, pools of cornflower blue, were fringed with long lashes which swept over the tops of her cheekbones. A dusting of freckles decorated the bridge of her nose. Roarke's cock twitched in growing attention when Deanna's lips curved in a beguiling smile.

"Do ye want me?" Roarke asked. He needed to hear the words from her lips. He dared not put any more meaning to Deanna's proposal until she made her desire clear.

"Aye," she said softly, taking a step closer. "I love you, Roarke. I want to be your mate."

Roarke enclosed Deanna in a crushing embrace. His mouth captured her lips, his tongue tracing the seam of her mouth. He groaned when Deanna shuddered, opening for him. She placed her arms around his neck and pressed her breasts against Roarke's plaid clad body. With a growl, he swept her up and placed her on the bed.

Laying her down, he straightened up. His breathing was harsh and erratic, his pulse thundering in his ears as the woman he loved watched him undress.

He unlaced his cuarans and his hose before tossing his tartan over his shoulder to unbuckle his leather belt. Deanna purred when he removed his shirt. He looked down, chuckling as he watched her sit up, her eyes drawn to his erection. She looked back up at him, her gaze filled with heat. Moving to the edge of the bed, Deanna lifted her hand, fisting him in her palm.

Roarke inhaled sharply, closing his eyes.

Deanna never expected giving Roarke pleasure would bring her such joy. She felt elation coursing through her veins as he groaned his appreciation. She closed her eyes and leaned up to kiss his chest, right over his heart. Her lips tingled as she felt the pounding of his pulse beneath his warm skin. Caressing his shaft, she marvelled at how something so hard could be so smooth.

"Where did you learn to hold a man like that?" Roarke rasped, his lust filled gaze boring into her very soul.

Deanna smiled. "I had a very good teacher."

Roarke grinned before his face gradually showed his lust, his eyes becoming hooded with passion. "I need you." He pulled her to her feet. She went willingly, keeping his manhood in her grasp.

Deanna nuzzled his neck, using the tip of her tongue to lick him, making a damp trail along Roarke's jaw, tasting the salt of his skin before capturing his mouth in hers.

"You are a vixen, Deanna Logan," he groaned against her lips.

She laughed softly. "Which is why you chose me, Roarke Hamilton. I am the only one who can keep up with you."

Roarke threw his head back and laughed. When he looked down into her eyes, he smiled at the memory. "Who would have thought I'd find the woman destined to be mine walking through the fayre without a chaperone?"

"I was chaperoned," she said with mock indignation, but her eyes were alight with mischief. "My aunt just couldn't keep up with me. And who would have thought the man I'd give myself to would be the very man who threw mead in my face?" Deanna planted her hands on her hips, cocking her head to one side.

Roarke growled in protest when Deanna's hand let go of his erection.

"Deanna, Deanna," Roarke groaned, hitting his face with his palm, much to Deanna's amusement. "Must you always remind me of that day? I believe I've made up to you many times over."

"Aye," she said, continuing to stroke him. "That ye have and more."

Roarke smiled down at her, his gaze darkening with his need. "I want you verra much."

He framed her face firmly between his hands before he swooped to take her mouth. She felt the muscles of her sex clench when Roarke's tongue seared hers. It was a sensation unlike any other she'd ever felt in her life. Her heart raced as though she'd run through the hills surrounding Hamel Dun. Deanna gasped against Roarke's mouth when he brought his hands down to cup her breasts, to tease her nipples through her cotehardie. His touch sent tremulous quivers down to her mound, teasing her to wetness. Bolts of desire ignited her whole body, heating her blood. The tops of her breasts strained against the square neckline as she arched her back to his touch. She felt the delicious throb in her sex, yearning for the caress of Roarke's callused hands. "Touch me, please. I need to feel your hands on my skin."

He trailed kisses down the column of her throat while he unlaced her gown. "Your wish. My command." Slipping Deanna's gown off her shoulders, it pooled on the threshed floor at her feet. Roarke licked her collarbone, her shoulders, leaving a trail of exquisite heat everywhere his mouth touched. His hands continued their sensual exploration of every inch of her skin.

"You set me on fire, my laird," Deanna moaned in delight when Roarke's hot tongue flicked against her nipple. She held on to his broad shoulders when he teased her peak to an elongated arousal, while his thumb and forefinger did the same thing to her other breast. Her body trembled, and she felt a deep-seated ache she couldn't explain. "I want. I want..." She knew she needed something, but she didn't know exactly what. There was an ache in the middle of her sex that was almost a hunger. Instinctively, her hips nudged against Roarke's arousal, making him hiss. Her breath hitched at the unbridled desire she saw darkening his silver blue eyes. Her own eyes grew larger when she saw gold flecks dance around his pupils. "Roarke," she whispered. "Your eyes..."

He smiled, a smile guaranteed to make her weak in the knees. "It's part of who I am, Deanna."

Her fingers tentatively touched the corners of his eyes, then she frowned in confusion. "The flecks disappeared."

Roarke took her hand in his. He seemed to hesitate before he spoke. "Does it scare you?"

"No!" Her eyes widened with her vehemence. She heaved a sigh. "I think it's beautiful."

A low rumble came from Roarke's throat. "I've never been called beautiful, Lass."

Deanna laughed softly. "Well, know that you are, my love."

"You are the one who's beautiful, Deanna." Roarke's gaze darkened, raking her form and causing goose bumps to rise everywhere his eyes travelled. He brought his hand up to caress her nape, his thumb drawing sensual circles over the sensitive spot behind her ear and down to the pulse beating fast at the base of her throat.

"I cannae see myself with anyone but you," he said. "I want you by my side. Will you grant my request, Deanna?"

"Aye. Oohh."

"Oohh?" he asked with a chuckle.

"Roarke Hamilton," she said, desire coating her words. "You're teasing my privates."

Roarke leaned down to whisper in her ear. "Do you like it?"

"Aye," she moaned. Her legs spread of their own volition to allow him greater access. Her hips moved against his fingers. She gripped Roarke's shoulders and cried out when he slipped one finger inside her.

"And this?" The deep timbre of his voice wrapped around her in a mist of seduction.

"Oh, aye, always aye." Deanna's head fell backwards, exposing her throat. Panting loudly, she whimpered when Roarke's mouth found her neck. He sucked hard on the skin covering her pulse and she shuddered. The erotic kisses sent electric signals down to her vagina and it wept, coating Roarke's finger with her juices. "Roarke!"

His touch was a source of great pleasure. Her channel tightened around his finger, causing him to growl in approval. "How perfect you are, Deanna." Roarke kissed her, slanting his mouth against hers, plundering deeply. Their tongues twisted and mated with each other.

Deanna's arms encircled his neck, anchoring her to reality. Yet, she couldn't get enough of him. "I need you, Roarke." She mewled against his tongue as it imitated the same thrusting movement of his finger teasing her sex. In and out. In and out. Her heart pounded against her chest, almost in tandem with the pace dictated by his touch. She felt the familiar stirrings of release beginning to coil in her belly. She was about to spring. It was always like this. Even though they'd never completed the act, he had brought her to a state of bliss several times with his fingers and mouth. Roarke had promised to introduce her to more carnal pleasure when it was time.

And each encounter was better than the one before.

Still, Roarke always held back. Deanna knew he would be in pain if he didn't find his own release. His jaw always tightened and his breathing grew harsh. She couldn't stand to see him in need. So, she'd learned how to help him find release with her hand.

Now, she felt a similar ache. What he gave her with his fingers was no longer enough. She was reaching for something. If Roarke's shaft could satisfy this desperation, she wanted him inside of her. Now.

"Roarke, please," she begged. "Make me yours. Completely."

"Aye, Deanna," he whispered. "This night of the full moon, I will have you. You will be mine for eternity."

She moaned in protest when Roarke removed his finger.

"Very eager," he said with a lopsided grin.

"Is that bad?" She looked at him in alarm. Deanna wanted him desperately, but she didn't want him to think she was a wanton. It was hard enough not to throw herself at him.

"Nay, Deanna. I love the way you are. You are perfect."

Her heart raced in anticipation, her sex clenching sweetly at his words. She smiled seductively before slipping off her shoes. Then she took the end of her hose that stopped midway up her thigh and began to roll it down.

"Don't remove them." Roarke's voice was so low, Deanna almost didn't hear it. When she arched her eyebrow, he said, "Please leave them. For me."

Excitement curled in the pit of her stomach and made her pleasure nub throb. With one last look at Roarke, Deanna turned around to crawl toward the middle of the bed.

"Stop."

Deanna looked over her shoulder, perplexed at Roarke's groan. She gasped when she looked lower to see his rod standing proudly, framed by dark curls. "Roarke?"

"You're going to be the death of me."

"Why?"

"Stay, just like that."

Deanna looked at herself, completely baffled. "I'm on my hands and knees."

"Which is exactly how I want you to be."

"Roarke..."

"Stay still, Deanna," he commanded.

Her eyes widened. She faced front and wondered why Roarke was practically growling. His voice was so low and sensual as to make her heart skip a beat, but she did what she was told. Deanna jerked when she felt his hot hands on her hips. Slowly, he pulled her back closer to the edge of the bed. She gasped when Roarke's hands skimmed over her bottom, closing her eyes when he squeezed her cheeks. Her lust licked her in all the right places, making her feel wicked, wanton, and left her wanting more. Her breath quickened as Roarke caressed her outer thighs with his fingers until he slowly moved inward and upwards to her nether lips.

"So beautiful..." He whispered.

Her breath hitched, her sex quivered, liquid heat beginning to flow. Anticipation of what Roarke was about to do caused her sensitive button to swell. When his finger teased the sides of her mound and the crease of her thigh, Deanna's hips began to move involuntarily. She pushed against his hand, craving more. But Roarke moved away.

"My laird, you are merciless," she whimpered. "Why do you tease me so?"

"We are just beginning, my lady. Now stay still, Deanna. God knows how hard it is to keep my need in check. Your pleasure is what I want. So please, do as I say," he said, his voice strained.

Need. Pleasure. Those two words increased the ache inside her even more.

"Roarke." She gasped when he blew against her sex. She tensed, her breath catching in her throat when her mind registered it was Roarke's tongue parting the lips of her sex. This decadent sensation was new. Roarke was tasting her, making her even wetter. She was drowning in a lust filled pool, moaning her delight. Deanna's knees would have buckled beneath her had it not been for Roarke holding her hips up as he speared her with his tongue. She cried out, arching her back and throwing her head up.

"You taste so good, my lady."

Deanna mewled. Wave upon wave of ecstasy crested and receded in her sex, radiating out over her body. Pleasure spiked at the vibrations Roarke's voice made against her slit. She looked back over her shoulder and groaned when she saw her beloved's head moving up and down as he lapped at her opening. She closed her eyes, feeling every thrust of his tongue bringing her closer to the edge. In and out he went, tunnelling deep, driving her to madness. She spiralled in desire, crying out her release. A kaleidoscope of colour exploded behind her eyes. With one last lap of Roarke's talented tongue, she collapsed on the bed.

Chapter Two

Roarke was in an agony of pleasure. Deanna's honey coated his mouth. Her scent was on his tongue, his nose. On his fingers.

And he still couldn't get enough of her taste, how soft and pliant her feminine flesh felt against his mouth.

He turned her around. Deanna's eyes were closed, her chest rising and falling as her breathing calmed. The fire from the hearth glowed on her alabaster skin. When she opened her eyes, they were languid pools of hunger and awe. With her tresses like a fan of flame around her and her body open to his gaze, she was the most beautiful girl he had ever met.

And tonight she would become his woman.

Roarke crawled over her, leaning down to capture her lips in a kiss. Her mouth eagerly opened and sucked on his tongue. She hummed. "Is this how I taste?"

"Aye." Roarke's lips twitched. "Do you like it?"

"I'm not sure," she said, her forehead puckered.

A low rumble of laughter rose from his chest. He spread her thighs with his leg. His manhood throbbed as its bulbous head felt the wetness at her opening. His jaw tightened when she mewled, and he found it difficult to stop himself from spilling his seed. Roarke needed to be careful. If he could spare her the initial pain, he would, even though he knew it was impossible.

"My lady," he gritted.

"My laird," she said, her voice husky with desire. "I've waited so long for you to make me yours. Dinnae tarry any longer."

"It will hurt for a moment."

She gave him a tremulous smile and cupped his jaw. Her eyes shone, caressing him with her gaze. "I love you, Roarke," she spoke softly. "Please."

Deanna's hips adjusted to him as his erection prodded her. He bent down to lick and tease her nipples with his teeth. He felt a shudder go through her. Her arms went around him even as her hips bucked beneath him.

His tongue blazed a trail upwards to the soft skin over her collarbone, scraping his teeth against the sweet flesh, spreading kisses against the column of her throat before his mouth found hers. Roarke groaned as Deanna continued to raise her hips against him. She lifted her legs and the tip of his staff slipped eagerly into her sheath. He eased further inside slowly. Bracing his weight on his arms above her, he thrust into her completely.

Deanna cried out and tensed beneath him. Roarke clenched his jaw and groaned at the indescribable pleasure of being enclosed in her velvet softness. Her channel's heat singed his flesh, almost burning him with insatiable lust. He felt his balls tense and his rod jerked inside Deanna. She moaned. Slight disappointment rocked through him. It didn't matter. There would be other nights. Once they were married on the morrow, they would have their immortal lives to explore each other without the initial pain.

As he prepared to pull out, grimacing at the ache in his groin, Deanna gripped his waist.

"No, Roarke. Don't go." She gasped, trying to smile even as a solitary tear threatened to trickle down the side of her face.

Roarke looked at her eyes filled with trust and love. He inhaled sharply when she arched her back, lifting her hips. He didn't need any further prodding. The next time she bucked, he thrust inside. Her forehead furrowed as though she was trying to gauge what was happening inside of her, but the more he pumped, the more the expression on her face changed. Her eyes lost the pained look, and it was replaced by a look of growing passion. With each renewed thrust, Deanna's lips parted softly. Her eyes closed, her face became a mask of pleasure. She made small blissful noises which fuelled Roarke's own hunger. Soon they were groaning together. He rode her hard, lifting her legs to let them rest on his shoulders.

Their carnal moans and the sound of Roarke slamming into her filled the room. Deanna's whimpers came faster and louder until she arched her back, screaming her release. Roarke followed with his climax soon after, shuddering as his seed claimed her womb. He fell on top of her, his breathing laboured and erratic. As his breathing slowed, he opened his eyes and smiled.

"Roarke?"

"Hhmmm?"

"Does this mean I'm immortal now that you've had me?"

He grinned against her neck. He was going to enjoy teaching her what it meant to be a Cynn Cruor mate.

In and out of bed.

"Yes," he said. "Immortality is only granted to the woman a Cynn Cruor chooses as his wife and if the woman chosen willingly comes to him." He felt her face move against his as she smiled. He raised his head to look at her. "What is it?"

"Wife," she said the endearment softly. "I like the sound of that."

Roarke caressed Deanna's cheek, his thumb rubbing her lower lip. He looked at their bodies. An opalescent sheen covered them both, shimmering around their entwined limbs like an ethereal cloud. They were now inextricably linked. "What's the matter?" Deanna caressed his jaw, her voice languid with the effects of their afterglow.

"Are you not afraid of me?"

"Why should I be afraid of you?" she asked, startled.

"Because we're not exactly human."

Deanna sighed as she looked at the canopy above them.

She shook her head. "No. Tales of your existence have been whispered around the campfires for centuries. We mere mortals have heard about those who live side by side with us, yet are not like us." She paused. "I always thought it was nice to think there were angels sent from Heaven to watch over us on earth."

Roarke chortled. "Angels? We're hardly that. We're warriors."

"So was Saint Michael," she rebutted.

He barked with laughter. He liked that his mate was spirited and could carry her own.

"Roarke Hamilton," Deanna began, cupping his cheeks to face her. "You are my angel. My warrior angel."

In no time at all, he felt the familiar stirring in his manhood and groaned.

"I can't get enough of you," he said with a wicked grin before he thrust his shaft deep in her channel once again. Roarke's laughter rumbled out of him when she hummed as his cock moved on its own volition inside her. "Do you like that, Deanna?"

Her tinkling laughter filled the room. "Aye, verra much."

He held Deanna's waist and rolled her on top of him. "I think you'll like this even more. Ride me."

Her eyes sparkled with interest.

Suddenly, they heard angry voices, followed by a loud banging at the door. Deanna squealed and jumped back on the bed, separating herself from Roarke. She scampered to pull the sheet up to cover herself. Roarke swore before getting out of bed to storm toward the door, unmindful of his nakedness.

"My laird." His eyes widened in surprise at seeing his father.

The Hamilton had the same untamed black hair as his son and was of similar build. Broad of shoulder, tapered waist, muscular arms honed by constant training and fighting with a claymore in their hands, and muscled thighs and legs which allowed them to cover the ground they stood on. Few were the men who could push them from where they stood. Father and son could almost be mistaken for twins. They both had masculine faces with strong noses, wide foreheads and firm, chiseled lips. Where Roarke's eyes were silver blue, the Hamilton's were as black as a starless sky. This night however, they glowed a haunting red orange.

A sign of fury.

"The Scatha," his father said curtly before he inhaled sharply. He glanced at the bed and bowed his head curtly. "Deanna."

She could only nod, her eyes filling with apprehension.

"Come to the great hall, immediately," he commanded his son before his face momentarily softened. "Deanna has your scent, my son. Make sure she is safe. Her father and her aunt are already there with the rest of the Cynn mortals."

Roarke mutely stared at his father before he agreed. "Aye, Da." Then his sire was gone.

An unfamiliar emotion engulfed him, tightening his chest.

Fear.

The fear of the unknown was something he'd never felt before. And now that he had Deanna to think of, the emotion held him in a stranglehold. He closed the door and pivoted around to see Deanna kneeling in the middle of the bed. After a slight hesitation he walked toward his clothes and immediately began to dress. He tamped the uneasiness down and forced his hatred for the Scatha to the fore. So many Cynn Cruor warriors and their spouses had been killed by the Scatha and their leader, Dac Valerian. One of the most brilliant generals under Julius Caesar, Dac used to be known as General Gnaeus Valerius Dacronius. Roarke had no intention of allowing Dac to destroy his new found happiness. He was one of the best warriors of the Cynn Cruor. He would protect Hamel Dun Creag.

And Deanna.

Roarke sat down on the bed to lace up his boots. He couldn't look at Deanna as his hands jerked at the laces. He jerked when he felt her hand on his arm. Roarke sighed deeply before turning to her, capturing her mouth with his. His tongue speared through her lips, desperation and anger in his kiss. Although Deanna shared his fear, she poured as much love and hope into her embrace as possible. Their tongues mated eagerly, hungrily, stoking their common desperation.

Reluctantly, he ended the kiss and placed his forehead against hers.

"Roarke, you have to go," she said before placing her arms around him, her cheek resting on his shoulder.

He nodded, his face a mask of determination, the planes harsh with commitment to his Cynn Cruor brethren.

"Stay here," he ordered as he looked at her. She gasped, bringing her hand to her throat. Roarke knew his mate saw his eyes change to red-orange. His mouth pressed into a thin line. "I'm sorry if I frighten you."

She shook her head. "You don't. I know it's not the time to say this, but I like it."

Roarke's mouth twisted to a wry smile.

Deanna stood up when he did. Her hair covered one breast as if to give her a modicum of modesty, but she was unabashedly unashamed of her nudity, something which Roarke admired. He watched her as she adjusted his leather belt before putting the rest of his tartan over his shoulders. As she walked toward the chair by the corner of the room, the flames from the hearth danced softly against her body. She picked up Roarke's dirk and bent to try and pick up his claymore. Roarke tamped down the surge of lust firing his loins at the sight of her round bottom and swaying hips.

"You'll have to pick up the sword, my laird," she said with the barest of smiles as she handed the small dagger to him, hilt first. "I'm but a wee lass to carry the likes of that."

He looked at her, then gestured toward the dagger with a thrust of his chin. "Keep it. For your protection."

Suddenly, she flung herself at him. Roarke crushed her in his embrace, inhaling her scent of lavender and the smell of their recent lovemaking. Closing his eyes, he kissed her hair. He felt her shudder and give a soft sob. Roarke felt his heart tighten with pain.

"I will be back, Deanna," he murmured. "No one can separate us now. I have put my scent on you. You are mine."

Gently, he moved back to look at her. "If I die, so will you," he said. "In the same way, I will become just a shell of myself and eventually join you, should you pass ahead of me."

"I will wait for you Roarke," she said, caressing his face.

Roarke couldn't help the feeling of pride that filled his heart at her strength of will.

"I will wait for you to come back to me."

"Unless it's necessary, stay here," he instructed as he grabbed his weapon. "Dinnae open the door to anyone. Understand?"

Deanna nodded.

Roarke swooped down to give her a hard kiss.

Then he was gone.

****

Hamel Dun Creag was a fortress atop a hill. The Hamilton had chosen the spot for his Faesten, because it could easily be defended but was difficult to breach. He just hadn't counted on the fact that the siege would be led by the old Roman General himself. Dac Valerian had disappeared hundreds of years ago when The Hamilton had been one of the most trusted warriors and a member of the Cynn Eald's personal guard. They had searched everywhere for Dac after his assassination attempt, but could not find him. They presumed him dead from his wounds, as the Deoré, the Cynn Eald's beloved, had almost clawed the general in two.

They were wrong.

Now as he, his wife, his son and the rest of the Cynn Cruor warriors who'd come to the Faesten to celebrate Roarke's bonding to Deanna, valiantly fought and defended the fortress, The Hamilton realized this was one mistake he would have to live with for the rest of his immortal life. A mistake made all the more heavy by the death of so many of the Cynn Cruor under his protection, including Deanna's father and aunt.

They were surrounded by the Scatha before they even knew what was happening. Stones dipped in Greek fire were lobbed at the Faesten, destroying the inner walls of the fort. Fighting alongside The Hamilton, his son slashed and decapitated many of the Scatha who scaled and flew over the walls. Overhead, the Cynn Cruor archers returned volley upon volley of flaming arrows at the Scatha forces below. The screams of the injured pierced the air as the swirling dust created a cloud around them. With the blood of his wife inside him, The Hamilton easily healed, even as he continued to slash and kill with his claymore. Deidré, The Hamiliton's wife, fought with her husband and son. She too, healed easily. They both looked at Roarke. He was weakening because Deanna's blood still did not flow through his veins.

"Roarke, go back to Deanna," The Hamilton roared over the din of battle, his chest heaving to take in huge gulps of air. "You have done enough here."

"Nay!" His son snapped. "Deanna understands that I need to be here."

Deidré turned to face her son. There was blood oozing from a cut in her cheek which slowly closed as they spoke. "You have not completely bonded. You need her blood to regenerate. Go please. Your father and I will be all right."

A screech from a foul-jowled Scatha abruptly ended with The Hamilton decapitating the creature who flew over the wall behind his wife.

"There are too many and we have suffered too many casualties," The Hamilton shouted. "We have to retreat. Roarke, you have to tell the rest to escape through the passageway behind the dais. Lead them. We will follow."

Just then a trebuchet from the Scatha forces propelled a fireball toward the tower of Roarke's room, tearing a hole through the wall. Screams from within the tower and below the falling debris added to the terror gaining ground inside Hamel Dan Creag.

"Deanna!" Roarke roared. The anguish in his voice made several of the warriors pause. Their pain for a fellow Cynn Cruor gave them further strength to take as many of the Scatha down as they could.

With incredible speed, Roarke ran toward the crumbling tower, uncaring of the bruises and the bleeding cuts. Blood ran down his face to splatter against his chest. But even before he could leap and catch hold of the floor where his room was located, the entire tower collapsed, surrendering itself to a conflagration of greedy flames which singed and ate everything in its wake. Roarke skidded to a halt. "No!"

In an instant, The Hamilton and his wife were beside their son, stopping him from going through the wall of fire. Several Cynn warriors held Roarke back as well. He fought against the restraining arms of his brethren.

"Roarke," his father thundered. "Enough!"

"Deanna." Roarke's eyes were a bright angry red. Incoherent words spilled from his mouth. "I told her to wait in the room."

"With everything that's going on, I am certain she left the room to escape, Roarke. Roarke! Son! Listen to me!"

Roarke's head snapped toward his father. Slowly, the red subsided to burnt orange, then to silver blue.

"Go." The Hamilton nudged his head toward the Great Hall. "She might be there with the rest of those who are readying to leave."

They heard the collective screeches of triumph from outside the walls.

"Fall back!" The Hamilton commanded, his face grim.

Everyone swiftly escaped to the secret passageway behind the dais in the Great Hall. After everyone had passed through, two of their warriors lit the charges from the mouth of the cave. They were only a few feet away when they were thrown off by the explosion. Picking themselves up, they followed the retreating inhabitants of Hamel Dun Creag.

The Cynn Cruor made their way to the rendezvous base nearby. It had been built exactly for this purpose—the possibility of the Faesten being overrun. Through the centuries the warriors and their families, under The Hamilton's command and protection, painstakingly chipped away stone and rock to construct Hamel Dun Uiamh. With the Ancient Eald's help, along with the Cynn architects and mortals, the caverns now resembled an underground city.

The wounded were treated by the healers. The warriors who were bonded found stone rooms and other secluded areas so their spouses could help them heal.

The next day, scouts reported that the Scatha Cruor had left, leaving Hamel Dun Creag in ruins. Roarke finally found Deanna's charred body among the debris, identifying her from the dagger still clutched in her hand. He took her body from the rubble and carefully wrapped it in a shroud filled with heather and lavender. Then he walked toward the outcrop overlooking Hamel Dun Creag to give her a proper burial, a forlorn figure with the love of his life dead in his arms.

Chapter Three

Manchester, United Kingdom, November 2013

The Faesten was a hub of activity when Roarke entered. No one walking the streets of modern day Manchester would dream the building was full of immortal beings infused with the Kinare gene, humans whose blood had been strengthened by the amalgamation of both vampire and werewolf DNA. From the moment word spread that Dac Valerian, the leader of the Scatha, the Cynn's nemesis, was spotted in Manchester, hordes of Cynn Cruor had arrived, dispatched from Faestens all over the world. The Council of Ieldran, the body of elders who made and imposed the law, had issued a directive for the Faestens to assist the Manchester citadel and its leader, Roarke Hamilton.

Roarke greeted the warriors' acknowledgements with curt nods. He glanced to his right. The huge kitchen which overlooked the east side of the city was busy with warriors taking their meals. Adjacent to the kitchen was the Faesten's Agora, the formal dining room. Roarke had it opened and converted into a cafeteria with long wooden maple tables and bench seats. The crystal chandeliers looked incongruous in a room which was beginning to resemble a glorified mess hall. One of their own, a Michelin rated chef, along with his staff of Cynn mortals, provided a continuous supply of food.

There were two types of Cynn inhabiting the Faesten. Warriors and their mates, the immortal Cynn Cruor, sat side by side with Cynn mortals, siblings of warriors. The mortal kinsmen were accorded the utmost respect and affection, for their loyalty was without question and they helped insure the protection and security of the whole Cynn Cruor race. It was a good thing they owned another building adjacent to the Faesten, because they needed the room. In no time, it had been converted to comfortable lodgings. Some of the men were by the windows, looking down at the street below. When morning broke, the Roman blinds, which had replaced the heavier curtains of the past, would fall over the windows, protecting those inside from the harmful rays of the sun.

Most of the couples had decided not to have children until Dac Valerian and the Scatha were completely eradicated. Stories of families being torn apart had been handed down through the Cynn's oral and written annals of their history. The tragic tales were enough to make many prudent. Still, there were others who were willing to take the risk of bringing up a family and siring a warrior to add to the number willing to give up their lives to eradicate the Scatha once and for all. Those warriors who had to leave their mates to take care of their young families were housed on another floor which had been converted into several bachelor pads. Although their mates were not with them, they each deposited enough blood into the blood bank of the Faesten, should they need to heal.

Graeme Temple, a member of Roarke's inner circle would have whizzed by had Roarke not called to him. His hands were full of electronic equipment. Clean cut, he had a handsome face with a strong jawline covered in sexy stubble. Graeme was the Faesten's computer and security expert. Almost as tall as Roarke, he dressed in black denim jeans and a black T-shirt. He wasn't as bulked up as Roarke, but his body was still ripped and well defined. His dark brown eyes crinkled at the corners when he smiled in greeting.

"Roarke. Sorry, I didn't see you," he said before turning his attention back to the equipment in his arms.

Roarke took some of his load from him before they made their way to the nerve centre which used to only take a small part of the Faesten's huge walnut and oak panelled library. Like the entrance to the kitchen, the centre was a mixture of hardwood and glass. Because of the extra inhabitants, they'd added furniture. Two more leather couches and armchairs the colour of warm molasses flanked a marble fireplace as opposed to just one couch and the armchairs before Dac was discovered.

"Set the equipment on the table." Graeme instructed Roarke. "I need to do some minor repairs before I hook them up."

"Is it colder in here than usual?" Roarke asked, feeling a sudden change in the room's temperature. He relaxed when he saw the opened windows. For a moment, he thought he was developing a sense of foreboding.

Graeme laughed. "I think you're getting old."

"Older and wiser than you." Roarke snorted, taking the time to study the tapestry of the Manchester Cynn Cruor's coat of arms which hung above the fireplace. Like the knights of old, each Faesten was given the prerogative to create their own heraldic crest. On a red background was a pheon—a jagged arrow and a battle-axe intersecting over a crane carrying a stone in one claw. A griffin and a wolf faced each other to the left and right of the intersecting weapons. The two animals of lore were common symbols found in any Cynn crest. They represented all the qualities a Cynn Cruor warrior or mortal should possess, a rare breed of loyal guardians. Seeing this filled Roarke with regret. The Faesten in Manchester had been bequeathed to him by the Ancient Eald, a prize to hand over to his sons someday. But he would never have sons. He had no mate.

Graeme made himself comfortable at a large hardwood table strewn with old maps. It separated the seating area from the command centre located closer to the specially tinted windows. He had a mammoth task. Equipment was strewn everywhere, even on the bookshelves. One of the things he was attempting to do was track the heat signatures of all the Cynn Cruor warriors and mortals in Manchester.

Graeme looked to the left side of the room where shelf after shelf of first edition books framed the back wall. Many were first editions which the Faesten had accumulated down through the centuries. The room was a veritable treasure trove of information.

"One day, I'm going to come in here and actually read. After all, this is a library." Graeme said, glancing at Roarke before shaking his head.

"I didn't realize you could read. I thought you communicated only in binary language." Roarke teased his friend.

Graeme grunted in response, but continued with his task.

The noise inside the nerve centre drew his attention, the cacophony alien. Unaccustomed to so many people inside the library, or even the Faesten for that matter, Roarke eyed the other warriors in the room. All of them possessed computer technology skills. They were checking on the latest gadgetry which Graeme had acquired with the Council's approval. Many of the purchases were based on his recommendations and that of Eirene Spence, a human mated to Roarke's second-in-command and foster brother, Finn Qualtrough.

Finn turned to them as soon as he heard their voices. He walked toward his leader. He was tall and had almost the same muscular build as Roarke. Even though he looked as though he spent a lot of time in the sun, his Cynn Cruor blood didn't allow him to do so. Clean cut hair with a few soft spikes atop his head, he presently had a scowl on his handsome angular face, his midnight blue eyes flashing his irritation.

And jealousy.

Roarke grinned in amusement at his brother when he saw the scowl on his face. Finn's arms were folded across his broad chest as he watched his woman holding court surrounded by other Cynn warriors and mortals interested in computers. Eirene, his destined mate, had stumbled upon the Scatha Cruor's computer system which led to them finding Dac Valerian's whereabouts. With her help, they had confirmed Dac's involvement in white slavery and child trafficking along with his other nefarious deeds.

"They're not going to do anything to her Finn," Graeme said with dry humour. "She's just teaching them the rudiments of semiotics so they can locate them while reading computer codes."

Finn grunted. Graeme's shoulders lightly shook with laughter. He chose a piece of the equipment Roarke had carried in before approaching Eirene. When Eirene saw Roarke, her face brightened with a smile. Excusing herself, she made her way to them.

"About time," Finn muttered.

"Roarke," Eirene said, giving him a hug. "Welcome back."

"Eirene." He grinned. "Finn has been quite impatient waiting for you. And jealous, too."

Eirene's eyes lit up with mischief. "Oh, I'm sure I'm going to pay for that later." She sighed with feigned regret, causing Finn's mouth to twitch, his scowl gradually giving way to resigned amusement. He let out a long breath, held out his arms and Eirene happily entered his warm embrace.

"Must you stay with them?" Finn kissed her temple, caressing her nape underneath her shoulder length blue black tresses.

"I need to teach them, Babe," she reasoned. "It will help them in their own Faestens. If Dac disappears from Manchester, the system Graeme and I are putting up will make it easier for many to find the Scatha."

"I know." Finn sighed. "This bonding thing sometimes just messes with my head."

"Only because we're the first to be mated in this Faesten," Eirene answered, bringing her nose up to his neck, nuzzling and inhaling his special scent. "I'm sure the warriors who have their women with them went through the same thing we're going through."

Roarke's smile faltered at their display of affection before the strong resolve which marked him as the Faesten's leader kicked in. "What have we found so far?" he asked, his hands on his hips.

"Not much," Eirene said. Her shoulders slumped as she glanced at Graeme and the rest of the warriors by the computers. "Since Dac left the program in the club and it was destroyed, I'm still trying to track him down. Some of the Cynn have been helping me hack into computer systems to see if the codes raise any red flags."

Roarke nodded, though his expression was grim. "It's the best we can do under the circumstances."

"We'll find him," Eirene said. "I promise."

"And we'll find Penny," Roarke replied. "I'm going to shower off this grime." He glanced at Finn. "Call me if anything comes up."

"Will do." Finn looked down at Eirene. "I have to check the weapons and see if we have enough with the multitude that's come in. I know they brought their own, but I have to make sure there's enough room for all of it in the armoury." Finn kissed her. "I'll see you in a while."

****

Roarke left as Graeme instructed the Cynn warriors as to where to put the other computer equipment. Eirene returned to the main console to resume teaching her students about semiotics. He took the main flight of stairs to the second floor before veering to the left corridor to get to his quarters. As he entered his suite of rooms, the lights automatically switched on. He sighed in relief. After the buzz of activity downstairs, the silence of his rooms was a welcome respite. His suite had a monochromatic grey scheme of the Hamilton tartan. There was no point in adding colour when his immortal life had become empty since Deanna's death. His Deanna. Cruelly taken from him after their one night of passion when Dac Valerian and the Scatha Cruor besieged Hamel Dun Creag.

Roarke thought she was lost to him forever—until he'd seen her ghost in the club a few weeks ago when they'd tried to capture Dac and bring him to justice.

After seeing Deanna's apparition, Roarke had resorted to taking a shot of scotch every night for the last few weeks. The effect of the strongest alcohol for a Cynn Cruor was to make their minds razor sharp. Roarke wanted to know if it was Deanna he saw or a doppelgänger, but after another fruitless search, he was beginning to think he had just truly imagined her.

The weather was getting colder, laying its claim on Manchester, the temperature dropping. The city centre had begun to prepare for Christmas with Deansgate already ablaze with lights. Restaurants and cafés along this part of town, as well as shops closer to Market Street and beyond, had started to extend their hours for office workers who had their early Christmas parties or who opted to do their Christmas shopping in the shops instead of online. The Christmas market was also in full swing. Albert Square, which faced Manchester's Town Hall, St. Anne's Square, and the walkways between Brazennose Street, in between Sefridges, Zara, Harvey Nichols and L.K. Bennett to name a few, were now chock-a-block filled with stalls of food, chocolates, glass jewellery, and other possible Christmas presents. Men, women, and children wore thick coats, mittens, beanies, and ear muffs, hunkered down in groups to keep warm while drinking mugs of mulled wine. It was a chance to bring drinks outside the confines of the pub which was more of an exception than the rule.

Roarke was tired in body and soul. He poured himself a drink before sitting down in front of the unlit hearth, staring into it without seeing. He wasn't interested in the festive atmosphere. He was more intent on finding the one person who had made his life complete. He searched each and every face he encountered, hoping against hope he wasn't going out of his mind, because he'd buried Deanna himself.

After hundreds of years, why was she haunting him?

And for that matter, why was he still alive?

Deanna. Even after all these centuries, her beauty haunted him. From the moment he'd seen her walking down the muddy path through the traveling fayre which arrived just outside the walls of Hamel Dun Creag, he couldn't stay away. He'd liked the way her hips swayed as she walked. The lightness in her step and her gracefulness was so natural, it made Roarke wonder if she would be as graceful writhing in bed as he brought her to a climax. Pretending to inspect the wares displayed at the stalls with his men, he had feigned indifference, but couldn't sustain it when the muscle between his thighs tented against his kilt. Like a dowsing rod it was attracted to hidden things, only this rod wasn't attracted to water. It was Deanna.

It was unusual for a maiden to be left to walk alone, but Roarke didn't care. He swaggered about, bringing a quizzical look from his father who happened to be speaking to a group of tradesmen. Roarke just grinned. If Deanna noticed his antics, she didn't show it. Resolving to get to know her, he took two tankards of mead before walking toward her. Just then, two young children hurtled themselves at Roarke. Unable to stop the unexpected force, he had thrown the mugs' contents right at Deanna. The liquid splashed against her incredulous face and ample chest, and Roarke had to stifle his groan when Deanna's soaked cotehardie hugged her breasts. Her aunt had arrived then, scandalized. The Hamilton had intervened, taking Deanna and her aunt back to the Faesten. Roarke later got a telling off, but he didn't care. He was smitten and immediately set to wooing Deanna, who had felt the same way about him. Those carefree days were some of the best moments of his immortal life. He had initiated Deanna slowly into the intimacies which would bring them both heaven on earth.

But Dac Valerian had dashed it all.

He could still remember the carnage and destruction wrought by Dac and the Scatha Cruor at Hamel Dun Creag. The Cynn mortals who died during the siege were taken and prepared for burial. Everyone who returned to see what could be salvaged had helped put the dead in shrouds before laying them to rest in their graves. The ashes of the warriors and their beloved who were killed in the defence of the Faesten were swept and gathered together before being given to The Hamilton. He, his wife and his son went upon the hill where Roarke had made a funeral pyre for Deanna, and there they scattered his warriors' ashes to the four corners of his land. The Scottish winds would take them up to become part of the pantheon of Cynn Cruor heroes. They were now immortals in the afterlife as they were on earth. Forever they would guard the lands and Hamel Dun Creag.

The Hamilton decided not to rebuild the Faesten. It would stand as a memorial for their beloved dead, and a reminder that their existence, as well as the safety of mortals, was still perilous.

After the massacre, Roarke requested he be included in every dangerous mission the Cynn Cruor had against the Scatha, much to The Hamilton's and his mother's dismay. He wanted to die quickly so he could be with his Deanna. He appealed to the Council of Ieldran and the Ancient Eald. Roarke was given leave to do so. The Hamilton and his wife had no choice but to acquiesce. They would never go against the Council's wishes.

So began Roarke's rise to legendary status. He led every difficult mission anywhere in the world, placing himself in very dangerous situations, but always returning unscathed. He always considered each mission to be his last. Yet centuries passed, and he was still alive. Without his mate, physical changes were evident in his bearing. His hair, now cut short, was grey at his temples, but the rest remained black. His body, now more chiselled and ripped, resembled that of Lacoön, the Trojan priest of Poseidon. In less than a century, Roarke Hamilton had become the youngest Cynn Cruor Dux to become responsible for a Faesten.

And the only one of his generation to have access to the Cynn Eald, also known as the Ancient Cynn.

Roarke replayed a scene in his mind, something which happened a few months before Finn had met Eirene. He was commanded to attend the Cynn Eald in his Faesten located in Wales. It was a custom which had stopped since Dac's assassination attempt a thousand years before, but now he had been summoned.

The Cynn Eald's Feasten had been converted to a massive, yet elegant fortress. The castle walls still remained intact, but inside it was filled with all of the technology the 21st century had to offer. Security cameras were installed in every room, except the private chambers of the Cynn Eald. The foyer was spaciously decorated in cream and golden green. Several warriors sat on the couches, their drinks placed atop the wicker and glass tables. When Roarke arrived, they sat straighter in his presence, greeting him with awe and respect. He acknowledged them with a smile and nod, unused to the adulation of the young warriors.

As he walked through the grounds, he took in all the beauty. Tall columns reaching toward the sky were made of marble, while slim curtains flowed around them like nymphs' gossamer gowns floating in the breeze. At the far end of the huge lobby were massive glass doors which opened out to a manicured garden filled with different flowers and trees, and beyond it was the Irish Sea. Roarke could hear the soft lap of the waves against the shore. He inhaled deeply and smelled the hint of saltiness in the air, but the tang was overshadowed by the fragrance of the garden's blooms.

After being checked by the Cynn Eald's personal guards and depositing his weapons with them, Roarke crossed through the massive oak doors leading to the Ancients' quarters.

The Ancient One welcomed him warmly. For a man, whose age was almost as old as time itself, he looked no older than a gentleman of fifty years. His sharp green eyes were the colour of dark moss. His cropped hair was salt and pepper grey. His body was all lean muscle, but his skin was smooth and had a golden sheen. He wore a polo shirt, windbreaker, a pair of chinos, and topsiders as though he'd stepped off the deck of a sailboat.

Roarke knelt before him.

"No need for that, Roarke," the Cynn Eald said as he held Roarke by the shoulders to gently stand him up. "It is I who should be kneeling to thank you for helping keep Dac and the Scatha Cruor at bay."

"My liege." Roarke's voice held a tinge of alarm. "You can't do that."

He raised a mock brow and Roarke felt himself flush.

"Your pardon, my leige. I spoke out of turn."

The Cynn Eald merely chuckled.

Roarke relaxed and allowed himself a grin. "Though I have to say, it is just regretful we have not found Dac."

"Let us not talk of Dac." He waved his hand.

Roarke looked at him, confused. "Wasn't that why you summoned me, Sire?"

"No, Roarke. I wanted to talk to you about Deanna."

Roarke blinked, unsure if he heard right. "Deanna?"

The Cynn Eald nodded.

A dull ache in the centre of his chest bloomed outwards toward his heart and through his veins. After all this time, Roarke hadn't expected the pain to be as fresh as the day Deanna died. For his liege lord to talk of her was painful, to say the least, but he couldn't voice his resentment.

"She is dead, my lord. What else is there left to say?" Roarke said without rancour. "I buried her myself when I found her body among the ruins of Hamel Dun Creag."

His liege lord indicated the chair behind Roarke. They both sat down.

"I don't mean to be uncouth, Roarke, bringing her up after all this time. If she's dead, you should also be dead by now."

"I know that, Sire," Roarke agreed. "And I have been waiting for death to take me. Must have lost its way."

The Cynn Eald's mouth curled to one side in a half smile at Roarke's attempt at macabre humour. "It was stupid of me not to anticipate this," he murmured. "When our race began it was always under the assumption that a warrior bonded to his mate will live only while the mate lived and vice versa."

Roarke remained silent.

"Unless..."

"Unless what, Sire?"

"The woman you buried was not your mate and she is still alive." A lyrical voice completed the Cynn Eald's sentence.

Roarke looked up startled. He was about to kneel on one knee in front of the Deoré when she approached and held him by the shoulders to stop his descent.

"Like my husband, you should not kneel before me," she spoke with a soft smile. "We are deeply indebted to you."

Roarke wasn't used to such praise and felt himself redden. "It's my duty as a Cynn Cruor warrior, my lady."

The Deoré could have passed for Cleopatra. She had long straight hair, black as night which brushed below her shoulders like a silk curtain, while a fringe framed a heart shaped face. Like her mate, she looked as though she was in her fifties even if she was a hundred years younger than her husband. Her eyes were also a deep moss green, and kohl rimmed. Apart from the liner and her dark red lipstick which enhanced the cupid's bow shape of her mouth, her face was devoid of any make-up. She was svelte, and as tall as the Cynn Eald. Her soft cream silk dress showed her hour glass figure to perfection.

She arched a brow at Roarke.

"Forgive me, I didn't mean to stare," Roarke said, feeling like a schoolboy caught looking underneath a girl's skirt.

"Ah, yes, my beloved does have that effect on our kind and even on mortals," the Cynn Eald said, his eyes twinkling. He extended his hand to the Deoré, who took it, sitting her down beside him. "What did you mean, my love? Where can Roarke's mate be?"

She shrugged. "That I cannot know," she replied as she trailed a perfectly manicured red nail over her husband's thigh.

Roarke wished he could leave to allow them some privacy.

"You have nothing to be embarrassed about, my son," the Cynn Eald said.

They both smiled at him.

"I buried Deanna myself. You heard that as well, my lady."

"What about the possibility that Dac might have her?"

Roarke felt pain like a claymore hacking toward the centre of his chest, so sharp he had to grip the sides of his chair.

The possibility of Dac having Deanna brought a tidal wave of fury through his whole being. He found it hard to breathe. He wanted to rant and give in to the violence consuming him, to hell with his progenitor and his mate. The thought of Dac having his hands on his mate was more than he could bear. His breathing increased, his chest expanding to take in huge amounts of air, uncaring if what he was doing was becoming uncomfortable. He closed his eyes, wishing with all his heart to be in the battlefield at this very moment, to vent his rage. But he was not a Cynn Cruor Dux for nothing. He stilled his mind, beating the beast back inside him. He jerked when he felt hands gently touch his shoulders. He felt as if he was close to jumping into a ravine when he was pulled gently away from the jagged edge. Gradually, a sense of peace pervaded him, calming his senses and soothing his pain. He opened his eyes. Both his liege lord and mate were holding him, their strength and joined immortal healing gift seeping into his skin. Into his being. He heaved a huge sigh, feeling the raging anguish slowly dissipate until only his heartbreak remained. He jerked his head, nodding his thanks.

"If that were so, my lady, then Deanna is truly dead." Roarke's voice sounded strangled even to his own ears. "We had already mated," he continued. "My scent was on her. My father attested to that. Dac would know as well."

The Deoré nodded before she and the Cynn Eald removed their hands from Roarke's shoulders. No sooner did they do this when a wave of desolation descended on him. He clenched his jaw, holding on to his centuries of training not to give in to the pain.

"I am sorry, Roarke," the Deoré said, her voice filled with sadness. "We asked you to come here to see if we could help you. But as you have already mated, and nothing we say seems to assuage you, I too cannot understand how you have lived so long."

"Sire, would you know why?" Roarke asked, troubled.

A frown marred the Cynn Eald's forehead, eyeing his mate thoughtfully. His fingers formed a steeple against his mouth. "Did you complete the three stages of the mating ritual?"

Roarke started in surprise. "I didn't realize there were stages to the mating ritual, Sire."

"The Hamilton did not tell you?" The Cynn Eald's brow arched.

Roarke was too stunned to reply. The Ancient One's mouth lifted to one side.

"Joining together with a woman doesn't make her your mate unless she has been chosen and she accepts," he began. "You should know that, especially during the nights close to the full moon. If you stamped your scent on every woman you had sex with." He chuckled. "I cannot even begin to imagine what would happen to all the females and how a disagreement between any of them could be resolved."

"Careful, my love," the Deoré growled low in her throat. Her mate arched his brow in amusement.

Roarke bowed his head to hide his grin the reluctantly pulled at his lips.

"The second stage of the ritual happens after you have marked her with your scent," his liege continued. "You would know she is your mate and betrothed when your auras become conjoined."

"You and the female will be covered with an opalescent glow. Those are the auras uniting to prepare you both for the last ritual." The Deoré added.

"When she gives me her blood." Roarke finished.

"Yes."

Roarke sighed as he raked his fingers through his hair before rubbing the back of his neck. He'd never felt so defeated in his entire life. This was one battle that didn't seem to have an end in sight.

"We didn't finish the mating ritual. We only reached the second stage," Roarke said flatly.

"I see," the Deoré murmured before walking to stand at the back of her beloved's chair.

The silence which followed was pierced by the sound of the flames in the hearth as they popped and lapped the oozing resin of the pine logs.

"Have you ever considered she might not have been your mate at all and that she's still out there?" the Cynn Eald queried.

"She was destined for me, Sire," Roarke replied heavily. "I saw the iridescent glow. And even if there was no glow, I felt it in my heart that she was mine."

Finally, Roarke stood up. "Sire. My lady. I know where this conversation is going. Deanna was my mate. I knew and felt it deep in my soul in the same way I know without a doubt I am your warrior and a Cynn Cruor."

Eventually, the Cynn Eald nodded, his face sad.

"I beg your leave. We have found a nest of Scatha by the Borders and we have to prepare." Roarke gave them both a slight nod before he turned on his heel toward the door.

"Roarke?"

He turned back. "Yes, my lady?"

"What if you don't find your mate?"

Roarke's jaw clenched. Slowly, his face hardened.

"Then I will come back and ask you both to end my life."

Chapter Four

A knock on his door broke Roarke's reverie. Leaving his glass on the floor, he went to open it. Finn was standing on the other side, a grim look on his face.

"I think you'd better come to the library. Eirene noticed something on the CCTV," Finn said before turning on his heel.

"Why?"

Finn turned back and scowled. "Just because," he said, not giving Roarke a chance to retort as he left his brother at the door.

Slightly annoyed by Finn's cryptic statement, Roarke left the room, his frown not leaving his face even after he entered the library. "Eirene, what's this that Finn can't tell me?"

Except for Eirene, Finn and Graeme, who stood to one side with his arms crossed over his muscled chest, they were all alone in the nerve centre.

"Where are the others?" Roarke asked puzzled.

"I told them to take a break and see what Manchester has to offer," Graeme replied. "I've called Zac in. He'll be here any minute."

As if on cue, the glass doors whooshed and Zac McBain strode confidently into the room.

"Roarke," Zac greeted his leader with a handshake and a warm smile. "Good to see you back from your city centre recon."

"Good to be back, Zac. Don't like crowds too much." Roarke smiled briefly before addressing the entire inner sanctum of the Manchester Cynn Cruor. They were one man down. Blake Strachan, the youngest of the group, had left shortly after they raided Dac's club almost a month ago. "Now what's this all about?"

Zac shrugged. "I'm in the dark just like you."

Roarke raked his hand through his already dishevelled hair. "Eirene?"

Eirene's fingers flew over the keyboard. From the small console, the CCTV real-time footage of the pavement across the Faesten's building transferred to the huge LED screen on the wall. There were several people weaving their way along the pavement.

Some held bags with the names of the High Street store emblazoned on both sides. Others walked briskly, the collars of their coats upturned over their necks to ward off the cold of the early evening air.

However, that wasn't what caught Roarke's eye. All colour drained from his face. His mouth dried and he found it hard to breathe. His hands fisted so hard by his sides, he wouldn't be surprised if his knuckles tore through his skin.

A woman wrapped in a thick woollen coat watched the Faesten from across the street.

"Get me a close up, Eirene," Roarke ordered, his voice strained.

Finn stood by his side, his eyes narrowing as the camera zeroed in on the woman.

The silence in the air was palpable.

How did you know? Roarke asked Finn telepathically, automatically switching to the Cynn Cruors' form of communication. All of them, including Eirene, could hear him.

I didn't, Finn replied. *I vaguely remembered you describing her to me after we raided Dac's club. Am I wrong?*

"No, you weren't wrong." Roarke's voice was death vocalized. "That's Deanna."

****

Deanna stomped her feet lightly on the ground to get the circulation back in her legs. She turned against the sudden gust of wind so she could remove the strands of hair which softly whipped against her cold face. She burrowed further into her beige woolen coat as she clenched her gloved hands inside her coat's pockets. She turned her attention back to the tall red building.

Henry Heaton, the very expensive private investigator she'd hired was adamant that the building across the street from where she stood was the place she'd been looking for. When she asked him how he could be certain, Henry gave her an enigmatic smile before saying he had his sources. Deanna suspected his source was a man called

Devon. She had eavesdropped on Henry Heaton's telephone conversation without meaning to. Moments later, she'd been ushered into the private investigator's elegant office. It was another instance where she could hear what was being said from several feet away, even if the conversation was being conducted in hushed tones. She didn't know how she'd acquired such sharp hearing. Eons had passed and the possible reason was now buried deep into her psyche.

Deanna scanned the building's facade. According to the file compiled for her by the private investigator, the building had been an eyesore before it was bought by an anonymous buyer who renovated it completely for an undisclosed amount. While the building was under renovation, the new owner bought the building next to it and lived in it until the older building had been completely restored.

On the frontispiece of the first building was the name *Sawyer & Bean 1857*. The file said they had been cotton merchants who made their fortune during the textile boom in Manchester before falling on hard times. Both buildings were made of red brick with red sandstone dressings which characterized many of the buildings in the city. The architecture was a simplified palazzo style of arched windows and large pediments so prevalent in the middle of the nineteenth century. But unlike other palazzo inspired buildings, the first floors of the Faesten didn't have colonnades, but resembled the walls of a fortress. It may have looked incongruous, if not for the skill of the architect employed to restore the facade.

Deanna looked up. The last three floors of the buildings were ablaze with lights, but they were muted by the tinted glass windows which would have filtered much of the sun's rays during the day. She knew the windows were meant to protect everyone who lived inside. After all, it was the headquarters of the Cynn Cruor, warriors with human, vampire and werewolf DNA in their blood. Deanna always thought it was a mouthful to say. She'd wanted to ask Roarke more about the Cynn Cruor, but the assault on Hamel Dun Creag had changed that.

Actually, it had changed everything, and Deanna wasn't a fool to believe things could be the way they used to be. She sighed as indecision swept through her. For centuries, she'd dreamed of this moment and now that it was here, she didn't know what to do. She didn't know what to say.

And she didn't know how Roarke Hamilton would react to seeing her alive again.

"Oh, damn it all," she muttered. "At least I know where they are."

People who passed glanced at her surreptitiously. Deanna quirked her mouth sideways. 'They probably think I'm a prostitute,' she mused. She sobered. It wasn't actually far from the truth, since after her capture all those centuries ago; Dac Valerian had turned her into one.

"Hey you," a sexy voice drawled behind her. Deanna stiffened. The owner of the voice was so close to her, Deanna could feel his body heat seeping through her coat. "Are you waiting for someone?"

"It depends," she said.

Deanna turned around. She sucked in her breath at the sight of the stranger. He was one of the most handsome men she'd ever laid eyes on. He wore his wavy hair slightly longer so the edges brushed his nape. The lights from the bar's entrance behind them threw his face in sharp relief when someone opened the door. It made his face more angular when the light was replaced with shadows. Dark brown eyes twinkled with interest while one of his thick dark brows rose in question. His sensual mouth opened in a smile, showing perfectly formed teeth.

The stranger chuckled as he turned to idly watch the people come and go around them. "You shouldn't be on your own."

Deanna smiled in amusement. "I didn't realize gallantry existed in the twenty-first century."

He grinned. "It doesn't hurt to bring it back again." Extending his hand, he greeted her. "Luke Griffiths."

Deanna shook it. "Pleased to meet you, Luke Griffiths."

Luke chuckled. "You don't want to give me your name."

She smiled again, not saying anything.

"So who stood you up?"

"You presume too much, Mr. Griffiths." Deanna cocked her head to one side. "An unusual pick-up line, don't you think?"

Luke laughed, a rich timbre that reverberated through Deanna's insides. A ghost of a smile flitted across her mouth. The last time she felt this way Da Vinci hadn't even been born yet.

"Well, it's much better than saying, what's a nice girl like you doing in a place like this. You and I know that's worse than a cliché."

"Touché, Mr. Griffiths," Deanna said with a wry grin. She looked around. "But if you must know, I feel safe here."

Luke cocked his brow, giving their surroundings a similar assessment. "Canal Street?"

"No one would dare accost anyone here," she replied, giving him an appraising look. "You're not from Manchester."

The smile he gave her didn't reach his eyes. "No. I'm not."

Deanna decided not to pry. Everyone had secrets. Centuries of merely existing and always watching her own back had taught her that.

"You should be on your way," she said.

"And you?"

Deanna sighed. "I'll be fine, Mr. Griffiths. Thank you."

"Why don't I wait with you until someone shows up?"

Deanna stiffened. "What are you implying, Mr. Griffiths? Tread carefully, Sir, or you'll find yourself on the other side of the law."

Luke flushed. "I wasn't implying anything at all, Ma'am."

"American?" Deanna raised a brow in interest.

"A long time ago." Luke gave her a slight frown. "You're pretty good. I didn't expect anyone to notice." He paused, raking his hand through his hair. "Forgive me. This isn't going too well."

Deanna watched him with wariness. "Mr. Griffiths, you appear to be a nice man. I appreciate your concern, even for a stranger like me. But I have no interest in you or anyone for that matter. So you can practice your lines on someone else."

"And why is that?" he asked.

"Because she's with me."

****

Several emotions ran through Roarke at seeing Deanna alive. The shock rippled through him, making him both fiery hot and stone cold. For a long time he'd just stared at the CCTV. She was covered up against the cold and Roarke wanted to run down to her, to hold her in his arms and to warm her himself instead of the coat she had on. Then a man spoke to her. Roarke hadn't realized he'd emitted a low growl until Finn, Graeme, and Zac surrounded him.

"Roarke." Finn snapped him out of his jealous trance.

Chagrin washed over him and his shoulders sagged. "I'm fine."

"Go to her," Finn said, his eyes alight with understanding. "I think that's why she's here."

"Why now?" Roarke asked, his voice hollow.

"She might have been trying to find you. And if she has her reasons, then only she can answer your questions," Zac McBain spoke. A man of few words, he was the medic of the Faesten. He had blond hair and striking blue eyes which would make any girl swoon. "We'll watch you from here. I don't think you'd want us to eavesdrop on your conversation."

With a nod of thanks, Roarke whizzed through one of the windows and jumped.

"Well, that's one way to reach the ground floor without taking the stairs," Eirene quipped as she raised her eyebrows at all the Cynn Cruor.

Zac gave a lopsided grin as he braced his feet apart and crossed his arms over his chest.

"Find out what you can about the man talking to Deanna," Finn said, looking at Graeme, who was staring at the computer screen intently.

"Already did. I've come up with nothing," Graeme said, sighing as he straightened. He turned to meet Finn's gaze.

Finn swore under his breath in frustration and worry for his brother and Dux. Eirene stood up. Finn drew her close, rubbing his hand up and down her back absently.

"You need to be there for Roarke now, Finn."

"I know, Eirene." He kissed the top of her head before embracing her. "We all have to be. He's suffered long enough."

****

Roarke quelled the anger coursing through him at the sight of the stranger standing so near to his mate. His unnaturally sharp hearing allowed him to know the stranger's name.

Luke Griffiths.

And Luke Griffiths was hitting on his Deanna.

So when he approached them and made that categorical statement of Deanna being with him, it felt right.

Until he saw the alarm in Deanna's eyes.

Roarke had no idea whether the emotion was because he'd suddenly appeared from the shadows and startled her, or whether there was another reason for it. There would be time to mull over it later. Right now, he needed to move Deanna away from Luke and find out where she'd been hiding all this time.

"Deanna," he greeted her, relieved that his voice was smooth and belied his anger.

"Hello Roarke," she said, giving him a brief smile. She turned her attention back to Luke. "Mr. Griffiths was just leaving."

Roarke smiled. Inside, he couldn't stop the shout of triumph.

"Mr. Griffiths," he acknowledged Luke with a curt nod. "Thank you for keeping my betrothed company until I arrived."

"Betrothed?" Luke blinked and frowned, stepping back in surprise. "I'm sorry. I didn't realize you were taken...Deanna."

The pause before Luke spoke Deanna's name wasn't lost on Roarke.

Roarke felt Deanna's glare as he continued to assess Luke. Why was she glaring? What happened to her when she disappeared?

"I'd better go." Luke smiled. "No offence meant."

"None taken, Mr. Griffiths," Deanna said, returning his smile.

As Luke weaved his way through the throng, an uneasy silence fell over them. Roarke drank in everything that was Deanna like a man drawn to an oasis. The smell of heather and lavender was gone from her skin. It was replaced by jasmine which tantalized his nose when the frigid breeze swirled around them. The sad thing was, he couldn't smell his scent on Deanna now. Deanna's long lustrous locks had been cut into a russet bob that brushed her shoulders and sported a fringe which artfully framed her heart-shaped face. She looked into his eyes and he was lost again in their myriad blue depths. Her thick lashes were curled delicately, making her eyes wider. Her cheeks were rosy, both from the cold and the light blush she wore. Her pert nose turned up at the end. And her mouth...

Roarke felt his cock stir inside his denims at the long forgotten memory of those ruby red lips closing over him as her head bobbed up and down while her hand caressed his sac. He'd had women after Deanna. It was but natural for the unmated Cynn Cruors to slake their lust with willing partners, especially during the days before the full moon. The night of the full moon was a special time for the Cynn Cruors. It was the only time that, should their mates agree, they could get them pregnant. The night of the assault on Hamel Dun Creag had been the night of the full moon. Roarke had planned on talking to Deanna about starting a family, but she was wrenched from him in the cruellest of ways. Now that she was here, his desire for her was still as strong as before.

His carnal thoughts soon disappeared as reason returned. "Let's go inside the Faesten. We'll talk there."

Roarke saw Deanna hesitate, looking anywhere but at him. "Deanna?"

"I'd rather not."

Roarke inhaled harshly. "Why not?"

Deanna looked at him. His pulse rate quickened at her haunted look. "Because I don't belong to you anymore."

Chapter Five

Deanna was expecting Roarke to explode or rage over what she said. The one thing she wasn't prepared for was to see him remain stoic. The only signs that betrayed his calm demeanour were the clenching of his jaw and the fury blazing in his eyes. Cold dread should have cascaded through her body. Instead, she only felt a sense of detachment and sadness.

"Come," was all Roarke said.

Holding her by the elbow, Roarke steered her across the street. Deanna's lips parted at the still familiar feeling of his hand on her body. A tingling sensation started from the spot in her elbow and spread slowly, languorously through her. It woke familiar feelings which Roarke Hamilton's touch always evoked. She was only too glad for the years of walking or half running in heels, or else she would have stumbled when the heat of Roarke's hand sent erotic signals to her core.

No other man had ever made her feel the same ways as Roarke. No one could.

Once they reached the front of the building, Roarke punched the code on the door lock. When it opened, he went in first, holding the door for her. The foyer was narrow and nondescript. The floor was art deco in design, but the elevator was state of the art. There was a panel with an infra-red sensor by the side of the lift where Roarke placed his thumb. A few feet above it was the iris identification panel which scanned his eye. A few seconds later the lift opened and they both entered. Deanna's heels clicked against the polished floor. She positioned herself in one corner, gripping the bamboo designed railing. As the lift closed, Roarke punched a combination into the console before pushing the button which would take them to the top floor.

She couldn't look at the man beside her. Even after all this time, she couldn't understand how she could still be so attuned to him. She sensed waves of confusion, hurt, and anger rolling off

Roarke as he stood. Deanna bent her head down, closing her eyes, trying to steady her nerves.

And yet at the same time a glimmer of excitement began to burn within her. She knew that with gentle prodding Roarke's anger could become unbelievable passion unleashed. The thought of lying underneath Roarke made her damp. Her pulse started to race at the mere thought.

She glanced surreptitiously at the man standing beside her, who literally exuded power. Her former beloved seemed to have bulked up over the centuries. His leather bomber jacket fit snugly across his broad shoulders, even as the T-shirt he wore underneath shaped his muscular chest and flat stomach. Deanna looked down at his hands which were clenched into fists and remembered that at one time those hands had caressed every inch of her body. Those fingers had played with her nipples and her pleasure nub before it claimed her core to bring her a little piece of heaven on this mortal plane. She'd been innocent then. She wasn't now.

The lift opened, stopping her appraisal of Roarke. She glanced appreciatively at the Faesten's sanctum.

The Faesten's foyer looked like the lobby of some of the expensive hotels Deanna had been to in her new life. She looked up to see a cupola made of tinted glass. The floor was made of Italian marble which complimented the wood and glass design of the entire area. A mandala with the phrase *Cynn Cruor* was in the centre of the marble floor. Several warriors who were crossing the foyer looked their way and acknowledged Roarke's presence before walking on.

Deanna's gaze continued to sweep over the place. Three marble staircases with black iron balustrades swept up toward the second floor. Men carrying platters of food came out of the kitchen located to her right before crossing to the opposite side of the foyer to enter another room. She caught a glimpse of others holding weapons and inspecting them before the door closed, hiding them from prying eyes.

Roarke was looking at her, his face inscrutable. She lifted her chin, an involuntary reflex. A flash of surprise crossed his face before it disappeared. She knew Roarke had never seen her this way. Defiant. She'd always given in and did as she was told.

Not anymore.

"Where do you want to talk?" she queried.

"Follow me."

Roarke left her to follow. She was used to following. Actually, she'd been forced to obey all of her captor's requests or they would have broken her. After a brief hesitation, she followed at a slower pace, her steps sounding sharp against the marble floor, echoing throughout the place.

Behind the central staircase, Roarke opened a thick glass door which led to a huge library. Close to the window at the end of the room was a bank of CCTV monitors and a huge LED screen showing a grid map of the entire city of Manchester. She spied the monitor that zeroed in on the street where she'd previously been standing before Roarke brought her into the Faesten. Deanna realized this was how they'd seen her.

Four people were inside the room. Three Cynn Cruor warriors and one woman. Immediately she sensed the woman was mated to the man who stood by the fireplace eyeing her with curiosity.

Deanna's hands balled into fists inside her coat pockets. She looked away, pretending to survey her surroundings. She didn't want them to see the pain she felt knowing she could never be bonded to a Cynn Cruor ever again.

"Impressive library." She was pleased her voice didn't falter.

"It's the nerve centre," Roarke replied before introducing her to the warrior by the fireplace. "Finn Qualtrough, my second-in-command."

Deanna shook Finn's hand. His handshake was firm. No nonsense. His eyes assessed her keenly. There was none of the lecherous stares she'd gotten before she escaped.

"My mate, Eirene." Finn introduced the lone female whose face coloured with a pretty blush at Finn's introduction. When Deanna smiled, Eirene's smile lit up her eyes. It was a warm and welcoming one, the type Deanna missed receiving after the woman who'd saved her passed away at the turn of the twentieth century.

"Graeme Temple."

Roarke introduced her to a man in jeans and a shirt which hugged his body in all the right places. His eyes twinkled as he shook her hand.

"Zac McBain."

Everyone raised their eyebrows in surprise as Zac introduced himself and approached her. Deanna looked inquiringly at Roarke.

"Zac is our resident medic and sage," he explained, his mouth curving into a lopsided grin. "He hardly introduces himself until someone calls him."

Deanna raised her eyebrows. "Pleased to meet you, Mr. McBain,"

Zac's grin slightly faltered after he took her hand. His eyes narrowed, not letting go of her hand. Then he inhaled deeply.

Deanna realized that he knew. Her heartbeat sounded loud in her ears as she tried to hide the apprehension which would show in her eyes. She searched his face for any hatred or disgust, but there was none. She blinked several times to keep her emotions at bay when Zac squeezed her hand in understanding. Zac let go of her and they both stepped back.

She heard Roarke exhale. "Everyone, this is Deanna. My mate."

Deanna sucked in her breath, her forehead puckering in a slight frown. She'd already told Roarke she didn't belong to him anymore. Must she even stand up to him? Couldn't Roarke let it go?

Are you willing to let it go? Her conscience taunted her.

Deanna's shoulders slumped a little. Knowing Roarke, he would get to the bottom of anything he set his mind to, and that included finding out what had happened to her. This was what she was afraid of. If Roarke knew, then this would be the end of whatever hope she had left in her. But why did she need to hope for anything when she'd firmly resolved that nothing more could happen?

She bit the insides of her mouth in irritation at herself. She wasn't thinking straight. She hated it when she couldn't think straight. To let him go or not to let him go? Hamlet didn't have this kind of problem.

She looked at the people gathered in the room. They didn't appear incredulous. They knew who she was. Her eyes flew to Zac who'd just nodded to her in acceptance. She faced her former betrothed.

"Roarke, we have to talk."

He nodded in agreement.

"We can talk up there in the mezzanine." Roarke pointed to the floor above them. "There's a reading room just along the corridor."

"Okay."

Deanna walked toward the bronze and wooden spiral staircase leading to the mezzanine. As she placed her foot on the first step a beep came from the bank of computers. She turned to see what she'd heard when her face almost slammed into Roarke's chest. She took a deep breath, inhaling his scent which she had sorely missed and her mouth watered, salivated, missing the feel of her tongue on his smooth skin. Her body almost arched toward him. In a flash, the memory of their last night of passion came unbidden to her. She desperately fought against Roarke's sensual pull. She looked up and saw his eyes dilate with need. God! How she missed seeing the gold flecks in his eyes. At that moment she knew he was feeling the same tug. She didn't know if he was thinking of the same night. All she knew was that they were affecting each other in the same way as before. If not more.

Deanna clamped her lips together to stifle the whimper wanting to escape from her mouth. Roarke's nearness seemed to siphon her essence and her body wanted to give in to the temptation. His heat caressed her like a mist, it made her breasts heavy and her nipples stand to attention beneath the clothes she wore. She wanted to undo her coat, but if she did Roarke would see she wore nothing underneath her black silk blouse. He would see her waiting nipples bead, wanting his mouth and tongue on them.

And Deanna wasn't sure whether she would be able to stop herself from yielding.

"Deanna..." The sound of his voice saying her name tingled down her spine to entice a sweet throbbing in the apex of her thighs.

She could feel herself becoming damp. Their ache and need for each other hummed around them, cloaking them from the outside world.

"Roarke!"

Finn's sharp call broke the spell that had weaved around them like a splash of water, Deanna moved away.

Frustration creased his face. He reached for his nape and slowly rotated his neck. "I have to deal with this."

"It's okay," she said. "I'll browse through the books."

"You won't disappear?"

Her heart almost broke at the worry in his voice. For a big hulk of a man who had no compunction against killing, it was such a revelation how vulnerable he could be.

She chuckled softly, looking around her. "That's pretty difficult to do here, don't you think?"

He didn't speak but merely looked at her.

"No, Roarke. I won't leave," she relented.

With a nod and a brief smile, Roarke walked toward Finn.

Chapter Six

Deanna turned and took the spiral stairs to the mezzanine. When she reached the top landing, she walked toward one of the shelves, her footsteps muffled by the Persian rug on the floor.

She smiled at the array of books before her. After her escape from Dac, her benefactor, Mrs. Emeline Montgomery Dalton had set out to give her an education. Mrs. Dalton was a rich widow and a suffragette whose late husband had invested in the American Steel industry, shipping and minerals, leaving his widow more than enough money for several lifetimes.

Deanna took out a first edition copy, a collection of poems by Emily Dickinson. She browsed through it, but not really reading the words. Her mind had drifted to how she escaped Dac.

Dac had brought her with him from his lair on the Isle of Man to Yorkshire in 1908. There was a suffragette demonstration in Woodhouse Moor in the Northwest city of Leeds, and the Scatha Cruor wanted to get more women to be sold into white slavery. Deanna had already ceased to be Dac's constant sex slave, but neither would he allow any of the Scatha to touch her. At first, Dac refused to take her on the Scatha's fishing expedition until Deanna gave him the best blowjob of his existence.

They arrived in Woodhouse Moor where thousands of women and sympathisers crowded the place to listen to the impassioned speeches of several suffragettes like Adela Pankhurst and Gladys Keevil, who stood on platforms espousing rights for women. As the Scatha spread out, Deanna was able to escape her guard who'd been flirting with one of the women in the crowd. Knowing this was her only chance to flee, she gave the guard the slip. She ran and shoved her way through the throng, the increasing panic in her chest threatening to paralyze her. But the taste of freedom spurred her on to find a place to hide. She almost had a heart attack and would have screamed when a hand stopped her from running. It was Emeline Dalton who'd seen her fleeing in fear. Mrs. Dalton ushered her into a waiting carriage. The rich widow drew the curtains of the carriage closed and hid Deanna in the hollow compartment underneath her seat. The Scatha who were looking for Deanna, wrenched open the doors of all the carriages leaving the moor until they were pushed away by the police.

Deanna smiled wistfully as she remembered the kind and extremely generous widow who had treated Deanna as though she was her own daughter. Mrs. Dalton's husband and only daughter had succumbed to cholera and no amount of medicine or medical expertise had been able to save them. Emeline had taken a liking to her and her eyes blazed in horror and fury upon seeing the long scars from a whip on Deanna's body.

To help Deanna disappear from Dac's radar, Mrs. Dalton made her cut her russet tresses short, wrap her ample chest to flatten it and pretend to be her nephew, Ellis Montgomery. Her trusted chauffeur and man Friday, Fitzpatrick, had been sworn to secrecy.

With Emeline's immense wealth, they'd tried to find the Hamiltons. They travelled to Perth in Scotland so Deanna could try and remember where the Faesten was, but the only thing they could find were the burned ruins and scattered rubble of Hamel Dun Creag. It wasn't one of the castles preserved and protected by Historic Scotland, so there were no documents chronicling what had occurred. They had reached a dead end. Whatever semblance of hope Deanna had in finding Roarke spurred them on. They looked everywhere, even to the point of Emeline buying a small house there so they could stay longer. But they couldn't find any trace of the Hamilton line of the Cynn Cruor. It was the widow who comforted Deanna in the dead of the night when she could no longer hold the tears or bear the pain of the knife which twisted in her heart at losing Roarke. Finally the tears stopped.

She had none left.

As the years passed, Emeline Dalton had noticed her ward didn't age. When she joked that Deanna might have found the fountain of youth, Deanna felt compelled to tell her the truth, despite her fear that her benefactor might think her a freak and throw her out. But the widow had been very open-minded. It also helped that the older woman had always been interested in the things human eyes were not fortunate enough to see, believing there were reasons behind even the most mysterious of things. Since she had no heir, and because Deanna had given her so many happy moments, she amended her will leaving everything to Deanna. They left for America to complete several transactions and transfer all of her interests to her new heir.

"He can never be mine, Aunt Emeline." Deanna had told her. "My blood is already tainted by the very man the Cynn Cruor have been fighting."

Emeline Dalton had smiled, a twinkle in her eyes.

"Pooh-pooh girl!" She had scoffed. "If this Roarke Hamilton truly loves you and is even half the man you tell me he is, what happened to you won't matter. He will continue to love you, body and soul." Then she had said in a gentler voice, "I know your heart is broken, my child. But promise me you'll keep looking for this Roarke Hamilton of yours, no matter how long it takes."

With a reluctant smile, Deanna had nodded as she replied, "I promise."

Six months later, Emeline Dalton was dead.

Deanna returned to England as the sole heir of Mrs. Emeline Dalton. There were hardly any pictures of her, as her face was always covered when she went anywhere, which was rare. She used the immense wealth at her disposal to continue looking for Roarke as she'd promised. But there was one thing she couldn't allow to happen.

She couldn't allow herself to belong to Roarke again.

****

"What do we have?"

Deanna heard Roarke ask, breaking through her musings.

"There seems to be a glitch in a system I came across by accident," Eirene replied.

Roarke snorted. "By accident?"

"It was because of an accident that I found your precious Scatha Cruor," Eirene muttered.

Deanna gasped. The book she held in her hands fell to the floor. Mortified, she saw the page she held had been torn from the tome. In an instant Roarke was beside her.

"Deanna?"

She let out a brittle laugh. "I was clumsy. The book slipped from my hands. I'm sorry about the book. I'll find one to replace it."

"It doesn't matter," Roarke spoke with quiet authority. Deanna opened her mouth, but he placed a finger over her lips. "Leave it."

That simple gesture unleashed the maelstrom inside her. She was so stunned at the effect he had on her, she backed away.

Confusion and hurt marred Roarke's face.

"By the Ancients, Deanna, what the bloody hell is going on?" he bit out. "Why do you shy away from my touch?"

"You don't understand," she said, her voice breathless at the sensations roiling inside her. Sensations which both excited and alarmed her.

"Bloody right, I don't," he said harshly. "For centuries I thought you were dead, only to find out you're alive."

"And you don't think I didn't try to look for you? I went back to the Faesten as soon as I escaped." Deanna hissed under her breath, her eyes flashing with anger over it all.

She saw the shock on Roarke's face.

"But the Faesten was gone and I didn't know where to find you and the Cynn Cruor. You're not easy to find."

"Escaped?" Roarke asked as though he didn't hear what she'd said, except for that one word.

She was tired. Really bone deep tired. Still, she needed to finish what she set out to do. "You'll have your answers, Roarke. I promised I wouldn't leave. Go. Your Cynn Cruor brethren need you. They're more important than I can ever be."

She looked down at the gathered Cynn warriors and Eirene. They were looking elsewhere, but at them. Deanna also knew they had heard every word of their conversation.

"Go," she said more gently. "I will be here when you return."

Again Roarke left her to jump to the ground floor. She turned back to the bookshelf to look at the tomes. She didn't want to destroy another treasure. Like the Cynn Cruor, her incredibly sharp hearing overheard everything they said.

"The system has a very similar coding pattern as that of Dac's," Graeme spoke. "Eirene is sure this system is part of a bigger computer configuration Dac uses."

"Valerian seems to be using different codes for different sections of his organization." Eirene added. "I'm hoping that Graeme, the other Cynn computer whiz kids, and I are able to break the codes in less time than before."

"What do you expect to find?" Roarke asked.

Deanna heard Eirene sigh.

"I honestly don't know," Eirene replied. "I'm hoping it will give us a clue in finding the girls Dac has kidnapped, including Penny."

Deanna closed her eyes. Her heartbeat gradually filled her ears, even as it plummeted to her feet. It wasn't the way she would have wanted to tell Roarke what happened to her. Neither was it the way she wanted Roarke to know why they could never be bonded. The aspirations of the Cynn Cruor to destroy Dac once and for all were the same as hers. So if what she told them could help the rest of the women who'd been captured before they were sold, it was worth giving the Cynn Cruor the information they needed.

Even if she lost Roarke in the process. But she had always known it would eventually come to that.

Deanna walked toward the balcony. "You don't have to waste time searching for Penny," she said softly.

Everyone turned to look at her. Finn cocked his head to one side. "Why is that?"

"Because I know where they are."

Eirene gasped, her eyes suddenly filled with hope. Finn and Graeme looked at each other before they narrowed their eyes. Deanna clenched her jaw when she looked at Zac, whose sad, grim eyes held a wealth of sympathy for her. She saw Roarke's face become blank before bafflement flashed across it. Then suddenly he stiffened, as though realization dawned on him. Clear and stark.

"How would you know this?" Finn asked.

Roarke didn't move. He looked as though he'd been turned to granite. Something shrivelled inside Deanna. What it was she had no clue, but for whatever it was worth, she would deal with Roarke's revulsion later.

Her eyes bored into Finn's.

"Because I was once like those girls. Until Dac made me his whore."

Chapter Seven

Roarke felt the blood drain from his face. It was as if someone had shoved him hard with such force, he unknowingly stepped backwards. Shock made it difficult to breathe. Pain lanced his chest, a pain that had no remedy. His eyes clouded. He saw Deanna gasp and step back, hand on her throat. There was fear in her eyes. Roarke knew his eyes had changed to red orange. He felt the bloodlust run through his veins even as his fangs began to descend. With every fiber of his being, he wanted to rip something apart. He welcomed the fury burning a trail toward the centre of his gut. The desire to kill tasted like the sweetest nectar, the same desire which kept him fighting on the battlefield. He welcomed it now.

The desire for revenge was the only thing which kept his knees from buckling underneath him. He wanted to roar with anguish, but it would do no good. Roarke closed his eyes. His Deanna, his mate. Defiled by Dac. Not only had the Scatha Cruor destroyed so many lives the day Hamel Dun Creag was razed to the ground, Dac had stolen the woman he loved and made her his own. Roarke couldn't adequately describe how he felt. The intensity was overwhelming, but he knew he was getting out of control. He tasted his own blood from the cuts his fangs made on his lower lip.

"Roarke!"

He vaguely heard Zac shout his name. Bands of steel encircled him, but he easily flung them away. He heard a scream then something crashed against the wall. Suddenly, he was tackled to the ground. He struggled against the weight, but couldn't push it away.

"Let me up," he roared as he twisted underneath the weight holding him still.

"Not until you calm down," Finn snapped.

A low growl rumbled up from his chest. A warning sign his brethren had no choice but ignore. Roarke gritted his teeth and forced the rising bile of rage down. He struggled to think straight against that fury which only the death of Dac could quench. Gradually, he felt his eyes clear and a feeling of weightlessness covered him. He tried to rise but couldn't, his lungs bursting with the effort. He struggled for air. "Release me," he gritted.

Quickly the weight disappeared.

"Okay, Hamilton?" Zac asked as he clamped a hand on Roarke's shoulder.

Roarke nodded, albeit grudgingly.

"I'll tell the other warriors to keep away from the nerve centre until I call them." Graeme informed them before leaving the room.

Roarke braced on all fours, still quivering with anger, before he knelt on one knee and doggedly tried to stand. He clenched his jaw against the new shaft of anguish which hit him. In the deep recesses of his mind he knew Deanna was right. The Cynn Cruor came first. He would not allow Dac to win by allowing his heartbreak to cloud his judgement. He gazed at Deanna. She looked like a goddess lording it over all of them. She remained rooted to the spot on the second floor, her face pale. Roarke turned away from her, disgusted at himself for having lost control. Yet, despite what just transpired, despite the images running through his mind of how Dac could have taken her, regardless of the fury he felt—God help him—he still yearned for her. An ordinary mortal would have judged Deanna and found her reprehensible, tainted. But Roark was no ordinary mortal.

He was a Cynn Cruor. A warrior with a different set of moral and ethical codes, whose mission in life was to eradicate that which caused his people so much pain and grief. Most of all, he was a man who wanted to avenge the woman he loved. Deanna belonged to him. She had suffered because of him. He had vowed to protect her. Instead, he'd led her to a fate worse than if he'd killed her himself. May the Ancients forgive him, but he still loved Deanna despite what she'd been forced to become.

There was no doubt in his mind that the attraction between them was still as strong as ever. Roarke could feel it like a thin line of silk from a spider, the tensile strength strong. Every time he was near her, his blood simmered, not like from the uncomfortable heat of the sun, but with the warmth of knowing they were meant for each other. The pull was still as unassailable as when they'd joined together in coital bliss long ago. Her essence still tempted him from afar.

He felt the rage curl again inside him at the thought of Dac's hands on Deanna. His face hardened as he struggled against the guilt which swamped him out of nowhere. If he'd remained with Deanna, then Dac's men would all be dead. He and Deanna would have been able to escape to the caves. Either that or they would have died together. The twisted nagging thread of self-doubt attempted to make its way to the forefront of his thoughts, taunting him, telling him that Deanna should be reviled. But could he blame her? If it was the only way she could survive, could he fault her for whatever methods she used to keep her life? He had battled with that question so many times. He had done a lot of things he wasn't proud of in order to eradicate as many of the Scatha Cruor as he could find. Taking all of these things into consideration, Roarke came to one irrefutable conclusion.

None of this was Deanna's fault.

It was his.

Roarke looked at her. "You said you were willing to help."

She nodded. That's when he saw the light dying in her eyes. Only grim resignation remained.

The silence in the room was pierced by the sharp sounds coming from the streets outside and the muffled laughter of the other warriors passing across the foyer of the Faesten. At that moment, Graeme returned. He entered the code by the door and the lock clicked into place. No one would be able to enter or even break the glass short of hitting it with an armoured piercing round.

"Can you show us where we can find the girls and women?"

Deanna nodded again. "I will need a map."

"I can do you better," Eirene spoke before facing the LED screen. Soon the map of the United Kingdom appeared.

Deanna descended the spiral staircase. Roarke noticed she had acquired an ethereal grace that hadn't been there before. Even bundled up in her coat, her graceful walk made her hips sway. Nothing had changed; their powerful connection still enticed him to want to hold her, to press her back to his front so she could feel his need. To heal his ache. To tame the beast in him the way only Deanna knew how.

To fill her and feel her warmth around him, making her his again.

He inhaled slowly as she approached him, unbuttoning her overcoat and shrugging it off. His eyes narrowed when he saw how her black silk blouse shaped her ample breasts. She wore nothing underneath. A wave of protection and a surge of jealously slammed against him. He caught her coat before it completely fell against the armchair. A low growl emanated from his chest. He and Deanna may have their differences at the moment, but he bloody well wasn't going to allow any of his brethren to see her breasts, even if silk covered them. He handed the coat back to her.

"Keep your coat on, Deanna."

A deep blush crested Deanna's cheeks.

"Please, my lady." His mouth curved to a semblance of a smile.

She nodded and wore it unbuttoned. Her all black ensemble complimented her russet bob and blood red lips. As Roarke's eyes devoured her visage, her scent permeated his nostrils, setting off an incandescence of memories, yearning, and lust.

"What is it with women and black?" Finn muttered underneath his breath.

Eirene made an unladylike snort and blushed furiously. Finn chuckled in amusement at his mate.

Roarke remained stoic.

"There are several possible places where Dac may have hidden the women and children," Deanna began. "Girls twelve years old and under are kept in a place resembling an orphanage. Other girls, aged thirteen and above are spread out in brothels that Dac owns. I only know of the orphanage, but I'm sure we will find answers there."

"We?" He raised a mocking brow.

"Yes, Roarke Hamilton. We. While I understand that I disgust you, my main concern is finding the women and children."

Roarke almost flinched like he'd been slapped. Graeme looked down in embarrassment. Eirene looked at him in dismay, while Finn grunted. The biggest surprise was Zac. His mouth was pressed into a thin line and his eyes were filled with disappointment as he looked at Roarke. It made him want to squirm under the cynosure.

"Once you find the children and the child you've been looking for," Deanna began. "I will leave and you will not hear from me again."

Chapter Eight

If Deanna still knew how to cry, she would have done so. She felt warm underneath her coat with the fire blazing in the hearth, but she abided by Roarke's request. Eirene smiled at her, making Deanna feel more welcome. Deanna smiled back and moved closer to Eirene.

"Are you able to get a satellite feed of the Isle of Man?"

She felt Roarke's eyes boring into her back. At that moment she didn't particularly give a damn and refused to acknowledge the sting invading the walls around her heart.

In no time at all the satellite feed of the Isle of Man dominated the screen. Situated in the Irish Sea, the island lay between the mainland and Northern Ireland. Without hesitation, Deanna approached the wall and pointed to an area north of Port Saint Mary.

"South Barrule," Graeme commented.

She nodded. "That's where Dac lived most of the time."

Eirene's fingers flew over the keys while Graeme fished out his phone and tapped it once. Then he started talking rapidly to the person on the other end. Eirene gave him a puzzled look, but continued on with what she was doing.

"There's nothing there," Finn commented.

Deanna's mouth curved into a half smile. "Oh, it's there. The Scatha's fort is immune to any detection."

"That's impossible," Graeme muttered, frowning as he spoke to the person on the other end of the line. "Are you sure about that Dan?"

"That's a new form of technology," Roarke spoke up. "He couldn't have had that ability all those years ago."

The ripple of pleasure at the sound of Roarke's deep timbre so close to her made Deanna want to melt. Her body just knew where he was. The heat his body produced covered her in gentle waves. Reluctantly, she brushed the sensory caress away and shrugged. "Dac has had some of the greatest minds throughout the ages in his pocket."

Deanna saw the slight hardening of Roarke's jaw, a sign of annoyance. Whether in anger that the Cynn Cruor couldn't find Dac, or because she challenged him, Deanna didn't know. At the moment, she was past caring. She just wanted this to be over and done with.

"Dan says there's still nothing there," Graeme said after ending the call.

"Who's Dan?" Eirene asked.

"A Cynn mortal working with NASA," Finn replied as he continued to look at the map. He scrubbed his hand over his face. "Bloody hell! Why didn't we think of that?"

"Because we were just too engrossed with capturing Dac, we let ourselves forget he was one of Caesar's greatest tacticians," Zac answered, sitting down on the arm of one of the couches, his arms folded against his chest.

Finn snorted which made Eirene softly giggle.

"Zac, were you a philosopher a long time ago?" Graeme grumbled. "With your one liner know-it-all come backs you probably pissed off a lot of people."

A rumble of laughter came out of Zac's throat. "You think?"

"Sometimes I feel stupid when you just deadpan something so common sense."

Deanna smiled when she saw Zac's shoulders shake with mirth as he shrugged. Her eyes flew to Roarke and saw he was watching her. His eyes were as flat as planes of glass. Her smile faltered. She bent down to check the time on her Chopard Imperiale. She walked to one side close to the bookshelves as she fished out her Vertu mobile phone. She spoke softly.

"Who are you talking to?"

Deanna jerked in surprise. Roark's voice drifted to her ear. He was near, so close she could feel his breath on her neck. As the sensual heat made her close her eyes, she allowed herself a moment to soak him into her system. "I told my chauffeur to pick me up on the other end of Canal Street."

She didn't turn around, knowing she was already holding on by a thin thread.

"We haven't talked yet," he said. "You owe me that."

She nodded as she heard the soft click of the glass door being unlocked.

"We'll leave you two alone," Finn said while he ushered Eirene out of the room, followed by Zac and Graeme. "We'll grab something to eat."

As soon as they left, Roarke moved to the window to look down at the street, leaving Deanna bereft of his warmth. Without the distraction of the other warriors' presence, she could continue her assessment of Roarke at leisure. His hair, now much shorter, had grey streaks at the temples. Her fingers longed to feel its softness again, to run through those short strands the way she used to when she held his head as his mouth and tongue made love to her mound. Her channel clenched at the memory, wishing for it to happen again. Roarke also looked older, as did she. Taut skin stretched over the harsh planes of his face. His dark brows slashed in what seemed a constant frown over his silver blue eyes. Those same eyes had once looked at her with tenderness, with laughter, with lust.

With love.

"I buried you." Roarke's voice was as cold as the present weather.

"I was as good as dead," she said, returning her phone inside her coat pocket. "I was on my way to you, but was caught by one of Dac's men."

If it wasn't for her sharp hearing, she wouldn't have heard what Roarke said.

"But the dagger was with the woman I buried."

She shook her head. "I don't know how it came to be with her," she admitted. "I couldn't stay in the room. The Hamilton said my father and aunt were in the hall, so I wanted to go to them first before I went to find you. The dagger was in my hand, but there were so many people running to and from the Faesten, I tripped and lost it."

The thought of her only family dying in the siege brought a wave of sadness through her. "I didn't even see my Da and aunt buried," she murmured.

Roarke slightly inclined his head toward her. "I'm sorry. They were buried together with the rest of my father's people. The moment you all entered the Faesten, all had The Hamilton's protection." A lot of good it did them, he thought with regret.

She slowly made her way to stand beside Roarke. He tensed. A smile flitted across her mouth, but she didn't flinch. "It was a good thing I lost your dagger."

Roarke kept silent.

"It they'd found your dagger on me, they would have known who I was." She paused as she stared at the dark sky. "Who I could have been."

The air between them became heavy with their heartache.

"I tried to escape several times, but always got caught. They finally chained me to one of the carts." She frowned at the unpleasant memory.

Roarke looked at her. "Carts?"

"There were many of us, Roarke." She faced him, her smile sad. "Some came from the Faesten, while the other women were from villages the Scatha had plundered."

And just like that she was ensnared again in the depths of his eyes. His silver blue pupils darkened to the colour of a stormy Caribbean sea. It seared her very soul as though he wanted to take the painful memories locked and hidden away inside her, and throw them into the deepest trenches of the earth.

"Don't," she said. She couldn't tear her gaze away. "Please, Roarke. Don't do this."

Roarke grabbed her by her upper arms. "Don't do what, Deanna?" His eyes blazed, darkening further. "Don't let me take away the pain that's covered you thicker than the coat you have on? I am not disgusted with you. I am disgusted with Dac and my fury knows no bounds. I am disgusted with myself for having left you to an unimaginable fate."

She inhaled sharply when she saw his eyes beginning to morph to red orange. His face hardened as he forced his fury down with difficulty, his eyes simmering to a stormy blue.

"I don't know how to deal with this," he said, his voice almost tender. He let go of her and his hands gripped the window sill as he stared beyond the tops of the buildings. "We were torn apart. I believed you were dead. By the Ancients! I cannot even begin to imagine what you went through." He turned to her, his face tormented. "The least I can do is share your pain. Let me, Deanna. Let me take it away."

The more his words fell from his lips, the more they became the healing balm to her wounds. She felt herself begin to melt, her constricted heart softening and fluttering like a hummingbird inside her chest. She sighed softly, even as her breath quickened. In the soft light of the library, she saw his mouth relax. Firm and sensually wicked, she remembered his lips on hers. She almost moaned, knowing she had to get away, but her body longed for him once more. It knew she belonged to Roarke. A puff of air whooshed from her lips when Roarke's mouth descended on hers. She raised her palms to his muscled chest and she felt his heart thud hard beneath her palm, a breathing muscle which pulsed with life and broke with the same pain she felt.

And she knew she was lost.

She closed her eyes, giving in to his teasing mouth. She'd allow herself one last kiss. A kiss to add to all her bittersweet memories of the man in front of her.

His mouth was gentle yet firm, just as she remembered. The kiss was tentative, halting as though he was trying to gauge whether he'd be accepted back. She gently nipped his upper lip, then his lower lip before the tip of her tongue trailed against them. A low growl reverberated through his chest. Her body heated at the familiar draw of desire in her belly. With a groan Roarke pulled her into his arms, crushing her painfully. She strained against him, opening her mouth to accept his violent invasion. His mouth ravished and plundered. His teeth grazed and ground against her own. And yet she welcomed it wholeheartedly, because she needed this pain. She needed to feel Roarke's agony so it could soothe her own. Sweet desire thrummed through her body like never before. Her blood sang along her veins and when Roarke captured her tongue, swirling and mating with hers, the wetness coating her sex made her delirious.

Her arms went around his neck and she moaned against his mouth as she finally ran her fingers through his hair down to the soft bristles on his nape. God, how she missed this heat! Ever since she'd escaped, she had denied herself the pleasures of the flesh. She felt dirty, thinking no man would ever want her again. Her thoughts had swung between Roarke being disgusted with her to Roarke still wanting her. And now, as he held her head with both hands and slanted his mouth deepening the kiss, she sighed. If his kiss was anything to go by, the pendulum had swung toward her dearest wish. She missed his taste. His scent. Of musk and spice. A scent that went straight to her head, making her lightheaded with a need which overwhelmed her.

But for how long?

Then the memories of her life with the Scatha came unbidden to her mind and the whisper of joy she felt dissipated. What a cruel mind she had. She couldn't do this. She wasn't worthy of Roarke's love or desire anymore. Dac had destroyed all hope for her.

The thought of the Scatha Cruor leader was more than enough to cool her ardour. She broke the kiss and moved away. The sound of their laboured breaths mixed with the sounds around them. Gathering her wits about her, she walked further away, her legs as stiff as stilts. With every step away from Roarke, the wall she'd built around the agony which had almost drove her to end her life crumbled. She sucked in her breath to brace herself for the pain she knew would soon engulf her. She had to leave before she fell apart.

"Where are you going?"

"I can't stay here, Roarke." Deanna hoped her voice didn't betray her. "I'll be back tomorrow."

"I can't let you go."

Risking everything, she faced him. She felt the unfamiliar prick of tears behind her eyes.

"It isn't for you to decide anymore, Roarke Hamilton," she said. "I don't deserve to be here. I am no longer worthy of you."

"Deanna—"

"Please, Roarke," she implored, her voice almost catching. "Don't make it any harder than it already is." She walked toward the glass doors. "I'll see myself out."

As she left and crossed the foyer, she looked into the kitchen. Roarke's inner circle sat around the kitchen counter and watched her as she waited for the lift to arrive. She entered and waited for it to close. Roarke stood in the middle of the foyer and watched her until the lift slid shut. Moments later, she walked through Canal Street and exited Minshull Street where Phil, her driver and bodyguard opened the door of the silver grey Maserati Quatroporte. As soon as she sat back, the tears she managed to hold back began to fall.

****

Deanna entered the flat, exhausted from crying. She was alone again, and in her aloneness she felt a modicum of peace. She flicked the light switch. Soon the entire loft floor basked in the glow of the halogen lights from the sconces in the corners.

She walked across the hardwood floor, her heels clicking alternately between sharp and muffled as she crossed the old wood floor and Persian rugs which covered the large living room in vivid colours of brick red, browns, black, gold, and dark blues.

Her flat, located at the top floor of an old cotton mill was a reflection of her personality. Deanna loved her home. Old wooded columns held up the beamed ceiling in the same burnished colour. Maybe she'd feel better if she ate something.

Deanna entered the kitchen and spotted a bottle of wine. That's what she needed. Taking a wine glass from the cupboard above the granite countertop, she poured herself a drink before moving toward the balcony. She passed through the living room, tempted to curl up on the brown leather sofa or prop her feet up on the glass coffee table. Deanna was tired, but she needed fresh air. If she sat down, her thoughts would drive her mad. On the way out something caught her eye. Memories assailed her. She walked toward the shelves that were drilled into the red brick wall behind the sofa. Several valuable first edition books and picture frames of places she'd been to during her incredibly long life graced the shelves. But the one thing she could never put a value on was the framed picture in the centre shelf. It was a grainy black and white picture of Emeline Dalton set against the backdrop of the ruins of Hamel Dun Creag. Deanna would forever be in her debt.

"To you, Emeline. I hope you and your family are happy wherever you are," she said quietly as she caressed the photograph.

Pivoting, she set her glass on the coffee table and unbuttoned her coat, draping it over the sofa before taking her glass and going out the French doors leading to her own private garden. She sipped from her glass and sighed as the liquid made its way down her throat. The cold air hit her hard after the coziness of her flat. Her nipples hardened against the sensual abrasion of her silk blouse, but she didn't care. No one was going to see her.

She walked toward the low wall which surrounded her garden and after taking another sip of wine, placed the glass on the ledge.

Deanna looked up. She could faintly decipher the dark clouds floating against the night sky. They obscured the stars and the half-moon in its waning phase. Her mouth curved on one side. Her ability to know how to determine the phases of the moon had helped her survive those agonizing centuries with Dac.

Her thoughts returned to Roarke. For once, her heart and mind were in agreement as a wave of melancholia washed over her. Shivering from the cold, she crossed her arms over her chest, rubbing her own upper arms to get warm. Still, it was better to be out here than be back inside, curled into a ball of misery on her bed.

Suddenly, she heard a rustling. She whirled around, her eyes boring into the shadows by the corner wall. The hair on her nape stood on end. Her mouth became dry when a figure detached itself from the shadows. She exhaled in relief, then scowled.

"Dammit, Roarke! Why can't you use the door like everyone else?"

Roarke's mouth twitched slightly. "But, I'm not everyone else."

Her pulse rate shot up at his double meaning, but she refused to acknowledge it.

"You're not," she agreed. "You're a Cynn Cruor warrior in the service of the Ancient Eald."

Someone I can no longer have.

"No, Deanna. I'm still yours."

"How?" she asked, startled that he'd responded to her unspoken thought.

"It's the Kinare gene. The vampire part of our blood," Roarke said, walking toward her. His eyes burned her with his intensity. She tore her own gaze away and looked at the city's eclectic skyline. Taking a deep breath, she willed her pulse back to normal. Her chest rose up and down with the effort. Damn Roarke for making her feel again!

It had been such a long time since she'd felt this way. To be able to join heart, mind, body, and soul again. Not to be detached as she had been when Dac had used her body repeatedly. To be able to cry out in unadulterated ecstasy and not have to fake it. The truth of the matter was that she missed Roarke, his touch, his scent, his possession.

Desperately.

"I am your mate, Deanna," Roarke said, trailing his forefinger down her cheek, her jaw, down the column of her throat and on to the exposed part of her collarbone. It sent delicious shivers up and down her spine, straight into the spot which needed his mouth the most. "Why can't you accept that?"

"And why can't you see I can no longer be yours, even if I wanted to be?" She looked at him with beseeching eyes. "I am tainted, Roarke! How can you take a Scatha whore and claim her as a Cynn mate?"

She moved away in frustration. Her mind was in turmoil. How could she convince him they couldn't be together when she couldn't completely convince herself of the same thing?

"Why did you come?"

"We never finished talking about what happened to you," Roarke replied.

She gave a mirthless chuckle. "What else do you want to know? Isn't the word whore explanation enough?"

Roarke swore underneath his breath. He ran both hands through his hair.

"You were mine before you were forced to be his." His voice was harsh with anger.

"And that should count for something?"

"Yes, it does!"

"How would you feel Roarke, if we fucked knowing Dac had used me as well?"

Roarke recoiled at the venom in her voice. Then, in two strides he was in front of her, his eyes blazing, but his voice dangerously soft.

"Why don't we find out?"

Then Roarke's mouth was on hers. Crushing them as his mouth punished and bruised. He possessed her lips as though no one would ever claim them again. All of his fury was poured into his kiss. She placed her palms against his chest to push him away. "Roarke, I don't think..."

He grabbed her wrists and pinned them to her back with one hand, causing her to arch into his body.

"That's right, Deanna. Don't think," he growled.

Her silk clad breasts slammed against his open jacket and his chest. Her nipples hardened at the contact and brought a bolt of lightning screaming down her spine, burning a coil in her belly which liquefied her sex.

"I can't help it. You just don't understand..." She was on fire and hot enough to make the cold air around them sizzle.

With his other hand, Roarke grasped her nape to keep her head in place as he continued his onslaught of her mouth, forcing her lips to welcome him home. She continued to struggle, then froze when his erection grazed against her belly. The sweet ache inside her bloomed, causing her to gasp. With a groan of triumph, Roarke's tongue slipped into her mouth, branding her. Desire lanced through her, heating her blood and sending more shots of pleasure down to her hungry core.

And she gave in.

She kissed him back, sucking hard on his tongue. Their groans filled the night air. She wrenched her hands from his grasp and moulded her body against his hard planes as her arms encircled his neck. His hand splayed against the small of her back to press her as close as possible.

"I want you, Deanna." He rasped before pulling out the ends of her silk blouse from the waistband of her slacks.

She mewled when his hot hands skimmed her belly, inching their way upwards to cup her breasts. Deanna gasped as night air cooled her heated skin. "Oh, God!"

Roarke arched her back and claimed her breast. His mouth and tongue voraciously laved and sucked on her nipple, making it harden while his hand played with her other breast before he alternated his attention. Her sex clenched tightly, sending delicious shivers in and out of her. She bent her head as she lifted Roarke's face so she could kiss him hard.

Soon, Roarke ended the kiss. Deanna gloried at the pleasure she felt when gold flecks materialized against his pupils. She touched the sides of his eyes.

"I missed seeing those," she whispered before cupping his face. He turned to kiss her palm. She sighed. "If only for tonight, make love to me again, Roarke. Make love to me so I can forget."

She saw emotion flit through his eyes before it was gone. Her heart was in her throat, afraid he would refuse. Then his head bent down.

He kissed her again, but this time it was soft and tender, even while his hand was wreaking havoc with her body. Her clit throbbed when he rolled her hardened nipples with his thumb and forefinger before palming her globes lovingly. She closed her eyes, giving in to the moment, her breath coming out in moans and gasps. Then her mouth opened in a silent cry, feeling his tongue flick and suck on her breasts again. She lost all coherent thought, holding on to his shoulders. Lust thundered through her, lighting her up like a fireball.

Roarke scooped her up and walked through the French doors and into the warmth of the loft. With her face against his neck, she inhaled deeply before flicking her tongue and sucking on the pulse at the base of his throat.

"Where?" he growled, his desire unsuppressed.

Mutely, Deanna pointed to the stairs which led to her bedroom. Instead of using the stairs, Roarke catapulted them to the open room's landing with one jump.

There wouldn't be any recriminations tonight. This moment would be for knowing each other's bodies again. To make up for all the lost time.

Chapter Nine

Without preamble she took Roarke's face in both her hands and devoured his mouth, laughing softly at his growl. She gasped when he tore her blouse from her body, the buttons falling like soft raindrops on the wooden floor.

"You too," she said as she pushed his leather jacket from his shoulders, letting it fall to his feet. "Now, your shirt." She helped him remove it, smiling when one of his buttons popped off, joining hers on the floor.

"Are you anxious?"

"Yes, Roarke." Deanna moved closer so she could run her hands along the hard planes of his chest and stomach, giving in to the urge to lick and nibble on his delicious skin. He groaned, entangling his fingers in her hair.

Slowly, her hands travelled down to cup his erection, bulging against his jeans. "Yes, touch me," he hissed, bucking his hips against her palms.

With an intensity which thrilled her, Roarke kissed her again, backing her to the bed. When Deanna felt the edge of the bed behind her, she eased herself on it, pulling Roarke down with her. When he parted her legs with his thigh, she sighed in pleasure and mewled when he cupped her mound and rubbed her clit. The friction of the slacks and the lace against her pleasure button made her arch in delight. She was in a vortex of carnal bliss with Roarke's mouth sliding down the column of her throat, his tongue flicking at the erratic pulse at the base of her neck, down to her sternum, then to her breasts. She unbuttoned the waistband of his jeans, and oh so slowly unzipped him. Roarke stood up to shuck his shoes and socks before he removed his jeans. She looked at his erection with hunger. It stood hard and thick and bounced a bit as he moved.

Slowly Roarke bent down to remove her slacks. She saw his eyes widen before his gaze scorched her with his lust. She lifted her buttocks and felt the material slide first against her lace underwear, then down to her lace edged stockings. She sat up to take off her hose.

"Leave them on," he growled.

Suddenly, it was as if they went back in time. His words gave her the oddest sense of déjà vu. He had said this to her before—before everything. Deanna panted, her entire body sensitized by the desire in Roarke's eyes. God, she was about to come and Roarke hadn't even touched her!

Roarke knelt down at the edge of the bed. He grabbed her hips and pulled her closer, his eyes never leaving hers.

"You're beautiful," he said. Slowly, he removed the tiny scrap of lace which covered her mound. Then he looked down, reverently. "Everywhere."

As a slow smile lit his face, so did the slow burn begin in her sex, making her hips writhe beneath his gaze. He held her thighs, spreading them wider before his fingers trailed a hot path toward the apex. She watched mesmerized as his mouth followed his fingers. Nipping, kissing, licking her inner thighs. Her womb tensed. Desire coiled toward her centre, and her whole vagina throbbed. This was the only man who'd ever mattered to her. All the pent up passion she'd had stored up in her heart for decades came pouring forth. Deanna bit down on her lower lip.

She was about to come.

Then Roarke's mouth was on her. His tongue parted her folds. He laved her from bottom to top, flattening his tongue against her throbbing clit before swirling it round and around. His hands gripped her hips, holding her steady when she just couldn't be still. He speared her sweet channel, dipping his tongue as far as it would go before going back to suck on her swollen clit and labia lips. She looked at him. His eyes locked with hers as he continued to pleasure her.

She threw her head back as wave upon wave of incredible bliss brought her closer to the edge. She panted and moaned, nearly delirious with ecstasy. She didn't know whether to hold on to his head or to grab the silk sheets into her fists. A powerful current in the centre of her sex threatened to drown her. Roarke's tongue and mouth were voracious and she loved every minute of it. His tongue made languorous flicks around her clit without let up. Then he inserted two fingers into her, rubbing hard and fast inside, and she combusted. Her cries of release merged with his growl of passion. His fingers and mouth continued to pleasure her until her orgasm subsided.

She floated in a cloud of bliss, boneless but not sated. She felt the bed dip. When she opened her eyes, Roarke was hovering over her. The gold flecks in his eye more prominent, and she knew his lust had grown. She purred as her hands caressed the hard planes of his chest.

"There is no one like you, no one," he said.

Deanna's mouth curved into a pleased smile when she heard his sharp intake of breath. Her hands continued to trace down the length of his body, lower to his rock hard stomach, his hips, circling around to clasp his taut buttocks before ever so slowly moving to the front to wrap around his turgid erection. She pumped one hand up and down while the other gently cupped his balls, rolling them between her fingers.

Roarke thought he'd stopped breathing and gone to heaven. As soon as Deanna touched his cock, he pulsated, becoming so rock hard he didn't know if he was feeling pleasure or pain. His stomach bunched at the intensity of the sensation. And her taste! Ancients! How he'd missed her taste. Her touch. Her scent. The only scent that could drive him out of his mind with lust.

"Kiss me," she begged, her eyes deep blue pools of desire. Her lips parted to cover him with her sweet breath, inviting him to partake of her mouth once more. He nibbled on her upper lip, her lower lip, then her entire mouth. Sensual. Languid. He felt her open up to him. Lust surged fast through him as she greedily sucked on his tongue, tasting herself on him. Roarke wanted her mouth on him, but that could wait. Deanna raised her legs, parting them wide and enticed his cock toward her opening. With one thrust he sheathd himself into her. Their mixed groans of pleasure filled the room, his cock enveloped in Deanna's wet warmth. He closed his eyes, giving a guttural growl when Deanna arched her back in ecstasy.

"Roarke," she gasped, her pupils dilated with desire. "Take me hard. I want you deep inside me. I missed you."

Roarke didn't need further prodding. He held her hip while his other arm held his weight. He groaned when Deanna encircled his waist with her legs allowing him to go deeper. He hissed as lust swirled around inside his bloodstream. Each thrust was a step up the passion ladder. He felt his wereblood pulsing through his cock, making him thicker. Harder. Longer.

"Oh, God, yes!" she cried out.

He watched Deanna as pleasure suffused her face. Her head thrown back on the bed, her breasts with their hard peaks arched as delectable offerings to him. Her channel, wet and wild, squeezed him.

"More Roarke! Please!" Deanna whimpered.

He rode her hard like she asked. His balls slapped rhythmically against her bottom as he thrust in and out of her slick heat. He groaned as his cock revelled in Deanna's velvet sheath, covering him with her delicious cream. Her whimpers spurred him on. In and out. Deeper and deeper. He rotated his hips, branding her.

Everywhere.

He kissed her hard. His tongue in her mouth imitated his thrusts between her legs. Suddenly Deanna pushed against his chest and rolled him onto his back. He looked at her in surprise, but pleased she was taking the initiative. In the glow of the lights from below, she looked like fire and desire personified.

Then she started to move. He closed his eyes as he held on to Deanna's waist. She rocked back and forth, making his cock move around inside her. She rode him. Up and down. His breath hissed from his mouth as the muscles of her sex milked him. Deanna rocked and rode him faster. He groaned loudly, closing his eyes as the feeling in his balls intensified. When he opened his eyes, he stared at her in surprise. She had cupped her breasts and was pinching her own nipples as a satisfied moan came from her. A slow smile curved her lips while she rocked. He watched her glow in her pleasure. He felt his orgasm draw close.

"Do you like me fondling my breasts and teasing my nipples?" she asked in between pants before her hand went down to play with her clit. Deanna's mouth lifted in a smile, but faltered.

He growled and held her hips so she couldn't move.

"Roarke, no!"

"Yes!"

At that moment, his hips bucked, thrusting deep inside her. Faster, he pistoned in and out of her, his balls tight against the base of his cock. Her sweet channel clung to him, squeezing him, begging him for his release. He closed his eyes, trying to prolong it, but Deanna suddenly screamed her orgasm, her head thrown back. Her sex pulsated around him and he gave a harsh shout as his orgasm drowned him. He felt his seed spurt forth into her womb. His heart stuttered as he felt more of his seed jet out. A kaleidoscope of colour burst inside his mind. In that instant, Roarke saw the thin opalescent glow surrounding her, connecting her to his body and binding them together. But there were gaps in the aura as though something was preventing them from becoming one.

Deanna was still his mate. No one could deny that, not even the Ancient Eald. She belonged to him and he would take care of her. What she did to survive all these centuries did not matter. The girl he fell for and the woman he bonded with, even for one night, was still inside her. With her, he felt whole. Without her he was merely a shell. She was his life and he hoped he was hers.

And at that very moment, Roarke made a decision to win her back.

****

Deanna stirred. She blinked several times to remove the sleep from her eyes. She was naked. A muscular arm kept her firmly back against a hard chest. A muscled leg pinned both her legs to the bed.

Her heart pounded so loudly it drowned out her breathing.

God, had Dac found her?

Who was this man behind her? She tried to still her breathing, but it came out of her parted lips in gasps. A wave of panic was close to cresting over her. Her mind went back to the times when she had been punished when she'd moved away from Dac.

No! Not after all this time!

"Sleep, Deanna. You are safe." The deep timbre from behind her startled her. He kissed her hair.

Memories of Roarke and the hours of lovemaking flooded her mind. The wave of panic which had nearly swallowed her slowly transformed into a blanket of relief. Instinctively, she turned to face Roarke, burying her face against his neck. The bad memories had no power over her as long as she was in his arms. She sighed. He made her feel safe.

Roarke had always made her feel safe.

"My lady, what's wrong?"

Roarke tilted her chin up. His eyes bore into hers, concern etched in them.

She snuggled more into his embrace, not answering him. Roarke adjusted himself on the bed to hold her tight. His hand moved up and down her back, down to the swell of her hip in a languid caress. "My lady, talk to me."

She smiled against his chest. "It's the twenty-first century, Roarke. No one says that anymore."

"I don't give a fuck." He scowled. "You will always be my lady."

Deanna giggled at his expression, then her smile wavered. Moving out of his embrace and laying on her back, she stared at the ceiling. The lights still glowed downstairs. The sky was still dark, but she knew dawn would be breaking soon, the same way she was attuned to the phases of the moon. She shivered, but didn't pull the sheets over her naked breasts. Her modesty had been lost long ago, especially after having been forced to expose herself to so many men, even if they'd been ordered not to touch her.

"Deanna."

"Do you really want to know Roarke?" Her voice was close to inaudible, but she knew he could hear her.

Roarke hesitated before nodding. "Only if you want to tell me." He paused. "You disappeared from my life. I searched everywhere for you, Deanna. You are my mate. It's the least you can do."

Deanna sighed, slightly frowning. She got up from the bed, but Roarke's arm shot around her waist.

"What the fuck is all of this?"

Her breath hitched at the sudden anger in his voice. From the consummate lover to a furious warrior in the blink of an eye. She looked over her shoulder and saw his eyes turning burnt orange and then it was gone.

"Didn't you see those before?"

"I was too intent on making love to you," he said in disbelief. "I didn't feel any ridges. Fuck!"

Deanna flinched when Roarke's fingers traced the lines criss-crossing her back, the skin reacting to his touch. He stopped. "Does it hurt?"

She shook her head, replying to him over her shoulder. "Only the memory." Her shoulders slumped. "It doesn't hurt anymore, Roarke, but it's my mark. Dac used the whip several times when I defied him. It should have left deep ridges on my back, but only the lines are left. I have no idea why."

Roarke enclosed her in his embrace. She felt him tremble with suppressed anger, even while he caressed her hair and kissed her forehead. "I have many regrets."

"I know." She could not read his thoughts, but she held him close, too. This was where she belonged. She knew this familiar place. But all she could think of was how the Cynn Cruor could turn against Roarke, a Dux and a well-respected warrior. The head of the Manchester Faesten. She longed to forgive herself, but she couldn't find the courage to do so.

She left his arms and walked toward her armoire. She took her black lace wrap from the satin hanger, shrugging into it and tying the silk ribbon before facing Roarke.

Her breath caught in her throat at the sight of his muscular form on her bed. She could see his gaze raking her lace covered form, searing her with those gold flecked eyes. Her body sang in tandem with the fire pumping through her veins. It made her breasts heavy and her mound, oh so ready, to welcome Roarke back in again and again.

But what happened between them earlier was enough, even as her body screamed for more. To have him again would make it more difficult for them to part.

"Dawn is fast approaching, Roarke. You have to go."

Roarke arched a brow before his gaze narrowed. He nodded. With effortless grace he got out of the bed.

Deanna exhaled, both in relief and disappointment. She knew it was the right thing to do. Her eyes feasted on Roarke's body. Broad shoulders and back, narrow waist, taut ass, before her gaze travelled down the length of his legs. He walked toward the loveseat, across from the bed where his clothes had been flung haphazardly earlier. Liquid heat fired her sex at the sight of his erection. The familiar ache in her sex intensified.

Even in anger he was magnificent.

But Roarke didn't pick up his clothes. He walked toward her, his gait slow, calculating. Like a panther stalking its prey. Her eyes flew to his and saw his carnal intent in the gold flecks that seemed to glow. Her mouth watered at the sight of his chest. Her tongue, remembering the salt on his skin and the erotic sensation of his flat nipple against her mouth. Her own nipples puckered underneath her lace wrap, the material further grazing and arousing the dusky buds.

Roarke stopped in front of her. He was hypnotic. Her senses sharper and her skin more sensitized by his mere gaze.

"Do you really want me to go, my lady?" His voice was soft. Was there a tinge of curiosity?

She swallowed and nodded, even as she moved slightly forward.

Roarke's gaze travelled down her breasts, her cleavage deep and narrow, pushing against the bodice. He lifted a finger and grazed her lace covered nipple. One sharp bolt of desire coursed through her and she couldn't stop the gasp which came unbidden from her mouth.

"Really?" he asked again.

They were just a foot away from each other.

"Yes, Roarke," she said, her voice betraying her need.

Another strangled moan came out of her as Roarke palmed her other lace covered breast, caressing the nipple with his thumb.

"Yes what, Deanna?"

Her channel was weeping. She could feel her heat making its way down her inner thighs. She writhed, feeling her sex swell.

Roarke moved closer so that the tip of his arousal gently scraped her lace covered belly. He hissed, but he kept his play on her breasts.

Her body thrummed in excitement. By taking a step forward, Deanna knew that Roarke had won. Again. His shaft ended up flush against her stomach. Roarke took possession of her mouth, his tongue tracing the seam of her lips before entering her sweet cavern to play with her tongue. He slanted her head to deepen the kiss.

Deanna's whole body was on fire. Her hands cradled his rock hard erection, moving up and down, teasing, gently twisting its length while Roarke continued to plunder her mouth and tease her nipples.

She smiled against his mouth. Roarke lifted his head and looked at her with lust burning in his eyes.

"I'm thirsty," she said.

"You want to get a drink, now?"

She laughed softly at his confusion.

Then his mouth curved into a slow grin when she went down on her knees. She heard his sharp and quick breathing as she continued to fist him. She sighed in contentment as her hand moved up and down Roarke's velvet encased granite shaft.

"Do your worst, my lady," he rasped, his hands running through her hair.

"My worst, my lord?" She arched her brow. "Oh, my lord, I intend to do my best."

She gently fisted his glans before she flattened her tongue to lick the underside up to his cock head. Her finger spread his pre-cum over the tip before she licked, flicking her tongue against the tip. His flavour exploded on her taste buds. He was huge. He was salty. And he was delicious. She always had a penchant for anything Roarke.

She kept her eyes on Roarke, enjoying the play of emotions on his face. She continued licking the underside, prolonging his wait. He groaned and held on as she teased the thick vein on the underside of his rod. As she reached the base, she opened her mouth wider and drew his balls into the wet haven of her mouth. Her lips sucked while her tongue laved. Roarke threw his head back, a guttural sound emitting from inside his chest. He looked back down.

"You torment me, my lady."

She fluttered her lashes and grinned, before she stiffened her tongue. If lust could get any hotter, it was in Roarke's golden eyes. She'd never felt this kind of power over a man.

It was very humbling.

Roarke's breathing came in gasps the closer her tongue got to his cock head. Then as though teetering close to the precipice, she slowly raised on her knees, her eyes still on Roarke before she enveloped as much of his entire shaft into her warm mouth as she could.

Roarke groaned loudly in pleasure.

Her heart felt like it was bursting from her chest. Her mouth and tongue revelled at the feel of Roarke's penis as she pampered him. Up and down. Sucking. Licking. Laving. The feel of his shaft's skin against her mouth's inner walls was exquisite. She relaxed her throat to take him as deep as she could. She closed her eyes and hummed.

"Deanna!"

She could feel he was close to the edge. Bobbing her head faster, in concert with her fist pumps, she sought to please Roarke in every way she could, rolling his tightening sac with the other hand, loving the groans coming from deep in his chest. Her forefinger slowly inched underneath the sac and she pressed on his perineum.

"Deanna! Oh, fuck!"

With a guttural shout Roarke erupted inside her mouth.

She closed her eyes as pleasure washed over her. She swallowed his essence, milking him for all he was worth. Her mouth continued moving up and down, even as Roarke buckled in front of her. Even on his knees, her mouth was still on him.

"Deanna." His voice was strangled as he removed her from his overly sensitive shaft. He lifted her face and gave her a long hard kiss. She moaned against his mouth, letting him taste himself on her tongue. "Now, that's one sexy way of feeding me."

"Hhmmmm..." she purred before she sat on her feet. Her arms loosely encircled his neck as he kissed a trail to the sensitive spot behind her ear and down the column of her throat. "You really have to go, Roarke."

"Deanna."

She placed her forefinger over his lips. She smiled. "I will tell you everything when I get to the Faesten. I'm not going anywhere."

Roarke hesitated.

"Roarke, dawn is breaking." She glanced at the French doors leading to the balcony. Tinges of pale pink and blue pushed against the horizon, moving over the purples and dark blues of the night sky.

She looked at the face of the only man who had ever captured her heart. Roarke was right and she'd give him the explanation he deserved. It was all clear cut anyway. Whatever she would tell him was the entire truth.

But even as she knew their impending talk would give closure to their past, it could never open a door to the future. Somehow she had to make Roarke understand how she felt about being tainted by Dac. If she agreed to take her place as his mate, rightful or not, there would always be questions from other Cynn warriors about where her loyalties lay. Roarke had a lot on his plate now that the Cynn Cruor had descended on Manchester. She couldn't add to that aggravation by asking him to defend her from those who suspected her intentions were anything less than loyal.

Roarke placed his forehead on hers as he cupped her face. She cupped his face also, her thumb running through the seam of his lower lip.

"Go, my lord," she whispered. "I will see you later."

"It's the twenty-first century, Deanna. No one says that anymore."

They both chuckled before she gave him a kiss.

"No matter what, Roarke Hamilton, you will always be my lord."

Chapter Ten

Gloom cloaked the Faesten in the early hours of the day as Roarke stepped out of the lift. The foyer was empty. His footfalls echoed on the marble floor. He looked toward the kitchen's glass doors where the Cynn chef and other mortals were busy preparing the Faesten's food. He hungered, but not for food. Having Deanna after all this time had awoken his dormant craving for her. Even now he longed for her to be by his side. A hollow feeling settled in his gut. Only her presence would make it go away.

But he also knew Deanna needed her space. She was hell bent on not becoming a part of his life. A misplaced sense of sacrifice because she'd survived living with the Scatha Cruor kept her from realizing her value to him. He needed to tread carefully and break through her conviction that she'd lost her worthiness to be his mate. But first thing's first. Finding the girls and women held against their will had to be the priority.

As he turned to one of the staircases to get to his quarters, he saw Zac come out of the kitchen, biting on a large sandwich.

"Roarke," Zac greeted him with a lopsided grin before chewing. "Tough night?"

"Not exactly," Roarke replied, his mouth twitching. "Where are you heading?"

"I'm on rota at the Emergency Department of the Manchester Royal," he answered and swallowed.

"I can never understand how you do that Zac," Roarke muttered, frowning. "Your blood doesn't boil when exposed to sunlight."

Their voices echoed in the silent foyer.

Zac shrugged. "I honestly can't say and I'd like to know why as well. I need to speak with the Ancient Eald, but I have no access to him."

Roarke grunted. "Give me a few hours and I'll see what I can do."

Zac's face lit up. "Thanks, my Dux."

Roarke's hand cut through the air. "Stop calling me Dux. I haven't been that for a long time."

"Dux just means leader, Roarke." Zac's eyes twinkled in amusement before he sobered. "Did you get to speak to Deanna?"

"Not exactly."

"I see."

Roarke scrutinized Zac's face. His eyes narrowed as the truth dawned. "You knew that, didn't you?"

The medic continued to chew the last bit of his sandwich.

"At first I wasn't sure," he admitted. "But her scent was not Cynn, nor Scatha. She was somewhere in between."

"You scented her?" Roarke asked with interest. "Neither Finn nor Graeme noticed. I couldn't smell my scent on her, either. Even if we were far apart my scent would have remained."

Zac nodded. "The Scatha's scent masked your scent. But it's there. She belongs to you."

Roarke looked up at the glass dome overhead where the watery sun peeked out of the clouds. Manchester was in for another day of rain which suited the Cynn Cruors well. It made their missions less painful and uncomfortable. He heaved a long sigh before allowing his shoulders to slump. "Why didn't you tell me?"

"You wanted to tear something apart. You didn't want to leave Deanna's side and I didn't want to embarrass her in front of Graeme, Finn, and Eirene," Zac admitted, his face grim. "Besides, it wasn't my place to say. And when she told everyone..." Zac left the statement hanging as he shook his head.

"She keeps on saying she isn't worthy of me." Roarke sighed, shaking his head. "But her body and blood sing to me."

Zac pursed his lips in understanding.

"It isn't easy for her, Roarke. She knows of the war between the Cruors. And with the length of time she was with them..." He shook his head. "I can't even begin to fathom what she went through."

"She had lash scars on her back, Zac." Roarke's voice filled with disbelief and hollowed with pain. "Dac punished her when she didn't do what he wanted. I want that Scatha dead."

"And he will be. Just as soon as we track his coordinates." Zac looked at his watch. "I'll be back tonight. Finn has already chosen warriors and mortals from the Leeds Faesten to do a recon of South Barrule."

Roarke nodded before Zac strode to the elevator. He then climbed the stairs toward his quarters.

Half an hour later, showered and wearing a snug T-shirt and jeans, he went downstairs to get something to eat. He'd almost finished his breakfast when Finn and Eirene entered the dining room followed by Graeme. Eirene giggled suddenly as Finn looked at his mate with amusement.

"Oh, go back to your room, people, and stop using telepathy," Graeme grumbled. "I'm eating food here."

Finn chuckled, looking at him. "Couldn't find someone to bed last night?"

Graeme grunted in response.

"Don't worry, Graeme. Your mate might just be around the corner," Eirene said before chewing on a bacon rasher.

"Where? In the community bins at the side of the building?"

Eirene shrugged, laughter in her eyes. "Anything is possible."

Graeme chuckled, shaking his head before wolfing down a huge portion of scrambled eggs.

Finn turned to Roarke, who was nursing his coffee. "Everything okay?"

He gave Finn a quick glance before nodding. "She'll be here later. Heard from Zac you've sent a team to the Isle of Man."

"Yes. They're going in, pretending to be a corporate group signed up for Laser Mayhem."

"When did they leave?"

"Last night," Finn said after taking a sip from his mug. He grinned. "They'll report as soon as they hit the ground. Colin Butler is leading them."

"Good," Roarke said, pleased that one of the best Cynn warriors was in charge.

"He's a damn good recon warrior." Finn chuckled. At Eirene's questioning look he said, "Colin, Roarke, and I were sent to Russia, then the Soviet Union, to help extricate a dissident seeking political asylum. He was about to be sent to the Gulag."

"Where is the dissident?" Eirene asked after cleaning her plate with a piece of toast that she popped in her mouth.

"He was brought here to the U.K. first before being sent to America," Graeme answered, smiling. "Blake and I stayed with him for a while before we were assigned to another mission."

At the mention of Blake's name everyone became quiet. Graeme paused in thought before he continued with his breakfast.

"Any word from Blake?" Eirene asked, sadness clouding her eyes. "At times, I think it might have been my fault."

"Stop that." Finn admonished before giving her a resounding kiss on the mouth. "You weren't even there."

"Eirene." Graeme took her hand that lay on the table. "It wasn't anyone's fault. I was surprised when he suddenly became cold to the touch and ashen grey. I thought he might have been hurt when Herod barged out of the room." He let go of her hand, seeing the growing scowl on Finn's face. He gave Finn a shit-eating grin.

"Herod?"

"Dac's second-in-command," Finn said, still eyeing Graeme before turning his attention back to Eirene. "I didn't know Herod was there. I couldn't see a damn thing from the rooftop of the other building."

Graeme straightened on the bench, nodding. He frowned at the memory. "He was. Blake barrelled into Herod and before I could launch myself at them, Blake suddenly let go. Herod could have shot him point blank, but just shoved him off and left."

"Scatha Cruors, especially Herod would never pass at the chance to kill one of us," Roarke agreed with a puzzled frown.

"Well, I wish Blake would come back," Eirene replied. "The Faesten seems incomplete without him."

"I agree." Roarke gave her a short smile. "Let's get to the nerve centre and check on Colin and the rest."

As they stood up, Roarke's mobile phone rang. "Hamilton."

"Roarke?"

"My lady," Roarke said, smiling. "You came."

"In more ways than one, my lord."

Her lilting laugh through the phone zinged down to his groin and his cock suddenly woke.

"I'll be right there," Roarke replied, then closed his phone. He looked at his second-in-command. "Deanna's here. I'll pick her up from downstairs."

Finn nodded and they split up in the foyer. Roarke wanted to just leap out of the building and get to Deanna fast. But people on their way to work would probably think he was a jumper and call the police. Something the Cynn Cruor would rather not happen. Besides, the sun had already risen.

As the elevator opened to the ground floor, he pressed the hold button before striding the few steps to the door and opened it, taking care that the sun didn't touch him. As the weak rays of the sun streamed through, he felt the gradual simmer in his blood. Uncomfortable, but bearable.

The scent of ylang-ylang reached his senses before Deanna appeared. Roarke closed the door and backed her against the wall. He claimed her lips in a searing kiss which burned a trail down to his sex. Deanna opened up to him, her tongue twirling against his. He groaned as their tongues duelled, each wanting dominion over the other. His hand curled around her neck while his thumb rubbed against the sensitive spot behind her ear.

Deanna's moan sent his lust rampaging through his loins. His cock was harder than it had ever been. He rubbed it against her hip, wanting to bury himself inside her sweet warmth.

"Roarke." Deanna gasped against his mouth. "Please, I need you."

In a flash, Roarke pulled her inside the elevator. As the doors closed he punched in several numbers.

"That's a longer code." Deanna observed.

He turned to her. "It's the code to switch off the camera feed."

Deanna walked toward him. She opened her coat. His breath hissed through his teeth. She wore a simple wraparound dress of dark blue which cinched her waist and pushed her luscious breasts up. He pulled her against his body and devoured her lips before trailing open mouth kisses down the elegant length of her throat. When he reached the base, where her pulse beat erratically, he licked it, eliciting a sigh from her before he sucked on the tender flesh.

Hard.

Deanna held on to him, her head angled so he could suck more. She whimpered and begged him to continue. Through her skin, Roarke drew a little of her blood. His body rejoiced. His cock strained against his jeans.

Deanna was still his mate. The sweet drop invigorated his senses. He felt more strength literally flowing through his sinews. But there it was. He also tasted something metallic and bitter. No one had to tell him it was the Scatha's taint. Inside his body, Deanna's essence mixed with his own. The combination of their blood was stronger than Dac's contamination. He clenched his jaw at the stab of pain in his system, and then it was gone. His body had battled the taint.

He licked at the spot and felt Deanna shudder against him. She faced him, her eyes aglow with desire. She shrugged out of her coat and parted the bodice of her dress, taking her breast out of her lace bra. Without preamble, Roarke latched on to her tit, kneading the breast as he sucked and nipped at the aroused bud. When he lifted his mouth, she moaned, until she realized he was moving to give the jealous twin equal attention. In appreciation, Deanna cupped his erection before quickly unbuttoning his waistband and unzipping him. Roarke backed her to the corner of the elevator and lifted her. Deanna's dress parted to show her black lace-edged stockings held by a lace garter belt over a lace thong.

"My lady," he rasped. "This will have to be quick."

"Yes, Roarke," she said huskily, nipping at his neck. "Quick, hard, and rough."

Deanna pulled her underwear aside for him. Her sex was glistening and wet. The scent of her arousal enticed him even as it mixed with his own. In one thrust he was inside her. They both cried out in ecstasy.

He was mindless with lust as Deanna's sheath clung to his cock. He rode her as she bade him. Quick, hard, and fast. The sound of his cock pistoning in and out of her and the sweet slickness of her fluids coating him drove him wild. His cock thickened with each thrust. By the gods, he loved how his shaft felt as it deliciously scraped against the muscles of her sex. Deanna's pants and moans became the fuel which propelled him on—harder and harder—until her cries became louder and she fell apart in his arms. With every twitch of her sex against him, he followed her, the guttural cry of his orgasm lost against the softness of her neck.

Their laboured breathing and the hum of their afterglow filled the elevator. Reluctantly, Roarke removed his cock from her wet heat. Kneeling down, he kissed her, pleasuring her until she orgasmed again.

Half an hour later, they walked into the foyer, meticulously dressed.

When they entered the nerve centre, both Finn and Graeme inhaled sharply. Eirene grinned and walked to Deanna to embrace her.

"Welcome back," Eirene whispered.

Roarke could feel the emotions swirling around his mate. This was where she belonged and he was grateful for Eirene's gesture, making her feel welcome. He walked toward his fellow Cynn Cruor warriors as they studied the two women talking. Deanna's soft laughter sent tingles down his spine to stir his manhood anew.

"No wonder you didn't die. She was really still alive," Graeme commented.

"She's been through a lot," Roarke replied. "But she's willing to tell us everything so we can help those women and children. Has anybody heard from Devon?"

Deanna looked at their direction. "Devon?"

"She's got sharp hearing too. Sign of a true Cynn mate," Finn remarked.

Deanna's eyes twinkled in amusement. "My hearing was not this good before."

"Before what?" Finn queried.

Roarke grinned when a blush stole up Deanna's cheeks.

"That's enough, Qualtrough. You know very well after what." Eirene scowled in gentle reproach.

Finn's shoulders slightly shook with laughter.

"Don't mind him," Eirene said, facing Deanna.

"Oh, I won't," Deanna replied with a wry smile. "But, who's Devon?"

"Devon is Eirene's partner in a law firm," Finn answered as he sat on one of the couches that flanked the fireplace.

"You're a solicitor?" She looked at Eirene with interest.

Eirene chuckled, shaking her head. "More like the computer geek," she said. "Devon is the solicitor. I pulled him out of the streets and helped him get his life back."

At Deanna's confused frown, Roarke spoke, "Devon's wife left him and brought their child with her. When we viewed the footage Eirene was able to get from the Manchester Airport, the people whom they left with were Scatha."

"Penny is Devon's daughter," Deanna confirmed.

Roarke nodded. "After that debacle, he didn't have the will to live anymore until Eirene made a deal with him."

"He agreed to get out of the streets and return to lawyering and I would help him find his daughter. That's how I met Finn," Eirene said.

"Eirene has been checking on the computer systems of almost every corporation in the Northwest," Finn said. "After getting the footage from the airport, every system was suspect. Until she stumbled upon Dac's."

"How did you know it was Dac's?" Deanna asked in surprise.

"I didn't at first," Eirene confessed. "Devon had asked me to keep him company when one of his clients insisted on meeting at ten in the evening at the office. He said there was something not quite right with this client."

"Eirene didn't know their client was none other than Valerian himself. I was following a Scatha Cruor and never thought I'd see Dac." Finn's voice hardened. "He's the reason my parents are dead."

"I'm sorry," Deanna said softly.

Finn shrugged. "It was eons ago. Anyway, there was a little misunderstanding during the meeting and a fight broke out in Devon's office. Dac escaped. And I met Eirene for the second time."

"The second time?"

"The first time Finn met his mate was when Eirene fought against three Scatha and killed one," Graeme spoke, grinning in enjoyment.

"Oh, don't look at me like that, Dee," Eirene mumbled, her face red. She squirmed in her seat. "You'd think I had grown another head."

Finn and Graeme laughed. Eirene frowned at her mate.

"But Eirene, that's incredible!" Deanna exclaimed, stunned.

Roarke chuckled. "Eirene beat the crap out of them, my lady. Her weapons of choice were a telescopic baton and the Philippine *balisong*."

"What's that?"

"A butterfly knife," Graeme spoke up. "It's always been attributed to the Chinese which is farthest from the truth. The knife was named after a town in the islands."

"Wow," Deanna mouthed, staring at Eirene. She sat upright, her face lighting up. "Can you teach me?"

"Deanna," Roarke warned, straightening his stance. It was his turn to scowl.

"Sure!" Eirene's frown gave way to a happy grin. "Now there'll be two of us against five of them."

"Five?" Deanna asked. "I only counted four the last time."

"Oh, Blake is on vacation," Eirene said unconcerned. "He'll be back."

"My mate is always the optimist." Finn looked at Eirene with tenderness. "Come and sit beside me."

"No, Finn. I'll sit in front of my computer."

Finn's low growl only made Eirene giggle.

"You'll pay for that."

She batted her eyelashes at him and swung her hair over her shoulder. "I know."

Finn sighed in resignation. "Okay. Back to work then."

Roarke drew in a huge breath, then exhaled. He looked at Deanna. She seemed flustered and bewildered. The smile she gave them was genuine but wary. An ache tightened in his chest. He could only imagine how difficult it was for her not to be able to feel the warmth or the camaraderie he and the rest of the Cynn Cruor shared. Eirene's generosity of heart might just be what Deanna needed. And Eirene had called her Dee. He liked that. He shook his head as his mouth curved into a grin. “Have a seat, my lady.”

Roarke stifled the grin, widening his mouth when Deanna blushed. Ancients! She was the most beautiful creature he’d ever laid eyes on. And sexy as hell.

He sat down beside his mate and waited until everyone was comfortable.

“You all know Deanna is here to help us find Penny and the rest of the women and children the Scatha has kidnapped. She also wants to let you know what happened to her during the time she disappeared.”

“I don't think that’s necessary.” Graeme interrupted. “What happened to your mate should be between the two of you, Roarke. It isn't the Faesten's business.”

“I agree,” Finn said, nodding before looking at Deanna. “Deanna, what you're going to tell us is something very personal. The Cynn Cruor doesn't choose a warrior's mate. A mate chosen is a mate respected, cherished, and protected.”

“Please,” Deanna spoke before Roarke could reply. She placed her hand on his knee. Roarke felt the warmth of her simple caress flow through him. “Thank you for being considerate, but I have my reasons for telling you.”

She bit down on her lip as she took a deep breath. “One day in the future, someone will find out who I was and where I've been all this time. When they find out I’ve lived among the Scatha for centuries they will question my loyalty. That knowledge will not only affect Roarke. The entire Faesten and all who belong to it will be compromised. I will not allow that to happen.”

Roarke couldn't help the anxiety coursing through his veins at what Deanna was about to say. He just hoped he was strong enough to withstand another bout of torment he knew would come out of her confession.

Finn looked at him as though asking his approval, but he refused to acknowledge the request. This was Deanna. This was her time to let go. He would respect her decision.

He saw Finn's shoulders slump slightly before he nodded imperceptibly. At Graeme's reluctant nod, Roarke sighed.

“Very well,” Finn said. “You have the floor.”

Chapter Eleven

Deanna took a deep breath before letting it all out. Fear knotted inside of her. She recognized the feeling, for it had been her constant companion when she was with the Scatha Cruor. She'd never told anyone of the terror she experienced living with Dac. Not even Emeline Dalton. This was different. She would learn to live with the humiliation of what she was going to say. But the children and the women? Deanna didn't think she could live with her conscience if she didn't even at least try to do something. She hoped that by telling them the whole story they might find a way to destroy Dac.

"After the Faesten was razed to the ground, I was taken to Dac," she began, looking at Roarke. "You spoke to me of Dac and the Scatha, but I didn't know what they looked like."

She shuddered. Roarke entwined his fingers through hers and squeezed her hand. She smiled, squeezing back.

"Dac realized I was a Cynn mate, but he didn't know to whom I belonged. I had no intention of telling him either. All he could talk about was destroying Hamel Dun Creag and the Hamiltons. He was furious that none of the Hamiltons had been captured or killed.

Deanna felt the familiar dread she'd experienced that fateful night trickle down her spine. Her stomach roiled at the memory. "The Scatha searched Hamel Dun Creag and the surrounding areas, but couldn't find any Cynn Cruor left alive. That's when Dac turned his anger toward me."

Deanna's eyes scalded with unshed tears. She refused to look at anyone, nearly balking at the shame of what she was about to confess. She drew a haggard breath before speaking. "He ordered that I be stripped and tied to a tree and took a whip to my back."

Eirene gasped in shock, her hand to her mouth. Deanna stole a glance at her and saw tears beginning to form in Eirene's eyes before falling down her face. Eirene could cry for her.

"Then he raped me in front of his men."

Eirene made a sound before sobbing softly into her hands.

Deanna felt the rumble beside her.

"Roarke," Finn warned, sitting forward, ready to launch at his brother.

Deanna could feel how Roarke was finding it difficult to keep his fury in check. She felt it thrum through his body as he sat beside her. She saw him close his eyes, his jaw clenched so hard it looked painful. But when he opened his eyes, they were still the colour of burnt orange. He looked at her, anger stamped on his visage.

And torment.

"I can stop," she whispered.

"No," Roarke said through gritted teeth. His Adam's apple convulsed as he swallowed. Finally, he exhaled. "I'll be fine."

Slowly he stood and walked toward the window. Roarke kept his back to them. "Continue, my lady," he said softly, not turning around. "We have to know everything."

Deanna looked at Finn for confirmation. Finn took a few moments before nodding, his face also stark with his own anger.

She swallowed against the lump in her throat. "After the first night and several nights thereafter, I finally realized I would never be able to escape and fighting Dac was futile. As soon as I gave in to everything he wanted, the whipping stopped. I became a body to be used over and over again. He raped me repeatedly until Dac convinced himself he'd removed the Cynn Cruor's scent." She paused, bowing her head to look at her hands on her lap. "I believed it too."

Everyone remained silent. Deanna looked up and tried to smile. "If there was any saving grace, Dac kept me for himself. He didn't allow anyone else to touch me. But neither did he allow me any clothes. I remained naked all the time."

Deanna bit the inside of her mouth to stop the whimper which begged to come from her lips. "I thought I wouldn't be able to bear the humiliation. When Dac wasn't around, his men jeered at me and made statements I'd rather not repeat. I wanted to die, but I had no means of killing myself." She looked at Eirene's tear stained face and gave her a smile of sorrow.

"By the time summer arrived, I was so used to parading naked, it didn't matter anymore. I had been reduced to a piece of property, a possession, existing solely for one man's depravity at any time and any place."

She looked at Roarke's rigid back. He hadn't moved from the window. He looked like a statue of a sentinel surveying the city below. She didn't know if he was still listening or if he was just trying to hold on to his own thin line of sanity.

She continued. "By then, we'd arrived in South Barrule on the Isle of Man. Soon enough, Dac tired of me. With the women he captured, there was always fresh meat he could taste before he sold them."

She suddenly stood up, too agitated to remain seated.

"Because I had not tried to escape, I was given more freedom around the stronghold. But there was always someone guarding me. During one of my forays into the woods, I told my guard I had to relieve myself. Not wanting to feel the brunt of Dac's anger, he allowed me my small amount of privacy. I was only a few metres away when I stumbled over what I thought was a fallen log. But it wasn't a fallen log. It was a small trapdoor."

This time Roarke turned. Gone was the man who'd ignited her passion and brought her to heights of ecstasy she never knew existed. Her heart sank as she resumed.

"For several days I visited the place until my guard got so used to my comings and goings, he didn't care what I did. Once I was able to ply him with enough drink that he passed out. When he did, I went to work finding out where the opening would take me. It took me to Herod's room."

"Finn, has Colin checked in?" Roarke asked, looking at his brother.

"Not yet," Finn replied, as Graeme faced the bank of computers to check on the Away Team's current location. "Do we tell them of the secret passageway?"

"Yes, but not to begin the attack," Roarke replied. "That's the Scatha's territory. They will be outmanoeuvred and out-gunned. Tell them to do a thorough recon."

"No one knows about the passageway, Roarke," Deanna said. "Only I do. It took me a good two days to even make the door move on its hinges. I always covered it when I left."

"Even so. They might have found it already. And knowing what we know of how Dac cloaked his location, I wouldn't be surprised if the entire area is littered with cameras."

"Understood," Finn agreed.

Just then the phone rang. Graeme answered it before returning it to its cradle. A moment later, the map of the Northwest was replaced by the face of Colin Butler. The tension in the room slightly abated, everyone taking deep breaths.

"Speaking of the devil," Finn drawled.

Colin gave out a hearty laugh. "Quite close, Qualtrough. Just checking in. We arrived safely."

"Colin."

"Roarke." Colin acknowledged him with a grin. "Good to see you, my friend."

"Likewise." Roarke smiled in return. "We've received new information about the location of a secret passageway to get into Dac's stronghold."

"Really?" Colin raised both his thick eyebrows. He smiled, but this time it didn't reach his eyes. "Where is this secret passage?"

"By the forest in South Barrule," Deanna spoke, moving closer to the wall.

Colin whistled when he noticed Deanna.

"She's with me, Colin, so don't get any ideas." Roarke's friendly voice had a steel edge to it.

Colin raised his hands up. "No need to be touchy, Hamilton. Point taken."

Deanna felt Roarke's eyes on her, because her heart skipped a beat. Steeling her nerves, she waited for Graeme to change to the terrain's feed. From above ground, she couldn't get her bearings.

"Graeme, can you zoom in?" she asked, walking closer to the screen. She exhaled, both to calm her nerves and to let go of some of the frustration that was starting to build inside her. "The place looks so unfamiliar looking at it from above."

"Graeme," Roarke simply said.

"Done, Dux," Graeme said, fishing out his mobile phone. "Dan, I need a favour. Can you check if you can get any forest view feed for South Barrule?"

"What are you doing?" she asked.

"If Roarke's assumption is correct, and there are indeed cameras all over the place, we might be able to hack into the system and get a feed from the ground," Graeme replied before his attention reverted to what Dan was saying. His face contorted with vexation. "Bloody hell!"

"You can't hack in, can you?" Eirene stated as she sniffed. She sat in front of her keyboard. "Can I speak with Dan?"

Graeme handed her the mobile phone. Eirene held it between her ear and shoulder, her face filled with purpose. "Talk to me."

Graeme looked at Finn, arching a brow. One side of Finn's mouth lifted as he shrugged.

Eirene's fingers flew over the keys. Everyone waited with bated breath. Finally, she pressed the "Enter" key.

The satellite feed was replaced by a ground view.

Graeme whistled. Finn's lopsided grin widened to a smile. He walked toward his mate, lifted her from her seat and gave her a resounding kiss.

"You never cease to amaze me," he said softly before encircling her in his embrace.

The woodland was all fresh green and reddish brown after the rains. Oak and Hazel trees dotted it. Narrow and thick trunks spread out over a wide area, but they were also placed where a copse struggled to remain together.

Deanna turned her attention back to the screen. Seeing the place of her prison over a century ago brought back images she'd rather bury in her mind. She puckered her forehead in concentration. "Eirene, can I manipulate the view on the screen?"

Eirene turned in Finn's arms. "Yeah sure, Dee. Here."

Deanna walked toward her. Eirene told her to sit down.

"Thanks," Deanna said.

Using the mouse, she made her way through the forest, imagining herself meandering through the trees of what was now called the Watertrough Park located north-east of the ruined fort. Her anxiety soon simmered to the surface and mingled with her frustration. She had to stand up and walk away for a few moments. With a hurried excuse, she left the library. No one stopped her as she left the nerve centre.

She couldn't stop her body shaking. Gritting her teeth, she forced herself to put one foot after the other. Her fear was beginning to paralyze her. Her legs were so stiff she wouldn't be surprised if they broke underneath her. Like a drunk trying to walk straight, she headed toward the kitchen.

The smell of freshly baked bread, sweet pancakes, sausages, and bacon should have made her mouth water, but it only made her nauseous. She hadn't had breakfast before she left her flat, because she couldn't wait to get back to Roarke. She smiled at the chef and those who turned their heads when she came in, but made a beeline to the dining hall. Grateful that it was empty for the moment, she looked around and spotted the beverage counter. She got a glass for water, but the hand holding the glass was shaking so badly, she had to put it back down on the table. She leaned her hands on the table's surface and closed her eyes, inhaling deeply to calm her nerves. She didn't know how long she stood there, but the sudden sound of bubbles expelling from the water dispenser brought her back to the present. Someone offered her the glass of water. She reached out to accept it, but the other hand did not let go. Instead, it held the glass and offered it to her lips.

The frisson of desire and tenderness which coursed through her from their hands touching did a lot to calm her nerves.

"Thank you," she said after drinking more than half the glass. A drop of water hung precariously in the middle of her lower lip. But as she stuck her tongue out to lick it, another pair of lips swooped down with the very same intention. Sighing, she opened her mouth, allowing Roarke's tongue to play with hers and to nibble on her lips. She melted into his embrace. Her arms encircled his waist and her mouth slanted against his to deepen his kiss. She didn't care who, if anyone, was watching them. She didn't care if Roarke had been cold and unapproachable in the nerve centre. She didn't care if he was only kissing her so she could gather her wits about her and continue telling them about the passageway's location. Because at that very moment, Deanna just needed him. She needed his warm body close against hers. To feel his entire muscular length sheltering her own soft one. And to regain her resolve from his strength.

Slowly, she broke the kiss and lay her cheek on his chest. She closed her eyes and concentrated on the heavy thud of his heart against her ear. Like a lullaby it reassured her. Everything was going to be all right. If only she could stay like this forever.

But forever was a myth.

"I'm fine now, Roarke. Thank you."

"Are you sure you want to do this?" he asked, kissing her hair. He lifted her chin before his hand curled around her nape. He swirled his thumb against the sensitive spot behind her ear. Deanna shivered at the sensual caress.

She nodded. "The sooner I'm able to tell you where the stronghold is, the better it will be for me."

Roarke looked at her as though he wanted to say something. For a brief moment, she thought she saw the passionate man reflected in his eyes. But it was gone quickly. With a curt nod, Roarke placed his hand on the small of her back to lead her once more to the nerve centre.

When she arrived, she was only too grateful that Roarke's inner circle treated her like nothing had happened. Returning to her seat, she took a deep breath and began to trawl through the forest. The coordinates showed on the lower right hand corner of the screen. She concentrated on where she was going, refusing to let the panic of seeing the familiar engulf her.

Deeper into the woodlands she went. Then she stopped the mouse. Remnants of a fallen log dominated the left bank of the screen.

"That's it," her voice was less than a whisper. "There." She pointed to the log. "Lift that log and the door to the passageway will be underneath it. The log should be hollow, and if you find a tattered cloth inside you will know it's the right one."

"It might have disintegrated already," Graeme said.

"It will be there."

Graeme nodded. With a push of a button, Colin's feed appeared on the lower left hand side of the LED screen and Graeme relayed the information to him. Roarke stood beside Graeme as he barked out orders to Colin.

Deanna slumped on the chair, completely drained. Her bones ached with the tension she'd put upon herself. Her neck was stiff and her back felt as though it had locked. Behind her, she heard Finn whisper sweet words to Eirene, asking her if she wanted to take a break.

"No, Babe." Deanna heard Eirene say. "Hopefully, we're close to finding Penny. I can take a break later." Then in a teasing voice, "Besides, you did say you were going to make me pay for my being sassy earlier."

"I didn't forget, Eirene," Finn growled softly.

Deanna heard Eirene's breath hitch. A smile flitted across her lips. That was how she felt when she was with Roarke. She looked at the screen again. In the distance, something moved in the forest. For a moment she thought it was just the leaves from the trees located further in the distance. But the movement became a shadow, and as it neared the screen took the shape of a man. Her breath caught in her throat and the blood drained from her face. She wasn't in the Faesten anymore. She was in the woodlands again and the Scatha Cruor was walking toward her.

She was trapped. She could feel the cold wind raising the fine hairs on her skin. Her breathing came out in shallow gasps. The smell of wet leaves and the damp earth assailed her nostrils once again. Her heart's pulse thudded to a heavy, slow and painful beat in her chest, her throat and her temples. She looked down. She was naked. Again.

The Scatha warrior still hadn't seen her. She looked around her. There was no place to hide. She was too far away from the cluster of trees. Dear God! Why was she here? How could she have been transported? She heard the roar of the waves from the Irish Sea. She frowned. The sea was nowhere close by. Why could she hear it? Her frightened gaze returned to the warrior. She whimpered. He was less than twenty feet from her.

Fifteen feet.

Ten feet. His gaze still searching for something in the woods.

Five feet.

He looked at her, sneering.

Deanna screamed.

Chapter Twelve

"Deanna! Deanna! Wake up!" Roarke said harshly. He held her in his arms, but she struggled. Her eyes were glassy. She couldn't hear him. The harrowing terror on his mate's face stabbed through him, almost robbing him of rational thinking.

"Finn, get Zac back here right away," he snapped.

"On it."

"What do you want me to do?" Eirene asked, her panic for Deanna etched on her face.

"Please help Graeme get the coordinates to Colin and the Cynn warriors," he instructed her in a gentler tone. "You are our eyes now, Eirene. Graeme will need to brief the rest of the Cynn."

He turned to Graeme. "Have everyone assembled in the Agora in thirty."

"Understood."

Roarke carried Deanna, even as she struggled. He leaped up to the mezzanine and rushed through the aisle toward the reading room. Beside it was another door which led to the second floor rooms. He opened the door and with supernatural speed, reached his quarters. Swinging the door open, he strode into the room and laid her gently in the middle of the bed. Deanna had ceased to be hysterical, but her body was racking with dry sobs. Roarke was about to leave the bed, when her hand shot out, gripping his shirt.

"No!"

Roarke's chest tightened at the fear in her eyes. "I'm just going to close the door, Deanna."

She didn't hear him, her eyes still panic stricken.

He leaned down and kissed her tenderly. She froze. Then, as though she was ice thawing, she yielded, encircling his neck with her arms. Deanna's tongue teased his mouth, desperately seeking entrance. Roarke groaned. His shaft was taking notice of the activity up north. Reluctantly, he ended the kiss. She gripped his shirt.

"Let me close the door, my lady. I will come back."

She searched his face for long moments before her fingers loosened their grip.

When he returned, Deanna was in a fetal position. Her dress had parted to show off her stocking clad legs and pert bottom. He lay beside her and pulled her to him. She rested her cheek on his shoulder.

"I thought I was back." Her voice was hollow. "I saw myself naked again and the Scatha grinning at me. I had nowhere to hide." Roarke felt her shudder. He held her closer.

"No one will hurt you, Deanna. No one can come here and take you away from me again. You're safe."

She didn't respond. Her breathing calmed and soon she was asleep, her face relaxing.

Roarke stared at the ceiling, his mind roiling with images of what Deanna had gone through. And for the first time in his entire immortal life, blood red tears blurred his vision. The helplessness he felt at the loss of his mate's innocence in the hands of Dac clamped around his heart like an iron chain. When he spoke to the Ancient Eald and the Deoré about the possibility of Deanna already being dead, he wasn't far from the truth. Dac had killed Deanna and left her with a wound so deep that it was possible she would never find herself again. He felt responsible for what happened to her. If Deanna had joined him to fight the Scatha, she wouldn't have fallen into Dac's hands and she would have been spared the horrors of what she'd gone through. If she had joined him and died while they fought the invaders, the horrors would not have come to pass and he would have joined her soon enough, instead of having lived a non-existent life until she returned.

He looked at her sleeping form. She was a fragile flower clothed with an armour of steel. But even steel needed attention, lest it rust. After what happened in the nerve centre, there was no way Roarke would let Deanna leave the Faesten. He would insist she stay within the walls of their stronghold. Roarke closed his eyes, dreading the possibility of even having to curtail her from leaving the premises. He hoped it wouldn't come to that. She would be protected and kept safe with the Cynn Cruor around. He traced her jaw with his finger before his thumb caressed her bottom lip. She stirred, but didn't wake. She wiggled herself closer to him, flinging her left arm over his chest and her left leg over both his legs. He grunted. Her mound grinding against his hip was enough for his cock to twitch to a hard-on.

A soft knock made him turn toward the door. Roarke exhaled. His lust would have to wait. Easing himself away from Deanna's sleeping form, he went to answer the door.

"Roarke."

Roarke sighed in relief. "Really sorry I had to pull you out of your shift, Zac. Something happened to Deanna when she was giving us the coordinates of Dac's stronghold."

"Yes, Finn briefed me." Zac's voice was grave. "The Cynn warriors are beginning to assemble in the dining hall. Can you ask Eirene to come over? I will stay here until she arrives. Your mate shouldn't be left alone."

Roarke nodded. He walked back to Deanna's sleeping form. A strong wave of emotion almost drove him to his knees. He was leaving his beloved again in a room. In his very own Faesten. The only difference was that history would not be repeating itself in the 21st century.

He bent down and was engulfed in her sweet scent. He inhaled deeply, taking part of her essence with him. He turned her chin with his fingers. Her forehead creased into a frown, but she didn't wake. Then Roarke gently covered her mouth with his.

He closed his eyes, savouring her lips' texture, their softness, their taste. She moaned softly in her sleep and when Roarke prodded her mouth with his tongue, she opened up willingly. Roarke groaned. Zac was waiting by the door, but he didn't care. He was making love to his mate's mouth, all of his desire pouring into the kiss. All of his hopes and dreams and promises were being transmitted into Deanna's heart, mind and soul. And Deanna welcomed him. She welcomed every touch, every caress. Until finally he had to drag his mouth away and bury his face by her ear.

"I love you Deanna," he whispered, before he stood up and left the room. Never had he felt so torn between staying with Deanna and taking his place as the Dux of the Manchester Faesten until now.

And for one brief moment he wished he could let go of the responsibilities of being a Cynn Cruor.

****

"I love you."

Those three words echoed through the caverns of her mind, bringing much needed relief by keeping the shadows at bay. Roarke had held her after she screamed, she knew that. But the sight of the Scatha Cruor walking through the woodland toward her broke the dam which held her fear. All of her terror came crashing down around her. The onslaught did not allow her to surface from her nightmare.

I love you. She heard Roarke's voice, but wasn't sure he had really said the words.

She rolled on to her back before she opened her eyes, blinking several times to chase sleep away.

"God, I'm such a wreck," Deanna whispered to the room.

"Oh, thank God, you're awake!" Eirene sat down on the bed to hold her hand. "Are you okay? We were so helpless earlier; we didn't know how we could bring you back. Roarke was shaking you, but you couldn't feel him."

Deanna swallowed and realized her throat was parched. "I need water," she croaked.

"I'll get it." Eirene strode to the bathroom and got her a glass of water, returning in less than a minute.

Deanna drank, feeling the cool liquid soothe her throat.

"Thank you," she said gratefully as she placed the empty glass on the bedside table. "Roarke?"

"He's downstairs with the rest of the warriors briefing them on the mission," Eirene replied. "Zac asked that I stay here with you. He said you shouldn't be alone."

"Zac's here?"

"Yes," Eirene said. "Roarke asked Finn to pull Zac away from his duty at the Manchester Royal Infirmary. It was just a good thing there were a lot of heavy clouds signalling rain, or else Finn's blood would be boiling."

Deanna nodded, understanding the Cynn bane of not being able to go out when the sun was too high in the sky. She plopped her head on the pillow. "I have to thank Zac. He's right. If you hadn't been here when I woke up, I would have remembered the last time I was left alone in Roarke's room. It was the last time I saw him, too." She took a deep breath and exhaled noisily. "I really lost it, didn't I?"

"No one blames you, Dee," Eirene said, a soft smile playing on her mouth. "You're a very strong woman to have survived your ordeal." Then she took a sharp breath.

Deanna looked at Eirene. "Go on. You were about to say something."

Eirene reddened. "It's none of my business."

"Eirene."

"Okay." Eirene let out her breath and it blew her fringe lightly off her forehead. "After what happened to you, you're still able to be with Roarke. I honestly don't know what I would have done if I were in your place. I probably would've killed myself."

Deanna's mouth curved into a humourless smile. She shrugged, but didn't say anything for a time.

"I came to that point, believe me," she admitted. "But I wasn't going to give Dac the satisfaction of breaking me. It's just fortunate I met Emeline Dalton. She saved me from going out of my mind. I just had to bide my time. I guess someone up there heard my prayers of wanting to escape the island."

"Who's Emeline Dalton?"

Deanna proceeded to tell Eirene about the woman who had saved her life. An hour later, Eirene whistled. "That's incredible. She must have been your guardian angel."

Deanna smiled. "Yes, she was. In more ways than one." She swung her legs off the bed. "Eirene, I have to do some errands. I've given the coordinates to Dac's lair, so that will help you."

"Dee..." Eirene hesitated. "Roarke wants you to remain here."

Deanna didn't stand up right away. Instead, she turned to Eirene. "Why?"

"After what happened to you in the nerve centre, he doesn't want you out of his sight." Eirene raised her hand to stop her from talking. "I know it's none of my business, but you were pretty hysterical earlier. Roarke is just worried about you being alone."

"So, I'm a prisoner."

"No, you're not. You'll just be among friends," Eirene said gently. "Wasn't that what you wanted all along?"

Eirene's simple statement brought everything home and Deanna couldn't find it in her heart to be irritated with Roarke insisting on making decisions for her. In fact, she was glad he cared enough to lay down the law to her. She'd been alone for such a long time, it felt good to have someone take charge of her well-being. Even just for a moment.

The word *prisoner* reared its ugly head in her mind, causing doubt to encroach into her thoughts. Whatever the case may be, she still had errands to do.

Her shoulders slumped from exhaustion. "Well, if I have to stay here...I'll need clothes from my flat." She stood up and ran her fingers through her hair to give it some semblance of order. Looking around, she found her coat draped on the armchair.

"Why don't I come with you?" Eirene suggested, standing up. They were almost of the same height with Eirene just a few centimetres shorter. "I'm a Cynn Cruor mate, so we're not breaking any rules." She winked.

Deanna chuckled. "I'd like that. I need to get away from all the testosterone for a while."

Eirene's eyes lit with amusement. "Uh huh."

Both women giggled.

Eirene led her back to the nerve centre, but as they walked, Deanna couldn't help but admire the wood panelled walls which flanked the hallway and the lush carpet underneath their feet. The Faesten was more like a luxurious boutique hotel than a fortress. Soft light from wall sconces illuminated their way. Then she stopped at the long tapestry dominating one wall which looked similar to the

Bayeaux tapestry. Covered in non-glare glass, it had several figures in battle scenes.

"Beautiful, isn't it?"

Deanna looked at Eirene and nodded.

"It's the Cynn Cruor's story," Eirene began. "How the Ancient Eald created them and how they came to possess a mixture of human, vamp, and werewolf DNA. The Kinare gene."

"What did the Ancient Eald hope to accomplish?" Deanna asked, her curiosity piqued.

Eirene shrugged. "Finn says the Ancient's reasons may have changed over the centuries. All he knows is that the Cynn Cruor were created to protect and contribute to human society."

Deanna murmured, "The Ancient Eald must have had a reason for creating the Cynn Cruor in the first place. Now there are two of them—good and evil."

"It wasn't like that before."

"I know," Deanna agreed. "Roarke told me about Dac turning away from all that they stood for and that he formed the Scatha after his failed attempt to kill the Cynn Eald and rule the Cynn Cruor himself."

"Saved by the Deoré." Eirene's mouth curved into a smile. "The mate who is chosen always protects her warrior." She looked at Deanna, respect in her eyes. "And you protected Roarke more than we can ever imagine."

"Let's go," Deanna said.

She saw Eirene stiffen, momentarily abashed.

Deanna relented. "I'm sorry, Eirene. I didn't mean to be ungrateful. I'm just not used to being complimented."

"Then we're no different." Eirene's mouth quirked as she nodded in understanding. "C'mon. Let's get to the nerve centre and I'll tell Finn where we're going."

Eirene led her through the same corridor that Roarke took from the second floor, so they didn't have to pass through the foyer. Deanna took out her phone as they walked, pressing the number for her driver and bodyguard, motioning for Eirene to go ahead without her so she could complete the call. When she left for the Faesten that morning, she'd decided to drive herself to the Cynn headquarters. She didn't want Phil to know where she'd gone and it was also for his safety that he didn't know.

"I'm hardly a bodyguard if you don't tell me where you're going," Phil said, concerned.

"I'll be fine," Deanna assured him. "Besides, it's time you took a holiday. I don't recall you ever having one."

"I travel where you go."

"That's hardly a vacation," she commented in a dry tone. "Take one without having to worry about me for as long as you like. I'll call you when I need you."

"Deanna, I don't think—"

"Phil, trust me. I'm in the safest place I could ever be."

"The people who are after you..." He paused, doubt still lacing his voice. "They won't know where you are?"

"Have they been able to find where I am now?" she countered, but Phil had nearly hit the nail on the head. The outcome of what she was doing to help Roarke and the rest could alert the Scatha of her whereabouts.

She heard Phil's long drawn sigh. "Fair enough."

She still sensed his uncertainty over the phone.

"Okay, I'll make a deal with you. If you still don't want to take your vacation, help Jenny with the Foundation. You can help spruce up security. I'll let Jenny know you're coming in, but the vacation offer still stands, Phil. I'm just rewarding you," she assured him.

"Vacation?" he teased.

"Old habits die hard," she said, amusement in her voice. "Besides, I can do that, you know? Not all employers are as generous as I am. Your salary will keep on coming. Have the travel agency book you to any destination you want and charge it to my account."

"Fine," he said. "I'll check up on Jenny and if I feel like it, I'll take that break."

"Excellent," Deanna said, pleased.

Completing the call, she pressed another pre-set number.

"Jenny? It's Deanna." Her voice reflected her sincere smile. "I'm sending Phil there to work with you. I'll be driving myself around and will be staying with friends. How have things been?"

"Hey, Deanna." Jenny's voice on the other end sounded tired. "That's no problem and things have been good and bad."

"Oh? Why?" Deanna frowned, slowing down. Eirene had already descended the spiral staircase.

"Good, because we're turning a profit from the crafts we've been making and each one of the women have received their share."

"That's great news!" Deanna was pleased. The women she'd rescued would be able to turn their lives around. "And the bad news?"

"We've been monitoring Scotland Yard. There's been a spate of women and children disappearing all over the U.K. again. And it looks like it's the same modus operandi of kidnapping them from clubs or children disappearing on their way to or from school."

"Shit! You're sure?" Deanna bit her lower lip.

"Afraid so."

"Why isn't it in the news?"

"Since when has Scotland Yard ever told the British public the entire story?" Jenny scoffed.

Deanna blew out an anxious sigh. Dac was on the hunt again. The Scatha were always on the prowl, but the full scale abductions only occurred periodically. This wasn't good. She had no way of finding out where the Scatha would strike next. Not once had she ever asked any of the women to track the Scatha for her. She was the only one who could do it since the Scatha didn't know how she looked anymore. Only Dac and his right hand, Herod knew. And when she did track them, she made sure she stuck to the shadows. Doing so had thrown the Scatha off her scent many times, but that didn't make her any less vigilant.

That was how she'd seen Roarke again. She'd tracked Dac and the Scatha in the *Dare You!* Club, looking for the women the Scatha had kidnapped. When she'd arrived, Deanna had meandered around inside, sticking to the shadows and making sure her face could not be tracked on the club's cameras when pandemonium struck. She had ducked when she heard an explosion, her sharp hearing picking it up from outside, even in the midst of all the loud music. Then she heard screams coming from the area of the door diagonally across the dance floor. She was jostled from side to side as she forced her way through the crowd, making a beeline toward it while the patrons squeezed to get to the only entrance and exit. Deanna had opened the door and was greeted by a dimly lit hallway with several doors flung open. She took her mace out, holding it with her right hand as she slowly looked into the rooms. They were empty, save for one, where she heard whimpering. When she looked in, there were two women huddled together in the corner, their hair unkempt, their eye make-up running down their cheeks in black tears. They screamed when they saw her, but she assured them she was there to help. She found two coats for them and told them to put them on. She'd asked if there was another way out and one of the women led her to a side door, opposite from the Club's door. Quickly, they left the premises. Toward the club's front, the screams of both men and women filled the night air. Her car was a hundred yards away in the shadows of the factories and industrial buildings which surrounded the club. As she turned to usher the women ahead of her, she'd seen Roarke. From his frozen stance and the way he was unmindful of the crowd that swarmed around him, Deanna knew he'd seen her. But she had to get the women out and bring them to the Haven Foundation so Jenny could start helping them heal from their ordeal.

Now, as she leaned back against one of the bookshelves with her mobile phone still by her ear, she thought of the women who could be the Scatha's next victims. There were so many of them and she was just one against many. But she had to do something.

"Thanks for letting me know, Jenny. I'll scout around the City Centre later."

"It's a weekday, Deanna. The crowd won't be as thick for any snatchings to occur."

Deanna shook her head. "We're not quite sure about that. Printworks might yield something. It's pretty chaotic there."

"Call Phil, then. He can back you up as he's always done in the past." Jenny suggested. "You'll never know what chaos you'll encounter."

Deanna chuckled. "So much for offering him some time off." She sighed. "Okay. I'm not scouring the clubs until later anyway."

"Be careful."

"Will do."

As she turned to follow Eirene, she locked her phone, but stopped mid-stride. Deanna felt like melting when she saw who was in the corridor.

Roarke slowly closed the gap. Deanna's face heated up beneath his gaze. Her neck slowly angled up the closer he came to her. His eyes darkened as he zeroed in on her lips. Her mouth parted as her heartbeat sped up her breathing. Then his mouth hovered over hers, their breaths mingling. Deanna closed her eyes at the invisible caress. Her lips involuntarily puckered as they felt the tip of his tongue flicking against them before his teeth grazed her mouth. Then his tongue was inside, inviting her own tongue for some erotic play. Deanna moaned, opening up to Roarke's slow, but heated possession. Their tongues swirled, teased, mated as their bodies moved against each other. Her hips cradled his long and hard erection. Her hands were on Roarke's hair, her palms enjoying its texture while his hands palmed her buttocks, squeezing them, pulling her against him. Deanna shivered as Roarke trailed a path of kisses against the corner of her mouth, up to her ear where he trailed the tip of his tongue over the shell of her ear and down to her earlobe. She pressed her breasts against his hard chest, a moan escaping her when he started another trail of open mouth kisses from the sensitive skin behind her ear, down the side of her throat, to the pulse thrumming at the base of her neck. She felt the familiar ripple of desire centering in her womb, causing her core to cry for release.

Then Roarke pulled away and took her hand. He opened the door to the reading room, closing it behind her.

"Turn around," he commanded softly into her ear, bringing delicious shivers to cascade down her spine.

"Lights." She gasped.

"No lights, Deanna." His deep voice brought tremors of lust to flood her bloodstream. Her body was so attuned to Roarke's, her buttocks were writhing against his hard shaft. He groaned at her erotic dance. "Just feel. I want you to feel everything when I make love to you."

Excitement filled her insides, making her senses sharper. Roarke tugged on her coat and she shrugged it off. She wanted to feel his skin against hers, so she started to undress.

"No, Deanna. I will undress you." Roarke's voice was so close to her ear, she jumped in reflex. A low rumble came from his chest.

She sighed when she felt his hands skimming her body, moulding them against her hips, her waist, and moving forward to cup her breasts. She gasped in pleasure when he palmed them, her head leaning back against his shoulder. Her channel flooded when he slipped his palms inside the lacy cups of her bra and started to tease her nipples, tweaking and pinching them until they became hard nubs of desire. She whimpered, throwing her head against Roarke's chest as she gave herself to the sensual experience of his fingers on her tits. She cried in protest when it ended so soon, but Roarke began to pull her dress down from her shoulders and planted kisses on her body as more skin was exposed. Her dress fell with a swish in a heap at her feet. He held her as she lifted one leg, then the other so that he could throw her dress over the stuffed chair together with her coat. She sighed as his hands moved up and down her legs slowly, moving to tease her inner thighs. Deanna widened her legs, welcoming his intrusion, but he didn't touch her. She groaned in frustration.

"Patience, my lady."

She turned to look at him over her shoulder. From the dim light coming from the frozen glass windows above the door, she saw Roarke remove his shirt and undo his pants, letting them fall to the floor. He undid his shoes and socks and stood. Deanna's breath hitched at the sight of his cock jutting out proudly. She turned to face him and removed her bra, then her thong before stepping out of her heels and taking her lace-edged stockings off. Her body burned from the heat of his gold flecked eyes. She was mesmerized when he palmed his erection, stroking it up and down, imagining her sex doing the stroking.

"Face the door." Deanna did as she was told. A heady feeling of unbridled excitement and lust boiled inside her, and automatically her buttocks inched a little higher in anticipation of his penetration. She gasped when Roarke fit his hard body against her back. He grabbed her hair and gently moved her head to one side so he could nibble on her neck. She sighed in contentment and then moaned when his other hand slid between her thighs to cup her mound. Her hips rocked sensually as his finger slowly slicked its way over her clit before moving lower to enter her wet channel. She reached back to hold on to his hard shaft while her right hand encircled his wrist as he pleasured her femininity. Roarke placed another finger inside while his thumb played with her engorged clit. Deanna arched her back, her hips gyrating against Roarke's hand. His finger thrusts became faster and she could feel the orgasm building inside her. She whimpered, almost in release, then Roarke stopped, but kept his fingers inside of her. He wasn't moving.

"Tell me what you want," he rasped against her ear, then gently bit her earlobe.

"I want to come, Roarke." She gasped. She continued to move her hips and play with his erection.

"As you wish."

Then his fingers moved, making a come-hither motion inside of her. It was a different, but pleasurable sensation.

"Oohhh..." She leaned forward, spreading her legs wider. She could feel the trickle of her juices coating her inner thighs. Then Roarke sped up his fingers, so fast, lending to the coil of desire tightening inside her womanhood. Her heart pounded in her ribs and the pleasure balled until it exploded inside of her.

"Oh, God! Roarke!" she screamed her release, her entire being exploding, her molecules rising like bubbles in ecstasy as her vagina twitched against Roarke's fingers.

Then his fingers left her heat only to be replaced by his hard shaft. Deanna angled her opening toward Roarke's cock head and they both moaned audibly when he entered her in one fast and deep thrust.

"You are mine, Deanna." Roarke's deep voice was husky with his need as he thrust in and out slowly. "Say it, my lady. Say you're mine."

Deanna's breath hitched, then she sighed. Roarke was telling the truth.

"I'm yours, Roarke. I always have been and always will be."

She turned her head to meet his lips, their mouths imitating what their bodies were doing. As her desire built inside her, she broke the kiss and faced forward. She rose up on her tiptoes to get Roarke in a better angle to reach her pleasure spot. Her hands were flat against the door. Roarke's hand moved toward her breasts, kneading and playing with her nipples, even as he thrust long and deep into her. His other hand splayed against her pelvic bone before his fingers teased and played with her nub.

Their bodies danced and held each other, while their sighs and moans fell from their lips. Their sensual and gentle love making brought them solace from the pain of their separation.

Deanna was lifted to a plain of bliss with each and every stroke Roarke made inside of her. As she felt his cock lengthen and grow, she opened her eyes and looked down. A shimmering opalescent glow surrounded them.

It was then she knew without a doubt that she was indeed Roarke's mate, to hell with the self-doubt and recrimination. No matter what had happened to her, she had been chosen to be by his side. It was a destiny she could not escape.

And a destiny she looked forward to.

Roarke began to thrust faster. Deanna moaned her approval, bending a little to give him more access to her core. Roarke held on to her hips as his strokes lengthened, then shortened before taking her quick and fast. A whimper fell from her lips, pleasure rising again. She closed her eyes, giving herself over to Roarke's possession, plunging into her heat, her core's muscles gripping him hard, intensifying both their pleasure.

"Oh, yes," she said over and over again. Her cries became shriller as the pounding lust inside her became a raging ball of fire. And as Roarke hit her womb, she cried out, succumbing to the explosion of sheer unadulterated pleasure that incinerated her body, cresting the wave of ecstasy on a high. With two more thrusts, Roarke bellowed his release. Deanna felt his seed flush her womb with its warmth, claiming it as its chalice.

She tingled all over, her toes curling on the floor as he continued moving and twitching inside her, prolonging their afterglow. Roarke leaned his weight on her back while they both waited for their breathing to slow down. She moaned when he unsheathed himself from her body. She turned around, kissing him, their tongues teasing, their bodies covered in the Cynn Cruor glow. Roarke leaned his forehead on hers.

"God, we smell of sex." She laughed, embracing him.

"Good," he growled. "So they'll know you're mine."

Deanna smiled. She felt the truth of those words deep in her bones.

"Yes, Roarke. I'm yours."

Chapter Thirteen

It took less than an hour for Deanna to get her things from her flat. Roarke refused to let her go alone. Finn refused to let Eirene go alone with Deanna either. It was now close to midday. The sun broke through the rain which bathed the streets of Manchester in a warm and humid glow. Of course, the Cynn Cruor warriors couldn't leave the Faesten until the sun had set. It was only when Zac volunteered to accompany the two women that Roarke and Finn relented.

When they returned to the Faesten, it was full of activity. Warriors and their mates flowed through the armoury and the kitchen. The Agora had been opened for easier access to the foyer. Roarke insisted that Deanna put her things in his room. She was, after all, his mate.

Outside the Faesten, it had started to rain again in torrents. The deluge could be heard like a roar of water overhead. Many of the Cynn warriors breathed a sigh of relief. The grey sky would ease their discomfort of having to move about during the day.

Colin Butler and his team continued to monitor the area of Dac's stronghold. True enough, the fallen log had yielded the passageway. It was agreed that Colin and his men would continue to pose as businessmen in search of laser fun before they returned to the Manchester Faesten. Roarke had briefed the rest of the warriors who had assembled in the Agora earlier. Until they were given the 'go' signal for the assault, everyone used the time to hone their fighting skills. More sparring sessions were arranged with Roarke and the rest of the Manchester Faesten pitching in.

Inasmuch as many of the Cynn wanted to begin the assault on Dac's stronghold, cooler heads prevailed. There were a lot of heated discussions in the nerve centre which overflowed to the dining hall, but through it all no personalities clashed. Roarke knew every warrior in the Faesten was hell bent on getting their hands on a Scatha. Each and every one of them had lost a loved one to Dac's men. The couples who opted not to have children wanted the Scatha eradicated so they could finally raise the family they longed for. Those who had families wanted a better world for their children to grow up in. With the death of Dac and the eradication of the Scatha Cruor everyone would have a lot to gain.

And also a lot to lose.

Roarke decided that Colin needed to tell the Cynn what he had unearthed on the Isle of Man. Graeme gathered everyone into the hall. Warriors from the main territories were there. Colin belonged to the Leeds Faesten while others were from Scotland, Ireland, and Wales. When news had spread about Dac's location, Cynn Cruor from all over the world wanted to join the fight. Roarke was aware that like their kind, the Scatha were also spread everywhere. If everyone descended on Manchester like a bloody D-Day invasion, it would leave the rest of the world vulnerable to a sneak attack from Dac and his transfuges.

He couldn't let that happen.

He made concessions for only one unattached Cynn warrior to join them and only if his own Faesten could spare him. Those who had spouses, but without any children could join the operation only if their Faestens agreed to it as well. The warriors must also agree to follow any orders given to them. From experience, Roarke knew this was a touchy point. Warriors were loyal to the Ancients first and their Faesten's Dux second. However, this was Roarke's ultimatum. Everyone complied. And so they arrived. Warriors from Greece, Spain, the Middle East, and even as far as Southeast Asia came to lend their muscle.

Once everyone made themselves comfortable, Roarke gave Colin the floor. Eirene and Deanna listened to the discussions from the nerve centre before they both decided to join the rest in the hall. Prior to leaving the library, Eirene made sure the feed was properly set up for Colin during the briefing and that he would come out on the screen which was set up in the Agora for everyone to see.

"We have found Dac's fort on the Isle of Man," Colin announced without preamble. "It lies south of the island, but north east of the ruined fort of South Barrule. Don't be deceived by the remnants of the tower. It has a sensor which can detect movement as far as a thousand yards."

Murmurs rippled through the hall, all of them excited.

"How did ye find his stronghold?" a Scottish Cynn asked.

"We received intel that South Barulle was where it lay. The Manchester Faesten has a reliable source and so I set out with my men to check it. True enough, it was there, though it has escaped detection all this time."

Someone whistled. A Welsh Cynn seated with his mate beside him said, "Impressive. How was Dac able to do that?"

"Money and influence. He's been able to draw some of the brightest minds in the world to him...that they also had to be perverted minds goes without saying," Graeme spoke with a wry grin. "This war has been going on for more than a millennium and in every war you try to find an advantage. Man is pitted against man." He cocked his head to one side. "The promise of prestige and fame is a very heady combination."

"Right." Colin continued. "For a thousand yards, any movement outside of that perimeter can be detected by the Scatha's security system. We need to find a way of disabling the sensor outside of that range."

"Eirene, Finn's mate and the first one to stumble across Dac's computer network, is working on a way to do this," Roarke added. Murmurs rippled as several heads turned to Eirene. Roarke saw others notice Deanna. His primal possessiveness made him clench his hands into fists, his eyes narrowing as he eyed each and everyone who looked at his mate with even more than a passing glance. He looked at Deanna. She kept her composure, not squirming under the cynosure of several stares.

"How?" The warrior who spoke earlier asked again. His mate had her arm draped over his shoulders. Roarke wasn't too keen on their nonchalant attitude. There seemed to be something off. He'd speak to Graeme about them.

"Dan Fowler, a Cynn mortal working for NASA will help us," Graeme said as he straightened from the wall close to Colin. "Once Eirene develops the code, it will be relayed to Dan and he can access a low orbiting satellite to fire a directed energy weapon to fry the sensors."

"Then we attack?" someone from the hall called out, his voice filled with anticipation.

Roarke's eyes narrowed, looking at everyone assembled. "Then we attack."

A roar erupted from the hall. Cries of jubilation and warriors thumping each other on the back added to the cacophony of sound. Roarke's mouth curled. He could empathize with his brethren. The assault on Dac's territory could be the end of the Scatha. The Cynn Cruor would finally be able to live in peace with the humans and raise the families they so longed to have.

Roarke searched the crowd for his mate again and spotted her beside Eirene and Finn. They stood by the door leading to the kitchen and breakfast areas. She had changed into black stretch denims which lovingly clung to her heart-shaped rear.

"Right, let's get back to business," Roarke said as he reluctantly turned his attention back to the assembled crowd. "We might have the element of surprise on our side, but we'll need to be ready when we finally battle the Scatha. They can be formidable warriors."

"The Cynn Cruor are better."

Cheers erupted again, together with the banging of palms and fists on tables.

Roarke's mouth twitched in amusement at the show of loyalty. And testosterone.

"Thank you," he said wryly, bringing about chuckles. "Nevertheless, we must continue to prepare. The three lower floors of the Faesten are dedicated training areas for every possible scenario we might encounter during the assault. Your team leaders have been briefed about the mission and they will let you know what you're supposed to do. Anything you don't understand or any suggestions to make the mission better, talk to your team leader and I will meet with you."

There were nods and murmurs of agreement.

"All right. Dismissed. Start training, Cynn Cruor. We only have three days before the assault."

The scraping of chairs, trestle benches and the din of chatter rose to a crescendo before it dissipated as the warriors moved like organized teams toward the elevator, emergency exits and toward the armoury where all of the target practice was done.

Roarke made his way to Deanna. She was talking to Eirene while Finn looked on with indulgence and a little exasperation.

"Anything I should know about?" Roarke asked, his brow arching.

"Eirene can't wait to teach Deanna to fight."

Roarke's shoulders shook with suppressed laughter. "And, well Eirene should. She is a Cynn Cruor mate, isn't she?" Suddenly a blush crept up Deanna's neck to her cheeks. The memory of their lovemaking in the reading room filled his mind and had his cock raring to go again.

When they'd made love, Roarke had felt his gums itching and his incisors lengthening. The time was so ripe to claim her and bring their ritual to the next level, but he had to let Deanna make the decision. She had to come to him willingly. He couldn't and wouldn't force the woman he loved to go through the ritual unless she came to him of her own volition.

And that was what he was worried about. What if she didn't?

"C'mon, Dee, I've got a lot to teach you." Eirene entwined her arm around Deanna's and pulled her gently away from the men.

Deanna threw her head back to laugh, her eyes twinkling in amusement. "All right," she said before turning to smile at Roarke. "See you in a while."

Roarke and Finn watched their women make their way through the rest of the throng in the foyer before waiting in front of the elevator.

"Thank you," Roarke said.

"For what?" Finn arched a brow.

"For Eirene." Roarke kept his eyes on the two women. "The first time Eirene arrived here and you refused to acknowledge how you felt about her, I knew her heart was pure. She had no guile and she genuinely liked helping people. I think that was what drew you to her. And now she's taken Deanna under her wing." He looked at Finn, who was both his Cynn brethren and step brother. “You have chosen well, Qualtrough.”

Finn gave a rueful laugh. “I wish I could take the credit Roarke, but it was Eirene who chose me. And I'm all the richer for it.”

“All the richer for what?” a voice asked a few feet away from them. Both of them turned to see Colin saunter toward them with a friendly grin on his face. Graeme and Zac followed close behind.

“Colin, good to have you on board,” Roarke said, his face breaking into a welcoming smile. He and Colin grasped each other's forearm in the Cynn Cruor handshake.

“If you were talking about wealth, I'm game,” Colin said. Cropped sun bleached hair with the most arresting dark green eyes, he looked like he would have been more at home surfing in Newport Beach than in the rainy U.K. Northwest. His body was bronzed and well defined. He had the looks girls would die for and he used his charms to make conquests. Yet, despite his sheer magnetism, Colin Butler couldn't be faulted for his attention to detail and his reputation of being one of the best Cynn Cruor trackers and reconnaissance experts.

“We were talking about our partners, Butler,” Finn said, crossing his muscled arms over his chest. “They are our wealth.”

“Ahh, the toughest Cynn warriors have fallen victim to Cupid.” Colin chuckled.

“One day, Butler, when you find your true mate, you'll never hear the end of it from us.” Finn grinned.

A rumble of humour came out of Colin's chest. “Not gonna happen. I like being a bachelor too much.”

After a round of laughter they all sobered.

“Care to tell me how your lady was able to get this intel?” Colin inquired before holding up a hand. “And no offense meant.”

“None taken,” Roarke replied. “She was Dac's prisoner.”

Colin's eyes widened with shock. “Seriously?” Then it dawned on him, his face filled with dismay. “All this time?”

“She escaped when Valerian took her to a suffragette rally at the turn of the twentieth century,” Roarke replied.

The rest of the Manchester Faesten warriors remained silent.

Colin cursed underneath his breath. “Man, I need a drink.”

“I'll get the scotch from the bar.” Graeme offered before returning to the hall and making his way to the stocked bar.

“Roarke, I need to make sure we have ample medical and blood supplies,” Zac said. “I'll also check on the warriors and their mates.”

Roarke nodded. “Let me know how it goes.”

Zac nodded with a short smile. “Will do.” Then he glanced at Colin. “Great to have you on our team, Colin.”

“A chance to kick Dac Valerian's stinking arse is always a pleasure.”

Zac laughed, shaking his head before leaving.

“C'mon, I'm hungry,” Roarke said, gesturing toward the nook by the window.

“So am I,” Colin admitted. “Didn't know talking could make you want to eat everything in your path.”

****

Luke Griffiths mingled with the rest of the Cynn Cruor. His gaze narrowed as he looked at the assembly. He made sure he wasn't detected. He needed to report back to who hired him. Knowing what was happening in the Faesten meant that much to them. It also meant he would finally become part of something. Something which he never realized was in his blood. Now that the Cynn Cruor was preparing for an assault against Dac Valerian, time was short. Not accomplishing his mission would jeopardize the entire operation.

He'd seen Roarke Hamilton and Deanna Logan together. The side of his mouth curved. Deanna didn't know that even before he spoke with her two nights ago, he already knew who she was. What he didn't anticipate was the presence of Roarke Hamilton. Why he wasn't told about Roarke annoyed him; then again, everything was on a need to know basis. Besides, he wasn't a man who asked questions. He did what he was told to do. No matter how distasteful.

It was how he survived.

Someone nudged him on the shoulder as they passed. Luke accepted the murmured apology with a grin which disappeared even before the warrior turned back to what he was doing. He looked around the sparring room.

He'd better get to work. He would need to report back soon.

****

Eirene taught Deanna how to use the telescopic baton. She was a hard taskmaster, commanding her pupil to keep on training with the baton and learning to click the butterfly knife with one hand. Eirene made sure Deanna knew how to use the weapons with both hands, so if one arm became unusable, she wouldn't be helpless. Within the day, both her hands had nicks and cuts from using the knife, but she continued practicing, gritting her teeth against the burning pain of her wounds. However, as the day progressed, the wounds were gone as though her hands had never gone through the ordeal in the first place.

For the next seventy-two hours, everyone was hard at work. Deanna and Eirene hardly saw their men. Every waking hour was spent going over strategies and sparring. The Faesten had become a full-fledged barracks. It fell to Roarke and Finn to make sure everyone was ready. Colin used part of the Agora to lecture on recon and intel. Graeme had several men with computer skills back him up in the nerve centre, teaching them everything he knew about security. Zac had three willing volunteers to help him with the medical aspect of the mission. In the Faesten's blood bank were several machines which accurately measured drops of blood and placed them into vials that a warrior could carry into battle. Zac had his volunteers man the machines, supervising them until they knew their workings inside and out. With all of the vials for the warriors matched and accounted for, Zac and his group left for one of the sparring rooms to practice. Each group was also given an hour for target practice. Finn taught them how to use the state of the art weapons housed in the armoury, training them to snipe at five hundred yards.

As long as the warriors stayed out of the sun, they had enough energy to last them several days, but their human mates needed sleep. Those who had no partners left the Faesten to savour what Manchester's night life had to offer, coming back before the crack of dawn to prepare for more gruelling hours of training. Still, Deanna knew Roarke was beside her in the middle of the night, spooning or cuddling her to his side. He didn't make love to her, allowing her to sleep, but as her body clung to him and her hand involuntarily travelled down his muscled torso to fist his erect manhood, Roarke obligingly gave in to her unspoken need, sending them both to the pinnacles of bliss, their bodies fusing in surrender before floating back to a satisfied slumber.

Toward the end of the second day, Deanna's arms were aching with the strain of using them to practice with the baton. Sweat trickled down her back and down her cleavage. Eirene had not only taught her how to use the weapons, she had been put through a round of exercises which stretched her limbs and taught her defensive postures should she be attacked from all sides. From Budokon to Kendo, Wu Shu to Taekwondo, Deanna went through all of the basics. Both she and Eirene had changed into exercise gear earlier, but it felt like she was in her swimsuit soaked after a dip in the pool. She couldn't remember when she'd had this much exercise, but it felt good. She felt invigorated. Fatigue which would have seeped into her bones immediately after the gruelling training was a thing of the past. Roarke's essence inside her made sure of that. Also, a sentiment she thought she'd never feel again blossomed in her heart.

Hope.

"Time out." She gasped at Eirene, making the "T" sign with her hands.

"I couldn't have said it better myself." Eirene laughed through her laboured breathing. "You learn quickly."

"I had to in order to survive," she said with a wry grin. "Besides, it seems to help a lot if you've made love to a Cynn Cruor."

Eirene giggled. "The easy absorption mode. I was surprised myself how quickly I learned from Finn, too."

Deanna gave a wide smile. "Looks like we've been imbued with part of what makes them unique."

They walked toward the bench where their towels, water bottles and mobile phones lay. She couldn't remember the last time she was this relaxed among people. It was a welcome feeling. She flipped the top of her water bottle and took long drags from it. As she and Eirene sat down her phone rang. She smiled at the name displayed.

"Jenny!" she greeted warmly.

"Deanna! Help!"

"Jen?" Her smile faltering, Deanna sat up. Dread fell heavy in her gut. Automatically she gripped Eirene's wrist. "What the hell's going on?"

"They're destroying the place." Jenny was sobbing.

"Jenny, calm down." Deanna tried to remain calm herself, but the look in Eirene's face pumped her heart into overdrive. "Where's Phil?"

"I don't know." Jenny continued to sob even as she whispered fiercely. Deanna could hear the hysterical screams of the women who were at the centre, which gave her an idea of the pandemonium happening at the Foundation. Her blood turned to ice when she heard a voice in the background she would rather forget.

"Jen," she said and then with a little more force. "Jenny, listen to me. Where are you?"

"I'm on the floor behind the office door," Jenny said. "Please Deanna—"

Then Deanna heard Jenny scream before a gun shot rang at close range. Deanna heard the phone fall. The call had not been disconnected.

"Jenny!"

Chapter Fourteen

Deanna and Eirene rushed out of the room, choosing the stairs over the lift. Their senses honed in on their mates. They looked at each other.

"The nook," they said in unison.

They stormed out of the stairwell, stopping just inside the foyer. They didn't even reach the glass doors before they saw Roarke and Finn striding out with Graeme and Colin close behind.

"Roarke, I need help." Her voice was laced with fear. "The Foundation. It's being attacked."

"Foundation?" he asked in confusion.

"I'm sorry, I didn't get a chance to tell you," she said in a rush. "I established The Haven Foundation to help women whom Dac had kidnapped so I could help them get their lives back. I'll tell you more later, but please, we don't have much time."

"Finn, call Zac. We might need a medic," Roarke commanded.

"He's on his way," Graeme replied. "I sent a telepath message."

Within the Faesten and in short distances, the Cynn Cruor could send messages telepathically with each other. When a Cynn took a mate, he had two lines of telepathic communication, one to communicate with his brethren and the other to speak with his mate, and he could manipulate the two however he wished.

Roarke nodded curtly. "You'll be in charge of the Faesten."

"Understood."

"Colin, I hate to do this."

"Shit, Roarke. You're not bloody keeping me here." Colin scowled. "You'll need recon even in the city."

"I wasn't going to ask you to stay, Butler. I was going to order you to come with us."

Colin grinned. "Right! Sorry, Dux."

Deanna's heart swelled with gratitude. She shrugged into her sweater, zipping it up while rushing with Roarke to the basement.

****

Deanna jumped out of the Range Rover even before it came to a complete stop, rushing up the steps of the building.

"Deanna!"

In a split second Roarke had his hand around her arm.

"Let Colin enter first," he said harshly.

"Jenny is inside and Phil might be there as well," she snapped.

"I know that," Roarke said, a scowl on his face. "But if there still are Scatha inside, they can take you away, too."

Deanna drew a sharp breath. What Roarke said put enough sense in her to get a grip. She jerked her head in a nod, feeling Roarke's hold on her slacken. The rain was now a fine drizzle, bringing a sweet, fresh scent to the air. It covered them in a mist of coolness and eased the blood simmering in the warrior's veins. Colin swept into the house with Finn following close behind. Deanna saw them disappear into the shadows. After what seemed to take forever, they came out, their face grim.

"Dux," Colin began.

Deanna rushed into the building even before Roarke, Finn or Colin could stop her. What she saw made her falter in her tracks.

Almost every piece of furniture in the lobby had either been turned over or ripped apart by someone whose fury knew no bounds. Papers, the computer and even the plasma screen television which used to be on the wall had been torn apart, the wiring pulled out of their casings. The beautiful Lowry painting which Deanna had bought hung by the edge of its frame, torn to shreds. Her footsteps dragged as she walked through the corridor by the side of the wall near the painting. She stopped in front of the door that said "Authorized personnel only". Her heartbeat was heavy as though it joined time to come to a standstill. She gripped the door handle and turned it. Her eyes closed, she didn't need to see what was inside, but her love and concern for the people who depended on her forced her to move into the room and look. Remnants of gunpowder were still in the air, mixed with the rusty, sickly, sweet smell of blood. Behind the door was Jenny's lifeless body slumped against the wall, a bullet hole in the middle of her heart.

Other women would have swooned, but she had seen so much bloodshed for such a long time that she just stood there. Numb. It was as though she was looking at the entire scene from outside of her body, before a gamut of emotions rushed into her, making her start and move forward.

She knelt down and stared at the face of a beautiful woman whose mission had been to help battered women, because she'd once been battered herself. Jenny had been the icon for the Foundation for women who had no hope. After having been forced to be a sex slave to fund her mother's crack addiction, Jenny had pulled herself out of the quagmire and rebuilt her life. Sadly, her mother had only recently died of an overdose, but Jenny was well on her way to finally making a life she could truly call her own. And now this.

Deanna reached out to brush away a tendril of hair which fell over Jenny's face before she closed the dead woman's eyelids for the last time.

"Rest in peace, my darling Jenny," she whispered before standing. When she turned around Roarke, Finn and Eirene were there.

"Let's sweep the entire area," she said, taking the three aback with her voice of authority. "Colin is looking around?"

Roarke nodded curtly. She saw the glimmer of admiration in his eyes, but now was not the time to acknowledge it.

"Zac must see if there are any survivors."

"Doing that as well," Finn replied.

"Okay." She nodded. "Let's do the rest."

Deanna swept through them and out of the corridor. She halted when she heard the voices in her mind.

You chose well, Roarke.

No, Finn. She chose me.

And Deanna couldn't help the slight smile on her face. Even in the face of all this tragedy, there was still something she could be thankful for.

****

They had found only two bodies. Jenny's and Phil's. The two people whom Deanna had trusted with her life. It looked as if Phil had struggled with those who entered the premises. He had cuts all over his body before succumbing to the blood loss from his wounds. Deanna had to turn away from his body when she saw the side of his neck had been ripped open. She and Eirene tried to salvage whatever they could. Eirene tackled the computers while she dealt with whatever records she could find about the women she'd rescued. She took out the hard drives from the CPUs to bring with her and inspect once they reached the Faesten. Zac and Finn called the Cynn mortals working for the Police and the Ambulance services to cordon off the area. Colin continued to search, going as far as a block around the place.

Now, hours later, they were sitting in front of the fireplace. The cheery flames didn't lighten their expressions which ranged from anger to determination and sorrow. News broke out about the murders in The Haven Foundation, but with the help of the Cynn mortals also working for the media, the report merely became a sound-bite, they would make sure everything would disappear within a short space of time.

"I've only managed to track a slight scent moving north of the building," Colin said. He nursed a glass of scotch in his hands which dangled between his knees. "It's the Scatha."

Deanna continued to stare at the flames. She felt so dead inside.

"Deanna."

She didn't hear her name being called until Roarke shifted on the couch beside her. "Sorry, what did you say?"

"We want to know more about Haven," Finn said, his voice kind, but firm.

She looked at him blankly. She understood what he was saying, but her mind seemed slow catching up.

"Finn," Eirene interjected. "Now is not the time."

Deanna saw Finn's jaw tighten, but he nodded.

"It's okay, Eirene," she spoke before looking at Finn and the rest of the assembled Cynn Cruor. She looked at Colin. "I don't know how much you know."

For once there was no ready smile on Colin's face. "I know enough."

She nodded, folded her hands and began to speak. "The Haven Foundation was established right after I came back from America at the beginning of the twentieth century. Emeline Dalton had died and she left her entire fortune to me. I never forgot what happened to me and to the women and children Dac imprisoned, so I built the Foundation. Since then, I've been going to clubs, looking for Dac's transfuges and the women they bring with them. When they're not looking, I take the women and bring them to Haven."

Colin whistled.

Roarke was furious.

"I didn't know where you were Roarke," she reasoned. "The Cynn Cruor are not easy to find."

Graeme and Zac bent their heads down to hide their grins.

Deanna continued. "It was only because of Henry Heaton's contact with Devon that I finally found you."

"Looks like our women are philanthropists," Finn said, his eyebrows raised. At Deanna's confused gaze he added, "Eirene and Devon founded the charity 'Kids Come Home'."

"That's why Mr. Heaton knew Devon. He's one of the private investigators we keep on retainer." Eirene gave a shy smile.

Deanna smiled. She already liked Finn's mate, and knowing they shared a common cause only made her like Eirene more. When there was a lull in the mission to bring Dac to justice, she would talk to Eirene about perhaps putting 'Kids Come Home' and a rebuilt 'The Haven Foundation' together. With the wealth she inherited, they could use their resources to track down the missing women and children and give those forced to sell their bodies a chance at a better life.

"The women shouldn't be far away." Graeme surmised, his hand running across his chin pensively. "How many women were in the building?"

"Twelve," Deanna answered.

"Where would the Scatha take them?" Roarke queried.

"Dac would want to see them. That is, if he wasn't part of this particular snatching mission."

"It's likely the prisoners would be brought to the Isle," Zac added.

She shook her head. "Perhaps, or if Dac is in a hurry to dispose of the women, he'd send them away immediately. The Scatha have something like a distribution centre. There is a boat off the coast of Heysham's Half Moon Bay. The women are taken there by motorboat."

The men swore softly.

"And you know all this because?" Colin queried.

"You're treading on thin ice, Butler," Roarke warned.

"Roarke, now is not the time, please," Deanna pleaded before releasing a sigh. She was dead tired, but her body wouldn't allow her to rest. She was running on adrenalin now. "Everyone is on edge and..." She looked at Colin. "I know you don't trust me and I don't blame you. I wouldn't trust myself either."

Colin had the grace to flush as he looked down at his drink. Deanna continued.

"The point is, we need to find those women. I know of the boat because I've been monitoring it for quite some time, since I realized that the disappearances of women and children were somehow connected to Dac."

She continued. "Some of the women will be shipped right away to the continent. The children are placed in an orphanage where they are trained. It isn't really an orphanage in the strictest sense of the word, but it has all the trappings of one."

"Where is it?" Finn asked.

"The Isle of Man."

No one spoke for several seconds.

"Right!" Colin's voice cut across the silence. He stood up as he downed his drink. "Looks like we have our work cut out for us."

"We need to spread out," Roarke added. "We have to be in two places at the same time."

"Not if I can help it," Deanna muttered.

Roarke's eyes widened at his mate's vehemence.

Deanna stood up. "I was supposed to hit the bars and clubs tonight to check on possible abductions," she said. "But after what's happened, the Scatha will want to concentrate on the women they've taken from The Foundation. We have to get to Half Moon Bay."

Chapter Fifteen

Luke sneaked out of the Faesten quickly, rushing across Canal Street and onto Minshull Street. The weather was wet and freezing, but the cold didn't bother him because it felt like a spring breeze across his skin. The people around him along the Gay Village gave him appreciative glances which he didn't return. Men and women, gay or straight flowed out of the bars lining the street. Luke passed the Velvet Hotel and Bar where people waited to get a seat inside. He continued on and stood under one of the trees which dotted the entrance to the parking lot.

There was a click on his phone.

“They are going to Half Moon Bay in Heysham. We have been told to stay and watch the clubs for possible abductions,” Luke said before pausing. “I assume you've heard about the murders.”

“Yes, such tragedy. Our police and media contacts gave me the full report, not like the bite size reported in the news. You should go with them to Heysham.”

“I can’t do that. Roarke and Deanna might have already seen me.”

“And you think the rest of the Faesten haven't?” The male voice chuckled in amusement. Luke bristled at the mockery.

The caller continued, “It is precisely because of your ability to be near invisible, to blend in, that we made the offer for you to be one of us.”

“And I’m still not convinced that’s the only thing you want from me,” Luke retorted.

“Agreed. But soon you will need to choose sides and I hope you make the right decision.”

Luke kept quiet, his mouth pressed into a hard line. He didn't have to be reminded that time was running out.

“I'll keep you posted when I learn anything new.” He ended the call. He had to get back to the Faesten to join the group of unattached warriors going to the clubs on Deansgate, The Printworks, and Northern Quarter. The clouds above covered the nearly full moon. He felt the stirrings of lust in his groin. A semblance of a smile coated his lips. He might as well make use of the perks of watching the clubs with several good lays that evening.

****

Dac Valerian paced the deck of the ship, looking at his watch almost every minute. He'd just finished the call from his spy and was furious. How dare the Cynn Cruor cover the murders at The Haven? He wanted to send a message to whoever owned the damn foundation that no one messed with Dac Valerian's property. Even on the pain of death, the only man they found with the women refused to divulge the identity of his employer. Calls to his contacts yielded another dead end. Names placed in the articles of incorporation for the safehouse were fake. And so was the name of the man they'd killed. Dac screamed at the night. His breath came in huge gasps of angry air until he was able to regain control. He consoled himself with the fact that the women they'd kidnapped previously had been in the building and were now back to where they truly belonged, with his organization.

It was only by sheer coincidence that one of the Scatha Cruor had dragged a woman he was about to rape near the building, when he recognized one of their previous kidnap victims go inside. The potential rape was forgotten as the Scatha immediately reported his find to Herod and Dac. Dac didn't wait another minute and ordered Herod to attack the place. Valerian followed a little later, and when the man they found inside refused to divulge any information, he'd asked one of the Scatha to rip his throat out.

"Dac! Over there!"

Dac whipped at the voice before looking at the shore. His sharp eyes saw there was scuffling close to the beach. He heard the women scream as spits from several guns with silencers filled the air.

"Take me there! Now!"

****

Roarke was surprised at the number of Scatha they encountered at Half Moon Bay. Despite the low temperature, the women were not given any coats to keep the bitter cold away from their shivering bodies. He looked at the assembled team. Their faces showed their anger. Then he looked at Deanna.

She was calm and serene. At that moment, she looked at him. Her eyes were the coldest he'd ever seen them, devoid of any emotion. He turned back to survey the scene in front of him. He had a good idea of what Deanna had become. He had been through the same situation so many times in his long life.

She had become a warrior worthy of being called a Cynn Cruor.

Colin, recon. Roarke used his telepathic line to send his commands. *Finn, you and Eirene take the east perimeter. Zac take the west.*

You're not leaving me here.

Roarke and the rest of the Cynn warriors were struck dumb when they heard Deanna's voice in their minds.

How?

I have no bloody idea, Hamilton, but I realized I could hear what you told Finn earlier.

Roarke reluctantly grinned when he heard Eirene snort. Everyone started to snicker in amusement.

Okay, we're not here to laugh, people. We're here to kill.

Kill joy, Hamilton. You always have been on every mission, Colin stated before sighing.

Roarke grunted. *Let's go.*

Now, ten minutes later, they were fighting a multitude of Scatha who seemed to be coming from everywhere. Part of the dust from what were formerly Scatha bodies did not swirl as much as they would have due to the slow patter of rain falling around them. He searched for Deanna. She and Eirene had their share of Scatha to fight, while at the same time protecting the women from being taken.

"Roarke! A powerboat has just left the ship," Finn roared, even as he hacked through the Scatha who came one after the other. Their faces contorted to jowls filled with razor sharp teeth, their eyes glowing dark green, and the stench of evil coating their bodies fell like a blanket over all of them.

Fuck! If there were more reinforcements they wouldn't be able to get everyone out. Roarke ran toward Deanna and Eirene. As soon as he closed in on them, he started hacking at the Scatha.

Deanna, Eirene, get the women back in the vans!

Finn ran toward them as Zac rushed to open the doors. Hurriedly, the women entered the vehicles, uncaring whether they sat or not. Their need to escape spurred them on.

"Go!" Roarke thundered.

Eirene and Deanna took to the drivers' seats and gunned the accelerator even before the doors were closed. When they left the Faesten, Finn and Eirene had taken one van while the rest followed in the SUV. This time, Eirene drove their van while Deanna drove the Scatha's Caravel.

"Roarke, let's go," Zac shouted.

"Where's Colin?" Roarke asked as they sped to the SUV.

"Hamilton."

He swung around. Hell! Colin was running after them, but he had four long slashes across his chest. He and Finn ran back and carried Colin by his shoulders.

Colin groaned in pain.

"Just a little bit more, mate." Finn gritted.

A few steps ahead of them they saw Zac aim the MP7A1 assault weapon behind them, the bullets spitting in succession as he felled the Scatha chasing them. That would stop them, but not for long. They all bundled into the Range Rover at the same time Zac entered the driver's seat. The Scatha roared their fury, training their guns at the bullet proof glass of the vehicle. The vehicle's tires screeched as they sped away.

"Graeme, I need coordinates," Zac snapped at the open line connecting them to the Faesten. "We can't get to the Faesten unless we lose the Scatha." He looked at the rear-view mirror.

"How many are after you?"

"Two Alpha Romeos."

Roarke's attention turned to Colin as Graeme gave Zac a different route to try and lose their tails.

"We're almost there, Butler."

"Dux, in the bag, there's a syringe filled with the serum," Zac instructed, not taking his eyes off the road. "Plunge it close to the wound. It will help close and heal it until we get back to the Faesten."

Roarke rummaged through Zac's messenger bag and found the syringe kept snug inside a glass container. He took it out and steadied his hand against the pitching of the SUV.

"Colin, it's going to hurt, mate, but it has to be done," Roarke forewarned the warrior who was turning ashen beneath his tan.

"Do it, Roarke. I've been through this be—bloody fucking hell!"

Roarke immediately pushed down on the syringe to shoot the serum into Colin's body.

"Graeme, what's Eirene's and Deanna's coordinates?" Finn asked as he took his weapon, a 50 cal. Barrett to check the chambers.

"They're on the M6 heading this way."

"Good," Finn said. "Dux, we need to cut them down."

Roarke nodded curtly. He took Zac's weapon. He didn't bring his gun, preferring his sword to kill Scatha Cruor.

Roarke and Finn slanted the backrests of the seats and steadied their rifles against the leather. Colin mumbled incoherently between them.

"Ready, Zac."

Zac pressed on the tailgate button. The back slowly opened.

"Steady on the driving, McBain." Finn's voice was calm and soft. Then to Roarke, "That's a V6. Centre."

"Supressing fire," Roarke muttered.

"Three, two, one," Zac said under his breath.

Even before the tailgate had completely opened, two tongues of flame from Finn's weapon hit the Scatha's car where the bonnet met the body. Flames erupted from under the hood. The car swerved to the right and Roarke raked it with the bullets from his weapon, hitting the wheels and doors. The car flipped over before it exploded. A ball of flame lit the cold night sky, briefly illuminating the rain drops before metal and debris became road hazards on the motorway. Behind the exploding car, the second Scatha car broke and swerved to the left, but was not able to escape the exploding ball and was incinerated as well. Other cars on the motorway screeched to a halt sideways to avoid colliding with the huge conflagration.

"We should stop making cars explode. People are dying," Zac muttered, glancing at the side and rear-view mirror. "We'll be all over the news, if we don't."

"Graeme—"

"Calling the police and media now, Roarke." Graeme's voice came clear through the speakers. "And I agree with Zac. But bloody hell, this has been the most action we've seen with the Scatha for a long time!"

Chapter Sixteen

When Deanna and Eirene screeched the vans to a stop in the basement car park of the Faesten, there were several warriors and their mates waiting for them. Several men ran toward the car park entrance, their weapons at the ready to make sure no one followed them. The Cynn mates helped the women out of the vans and waited with them by the elevator.

"Eirene, I don't know where to take them," Deanna began.

"Leave it with me," Eirene said. "The Faesten has its own clinic. I'll keep them comfortable until Zac arrives."

Fifteen minutes later the SUV came screeching through. Finn opened the door to help Colin out. Roarke exited from the other door. Relief washed through Deanna and she gladly entered his embrace, opening her mouth for his kiss.

"Later," he whispered in her ear, the deep timbre of his voice sending waves of erotic anticipation along her spine to tease her sex. Even at this time when all hell was breaking loose, Roarke still had the power to sexually thrill her.

Colin walked under his own steam, grimacing as he stretched a little to get a kink out of his back and protesting when Zac helped him. His skin had healed and the only remnants of his wounds were the rents on his shirt made by the Scatha's claws.

"I'm not an invalid," he protested.

Zac simply grunted and continued to help him.

Roarke and Deanna waited until everyone was safely inside the Faesten before they took the lift. Finn had gone ahead to supervise the warriors. Zac had taken Colin to the clinic as well as to attend to the women.

Graeme greeted them as soon as the lift opened at the Faesten's foyer. Behind him, the Cynn mortals helping the chef were busy taking out trays of food to be brought to the clinic.

"Dux, you look like shit. Sorry, Deanna."

"I look like shit too, Graeme, so no need for the niceties," Deanna said with dry humour. "We're at war here. Remember?"

"Everything okay?" Roarke asked.

Graeme nodded. "No one followed you. I asked Dan to track the Scatha. It appears Dac has returned to the Isle of Man. Dan has the feed of how you botched up Dac's operation in Half Moon Bay."

"Any news of kidnappings from the clubs?" Deanna asked.

"Nothing unusual according to the Cynn assigned there."

Deanna sighed in relief. "All right."

"I'll be right there," Roarke said as he caressed Deanna's face. "I need to see this."

"Go," she said before planting a kiss on his mouth. "I'll go to the women to make sure they're okay."

As soon as Roarke and Graeme left, Deanna re-entered the lift and pressed the button for the clinic's floor. As the doors slid open, the sterile smell of antiseptic faintly marred the air. The entire floor was awash with harsh fluorescent light. It looked more like a private cosmetic surgery clinic with luxurious appointments. She passed the empty nurse's station, looking from left to right until she came across the women in two wards on her left. To her right, she saw Zac talking to Colin. She walked toward them.

"How are you feeling?" she asked, smiling as she came in.

"Feel drowsy is all I can say. McBain put something in my drip."

Zac had his arms crossed over his chest. "It's going to make you heal faster. The serum punch is only temporary. With gashes that deep, you'll need several hours of sleep for them to completely close. Now..." Zac's voice held a tone of amusement. "If you want to axe some Scatha the day after tomorrow, you'd better get some sleep or I'm not going to let you leave with the team for the Isle of Man."

"Shit, Zac, I'm not a kid anymore," Colin muttered, turning his back to them, clinking his drip.

"Watch it, Butler. That drip falls and you're grounded."

Colin scowled and a low growl came out of his chest, but he said nothing.

Deanna placed a hand on Colin's bicep. He tensed.

"Colin for what it's worth, thank you."

Colin turned to look at her. His eyes searched her face, the look of mistrust slowly disappearing, replaced with grudging respect.

"You kicked some butt out there, Deanna." His mouth curled to a lopsided grin. "You're welcome."

She and Zac left the warrior to rest. "How are the women?"

Zac's forehead creased slightly. "They're not too bad. Shocked and frightened, obviously. They're all resting at the moment. I'll find out more tomorrow."

"Okay," she replied, letting out a tired sigh.

"You need rest yourself."

"Yes, Dr. McBain." She chuckled. "Will do, so I can kick more Scatha butt."

Deanna entered Roarke's room, the weariness finally seeping into her bones. She took off her leather jacket, groaning at the ache in her shoulders and arms. She tossed the jacket on the love seat before stripping while walking toward the bathroom. For once, she sighed gratefully at the coolness of the floor.

She turned on the tap and entered the cubicle. Steam slowly rose from the water as she stepped in, moaning in pleasure as the warm liquid began to do its magic. Then she felt his heat. Roarke encircled her from behind, his erection slowly pressing against her hip. He bent down and nibbled on her neck before licking the sensitive spot behind her ear. Deanna sighed. All he had to do was touch her and she melted.

"Aren't you tired?"

He chuckled. "You know sex strengthens a Cynn Cruor."

She smiled as she turned around to look at him. The gold flecks in his eyes stark against the now deep silver blue irises. "Yes, I do know," she said, before she moved her mouth against his, tracing the seam of his lips with her tongue. The weariness from her limbs could not stop the longing that only Roarke could quench.

Deanna revelled at the feel of his callused hands against her wet skin, skimming her waist before one palm slowly made its way between her breasts. Her breasts tingled; her nipples beaded, anticipating his touch. She moaned against his mouth when he cupped one breast, kneading it gently before swirling her areola with his thumb. Her own hands moved over his chest, playing with his nipples. She smiled as he let out a low, sexy growl. Nipping and licking his chest, she kissed him, finding his hard shaft with her hand, marvelling at the velvet covered steel. Thoughts of Roarke thrusting into her drifted into her mind. She heard him chuckle.

In good time, Babe, I'll pound you so good, until you scream my name.

Roarke inside her mind made her gasp. The sexiness of his words notched up her lust. She fisted him, pumping up and down while her other hand joined to roll his sac. With a growl, Roarke kissed her hard. Their tongues explored each other, swirled against each other, their mouths seared together in one hot kiss after another. Her sex clenched at the sensations his hands drew from her body. She purred when he cupped her mound, letting two fingers play with her clit. Swirling, teasing, pressing before they entered her.

"Roarke." She sighed, breaking the kiss, letting herself enjoy his finger play. God, it felt so good! Her juices flowed and coated his fingers when he bent down to suck her nipples, grazing and nibbling.

"You taste so good, Deanna." Roarke's deep timbre turned her on all the more. He flicked his tongue fast against her breast, then the other.

Deanna felt herself sucked into a storm of desire. Her mouth watered. She just had to taste him. Sliding down the wall she knelt in front of Roarke and looked up at him. One, two butterfly flicks and she covered him with her mouth, humming at the pleasure of his taste. Roarke groaned loudly, holding on to her wet hair as her mouth weaved its magic. Looking up, she saw Roarke fling his head back to emit a growl. He raised her up, lifting her legs to put them around his waist.

"Take me, Roarke." She gasped. "Make me yours...don't stop! Don't...oh, God! Yes!" She was unable to complete her sentence as he thrust himself deep within her.

"That good?" he asked, his breath harsh.

"Yes!"

Deanna looked at his gold flecked eyes. Every time he plunged into her, she jerked up at the force. Her lips parted, her breath coming out in soft pants. Roarke's cock inside her felt so good. Each jerk and pump sent ripples of euphoria all over her body.

And then he withdrew.

"No!" she protested.

Roarke placed two fingers inside her and she bucked her hips, crying out her pleasure when his thumb circled her clit over and over. Higher and higher she went, about to crest into rapture when he removed his fingers. Whimpering her frustration, she moaned when his cock head nudged the lips of her sex again. Then slowly, inch by delicious inch, Roarke seated himself to the hilt.

Deanna felt stretched and full. The burning was exquisite as her sex accommodated Roarke's thick shaft. Her vaginal muscles quivered, sending bolts of ecstasy through her body. Then he started to move.

She was at Roarke's mercy and she welcomed his domination with a full and open heart. No more holding back. No more thinking that hers was just a body which she could detach her soul from.

Now was the time for body and soul to come together. Roarke pistoned in and out of her, claiming her completely as his mouth delved into hers, his tongue keeping time with the thrusts of his cock. Her body sang, immersed in the delight of heated sex. Roarke angled his hips to reach her G-spot, knowing it would bring her untold pleasure.

"More, Roarke! Please!" She panted and moaned, long and loud when he touched her cervix.

Then she felt his cock thicken and lengthen.

In the deep recesses of her mind, something clicked. Her gums itched. She gasped and looked at Roarke's glittering eyes. They crinkled as they looked down at her mouth. She felt her incisors lengthen and sharpen.

Roarke slowed down his thrusts, but it was no less sensual and languid. It continued to stoke her in more ways than one.

I love you Deanna. The eons have not diminished the love I have for you. Now that I have found you again, you shall always and forever be the one who holds my heart.

She looked deeply into his eyes and saw the truth of his words. Her heart swelled as tears formed in her eyes before they fell down her cheeks.

At long last, she could finally cry.

Roarke continued moving inside her. Her body slightly lifted with each thrust. The friction of his shaft against her silken heat kept her within a whirlpool of unquenchable need for this man. He had bared his soul to her. She did not need to bare her soul to him.

Because he was her soul.

She didn't reply. Instead, she let her body tell him how she felt. With a tight squeeze, she clamped down on his cock. Roarke closed his eyes as the friction intensified. Her breath hitched as the stoked fire suddenly flared. Roarke moved faster, in short thrusts, filling her, stretching her, pleasuring her until she arched her back in ecstasy, crying out her orgasm for one brief moment before she sank her fangs deep into the side of his heart. She whimpered as Roarke thrust hard inside of her, causing another orgasmic wave to crash over her even before the first one had ended. Blood flowed into her mouth and instinctively she sucked. Roarke's memories came bursting through. From his guilt and pain of losing her, to his anguish as he searched for her through the decades. Deanna witnessed the numerous battles he fought, putting himself in harm's way so that he could die. She experienced the emptiness of his life, and the shock at seeing her again. Deanna closed her eyes more tightly as his last memory surrounded her. It was his encompassing love for her, his desire to win her back, to make her see she was worth being the Cynn Cruor Dux's mate and chosen partner.

She felt her blood flow from her gums into Roarke's heart. The muscle stopped, then seemed to beat faster and she knew that with her blood inside him, he would now be close to invincible. He was now hers, totally and completely.

And she was his.

Roarke felt his heart stutter. His cock twitched, and at that moment his balls tightened. He growled at the intense, but sweet pain of Deanna's fangs in his chest. He felt her blood again mix with his own. But this time, the metallic stain of the Scatha's blood was gone.

I love you, Roarke Hamilton. You were never far from my mind. I am yours willingly, irrevocably, completely. Be mine, too.

Roarke roared his orgasm. He felt his seed flow into Deanna, his cock throbbing at each and every spurt. Groaning, his heart thundered in his chest. He could feel Deanna's blood strengthening him as it flowed hot and silky through his blood stream. His entire body became incredibly attuned to hers, more than before. He growled softly when he felt Deanna unlatch her fangs from his chest and lick at his wounds until he felt them close.

His breath came out in a hiss.

When Deanna looked at him, her eyes held the same familiar gold flecks against her cornflower blue irises. He looked around them. The opalescent glow was now complete. No gaps showed around the aura.

Roarke licked at her mouth and her incisors as they receded, feeling her shudder before she moaned.

I didn't know fangs could be so sensitive. She telepathed.

They are. In the same way that making love will be much better.

"Oh?" Deanna arched a brow. "Oohhh..."

Roarke felt his cock harden inside her again. He lifted her and brought her down on his shaft. Deanna closed her eyes in pleasure, her channel's muscles tightening against him. His left arm slid around her waist, while his other hand lowered between them to rub her engorged pleasure centre. Deanna's breath hissed as he placed a little bit more pressure, loving the waves of bliss painted on her face. Her lips parted before her teeth bit down on her lower lip, whimpers slipping from them. She was close to coming again, and so was he.

"Look at me, Deanna," he ordered even as he swirled his thumb against her clit faster and thrust into her sweet heat harder and harder. "Wait."

Deanna's eyes flew open, the gold flecks dominating her eyes.

"Roarke." She gasped, holding on to his shoulders tightly. "I can't. I'm close."

At that, he thrust faster, making her almost cry out. He growled, feeling his sac tighten again, the line of desire pulsing inside him. He felt his incisors push through his gums and saw Deanna's eyes widen at the sight.

Mine.

Yes, Roarke. Yours.

Deanna cried out at the same time his orgasm came crashing around him. He lifted her and sank his fangs into the side of her left breast. She screamed in ecstasy as he growled his. Everything whirled around them as he experienced the most amazing release of his immortal life, knowing it would just be one of many. He drank from her heart at the same time he fed his blood into hers. Deanna held his head against her breasts, her ecstatic sighs filling the bathroom, the water showering them and cooling their joined sexual steam as her body shuddered against his, her sheath milking him again and again.

Nothing would ever pull them apart again as long as they lived. They belonged together.

They were now Cynn Cruor.

Chapter Seventeen

Isle of Man

The sound of the whip lashing at his lacerated body was drowned out by the tortured screams forcibly uttered by the man chained in the dungeon. Dac threw the whip away, his anger still unquenched. In the blink of an eye, he took a sword from the table and decapitated the Scatha. He moved away as the body turned to dust.

Dac roared. He glared at the people left in the dungeon and was about to slice through another transfuge when Herod, his second-in-command, spoke.

"You keep doing that Dac, and there'll be no warriors left to do your bidding."

Dac swung around and pointed the tip of the sword against Herod's throat. Herod remained stoic and did not move, his eyes trained on Dac's furious face. His mouth formed a smile which didn't reach his eyes. "If you kill me now, who will protect your hide?" Herod asked softly.

Suddenly, the sword circled in the air with a swoosh and fell to the ground. Dac looked around. His rage knew no bounds as he looked at the pathetic group of transfuges he had amassed. Yes, they were pathetic because he was the only omnipotent Scatha Cruor. Not even Herod D'Argyl, his second-in-command, was his equal. True, he owed his life to Herod after his assassination attempt on the Ancient Eald. Herod had remained steadfast and loyal.

But Dac was becoming wary of him. He believed that in time, Herod would want to take over his whole operation. When that time came, many of the Scatha Cruor would immediately shift their loyalty to the new leader. After all, they were all transfuges. Traitors. They had no concept of loyalty. Not that Herod had given him any sign of disloyalty. Except for the time his second-in-command had left him to battle Finn Qualtrough when the Cynn Cruor raided his club. Or when he disappeared for a while. When Herod had returned, he was a changed man—a man prone to violence in the same way that he sought the sweet release of pain. Dac had escaped by jumping out the window and when he landed, Herod was there to pull him into a waiting car and leave the club. His man Friday had a good excuse for being where he was. They were able to make a quick getaway.

Dac stormed out of the dungeon, knowing Herod would be right behind him. His fury remained unabated, but he grudgingly accepted that Herod was right. If he kept on killing his men, there wouldn't be any warriors left to battle the Cynn Cruor.

The Cynn Cruor. The bane of his existence. And now he added another enemy.

Deanna Logan.

His whore who refused to divulge the name of her mate even after he'd flayed her within an inch of her life. She was still alive and had found the Cynn Cruor. How she evaded his grasp baffled him. He had spies all over the world and yet he couldn't learn the whereabouts of one small woman. After she disappeared from the Suffragettes' rally more than a century ago, his transfuges had looked for her everywhere. It was as though she'd vanished into thin air. The number of women they'd kidnapped should have satisfied him, but the loss of Deanna Logan left a bitter taste in his mouth. He refused to believe that he, Dac Valerian, had been bested by a woman. His lip curled. It didn't matter. After how he'd used her, fucked her til kingdom come, no Cynn Cruor would accept her now. It didn't matter anymore that he didn't know the name of her mate. From the day his men dragged her from the ruins of Hamel Dun Creag, he'd set out to prove her true value. And he had. He'd completely ruined her.

But it does matter. She knew where the women were and she's put a damper on all your plans. His mind goaded him.

Dac growled and tamped down his anger with difficulty. He entered his room. It still looked like a medieval chamber with grey stone walls, a high ceiling and a huge fireplace which could hold an entire roasting pig. He walked toward the cabinet filled with bottles of brandy and cognac. He pulled out one of the cognacs and took a swig straight from the bottle.

As the fiery liquid coursed down his throat, his mind whirled. He needed to put his other plans into motion. He had buyers for the women they had abducted from the Haven Foundation. But now that they'd been snatched away from him again, he would need to use his contingency measures.

"Send five groups of Scatha to the bars and clubs in Manchester and start taking women. I don't want our clients to be grumbling that there's a delay," he ordered Herod.

"I'll see to it." Herod nodded, fishing out his mobile phone to relay Dac's instructions.

"Another thing," Dac said after taking another long swig from the bottle of cognac, smiling as he wiped his mouth with the back of his hand. "Take the children out of the orphanage. It's time they earned their keep."

Dac's smile disappeared as soon as Herod left. Taking another drink from the cognac, he stared morosely at the fire, wondering how long this war was going to last.

He once had been Cynn Cruor. Had once pledged his allegiance to the Ancient Eald. He'd carried the name of Cynn Cruor with pride, dedicating all of his battles to the Cynn even if the victories were claimed by the Roman emperors. He had been one of the Council of Ieldran's most trusted generals.

But there was the rub.

He wanted recognition for those Cynn Cruor feats of valour. Acknowledgement of their strength, their ingenuity, their courage. Like the mortals, he was part human and he wanted to celebrate his humanity by letting the world know of their existence.

But the Ancient Eald refused his request. Knowledge of the Cynn Cruor's existence could lead to chaos. Men who desired to live forever, to become masters of the universe were likely to capture a Cynn Cruor and use whatever means possible to find out how to become one of them. Even the Cynn mortals were under the Ancient Eald's protection. While he couldn't understand this, Dac relented and acquiesced to the Ancient Eald's wishes. But when he saw that mortal leaders had so much power, he resented the fact that he couldn't aspire to be more powerful than them.

Was it so wrong to demand recognition for what the Cruors had given to humanity? Shouldn't the Cruors share in the accolades that were given to men who had the minds of ants and yet held the reins of power? Dac believed the Cruors to be superior. They could teach the mortals many things. Those who were not up to the task, well, he mused, they had no place in his perfect world.

At the time of his conversion, Dac realized he experienced a certain kind of high whenever he saw people suffering. He thrived on inflicting pain and he relished feeling pain. It had given him so much pleasure to subjugate the peoples of the world in the name of the Holy Roman Empire. The Ancient Cynn hadn't realized there were other Cynn Cruor warriors who grumbled that they couldn't be recognized for what they had contributed to human society. Dac cultivated this resentment and soon he had developed a secret following.

When his exploits were reported to the Council, he was summoned and asked to explain himself. Dac, however, launched his appeal again for the Cynn Cruor to be recognized. As he expected, the Council refused. There was no point belabouring the fact, so that evening he'd asked to see the Ancient Eald with the pretence of apologizing to his progenitor. When he was at close proximity with the Ancient Eald, he attacked, almost hacking the Eald in two. What he didn't anticipate was the presence of the Deoré, who almost killed him. Had it not been for Herod who'd whisked him through a secret passage underneath the Ancient Cynn's fortress, he would be the one lying on the floor bathed in his own blood. It had taken time for him to heal. He didn't have any healers and for a long time, he had to depend on Herod. Later when he'd recovered, he trained hard to regain his strength while simultaneously plotting his revenge. Eight months after his near death, Dac became the leader of the renegade Cynn Cruor warriors, calling them the Scatha Cruor.

His eyes narrowed. It angered him that the Cynn Cruor couldn't be defeated. But one day he would and he looked forward to killing all of them in the most painful of ways.

The thought of so much suffering filled his heart with pride.

He sighed as he closed his eyes, imagining the torture. His blood-lust fantasies added to the copious amounts of cognac he had imbibed, relaxed his senses.

"Much better," he murmured.

Chapter Eighteen

Just outside of the Scatha Cruor's one thousand yard deep perimeter, sat a black Fleetwood Terra RV. Instead of containing the comforts of a home, it was kitted out as a mobile command centre for the Cynn Cruor. The left side of the vehicle's interior was a wall of consoles. The most important one tracked every warrior operating in the field. The cabin's right side had a huge rectangular table with several folding seats, a long couch, and the secret compartment which held the Cynn's armoury. At the back of the transport was the portable mess hall and field kitchen, and right behind this was a small first-aid station and refrigeration for many of the Cynn Cruor mates' blood.

Before leaving the Faesten, Eirene had called Devon, asking him to come over. She'd briefly told him about their plan to rescue his daughter, Penny. Had it not been for Eirene asking him to be strong, Devon would have crumpled to the ground. Deanna finally met Devon and told him about the women in the Faesten's infirmary. At that moment, Devon composed himself. He was able to access his computer files from the Faesten's computer and paired the files he had against the missing women. Several of the files he had matched the identities of the victims recovering in the infirmary. Now he had the unenviable task of talking to the parents, relatives, and partners of the women, and at the same time not letting them know who had rescued them. Devon would need Henry Heaton's help. But first, he would need to go through all the files and speak to them. He agreed to stay in the Faesten, together with those who had been rescued. The Faesten's central command had a real time data link with the mobile command centre. They would know what was going on instantaneously and provide the support necessary to ensure the safety of the Faesten and the people inside.

The clouds completely locked out the midnight sky. A slight drizzle covered the Isle of Man, adding to the frigid temperature. Everyone could see in the dark as though it was daylight, so it didn't matter even if their surroundings were pitch black. Every Cynn warrior worth his salt also knew in the depths of his being that it was also the night of the full moon. All of them had satisfied their carnal desires with their mates. Unattached warriors painted the town to find willing partners for a night of satiating their lust. No Cynn Cruor warrior would force himself upon a mortal. They followed a code stringently enforced by the Ancient Cynn. Any infractions of the code were dealt with severely.

Tonight, all of the warriors and their mates wore black or dark grey skin tight suits moulded to their body. The material was like a second skin, but was actually a type of intelligent amorphic aramid material. It could protect a warrior from a bullet fired at close range or a sword's slice. However, the injury would leave a bruise which would disappear in an hour because of the Cynn Cruor's ability to heal quickly.

The Manchester Faesten's warriors and their women, Colin, and the rest of the warriors inside the command centre were all suited up. Even the Cynn mortals who'd been brought to man the portable heat tracking monitors wore the armour. The only difference was the coat of arms embossed on the left side of the armour which signified their particular Faesten.

Roarke looked at everyone assembled. Finn, Graeme, Zac, and Colin stood side by side looking at the satellite feed, their muscled arms and thighs straining against their suits. Eirene sat in front of one computer, talking into the wireless headset. Deanna leaned by the table. He knew she felt as if her body was coiled like a spring. He sought to give her peace. Roarke closed all telepathic communication, except the one directly linking him with his mate.

I love you Deanna.

His message startled her. Then she blushed, looking at him.

I love you, Roarke Hamilton. You dinnae hae to shout.

Roarke chuckled. *But you're afraid.*

Deanna nodded. *I cannot help it. After all this time I'm back here.*

You know I will keep you from harm. Roarke replied. *If I'm not here, the Cynn Cruor will protect you.*

I know. But I'd rather it be you.

He walked toward Deanna and took her into his embrace. He closed his eyes as her essence washed over him. Peace, calm, solitude. Whatever Roarke called it, Deanna gave it. He kissed her hair before tilting her chin with his fingers to kiss her tenderly. Their brief interlude was cut short by the transmission coming from the consoles. Roarke kept his arm around Deanna's waist as she, in turn, kept her arms around his.

"You're on speaker, Daniel," Eirene said before she removed the headset.

"It's Dan, Eirene." Dan's voice filtered through with a sigh. "Hey, guys!"

"Daniel," Finn drawled, eliciting chuckles all around.

"Qualtrough. I'd flay your hide if I were there."

Finn's mouth pulled up to a grin. "Looking forward to it."

"Okay," Dan said, drawing the word out long. "Let's get this asshole. Eirene, are you ready?"

"Ready as I'll ever be," Eirene said, looking up at Finn, who had a predatory grin on his face.

"Okay, I've given you the frequencies and command lines of the telemetry signals," Dan began. "Were you able to create the code for the rogue program?"

"Already done." Eirene sat at the keyboard, the staccato sound of her fingers on the keys filling the room. There was silence in the transport; everyone waited with bated breath. Everything rested on Eirene's intervention and the low orbit satellite's timing.

"Daniel," Eirene spoke again. "I need you to help me bounce off the signals. Window of ten seconds."

"Understood."

Eirene took a huge gulp of air. "Okay, here goes."

Eirene's fingers typed the instructions, sending them to Dan.

"All yours, Dan," she muttered. Tension made her forget to call him by his full name.

Finn laid his hand on Eirene's shoulder. The strain in the cabin was palpable.

"En route."

Everyone's eyes were glued to the wide screen above the monitors.

Zac's eyes closed. "In three, two, one."

One hundred fifty miles above the Isle of Man, Eirene's rogue program positioned the top secret satellite weapon over the Scatha fortress. The x-ray laser beam pulsed for only one one-hundredth of a second and the Scatha's sensors, power and major line of defence blinked permanently off. The sensor lights on the van blinked once.

Colin's mouth twitched. "It's show time."

Chapter Nineteen

Herod made his way through the passageway underneath the fortress. His eyes adjusted to the dark. Several torches lit his way. Dac didn't want any electricity in the passage because he wanted to keep it as old as he was. Herod didn't need any light to find his way. After all, he also had the Kinare gene in his blood. But this was also the passage the Scatha warriors took to bring the children to the orphanage. He smiled. The sweet babes were like lambs being brought to slaughter. All wails and cries. All helpless in the end.

Suddenly, he stopped and scowled. A feeling of uneasiness trickled from the base of his neck to the middle of his spine. Herod lifted his head to smell the air. A growl emitted from his chest. He couldn't smell anything untoward, but when he faced front, an image materialized in his mind's eye. Drawing his breath in harshly, he began to walk again, but his legs refused to move.

"Fuck! What is this?" he said aloud.

His mind wouldn't let up. Pain spread out from the base of his neck to slowly meander through his brain, like a snake uncoiling after hibernation. Herod grunted. He thrived on pain. Why did this pain feel different? He wasn't enjoying it at all. The vision slammed against his consciousness again.

"No!" he roared. Herod's face contorted. His eyes darkened to green and began to glow. His fingers transformed to claws. His mouth widened into to a jowl to accommodate the long razor sharp teeth. Herod bellowed again at the pain as it excruciatingly moved from his head to cover his entire body. He crumpled to the ground.

Memories of his immortal life ran like a runaway train through his mind before it stopped at another face. The face of a girl. An innocent girl he'd loved but betrayed in the end. The more he thought of her, the more the pain began to lessen. He held on to that thread to prevent the pain from spreading further. He had a mission to do and he'd be damned if he didn't see it through.

Soon the face of the girl morphed to the face of a young boy. Herod kept his eyes shut, willing himself to bury the image in the deep recesses of his mind. His mind refused. It was as though his brain wanted him to acknowledge the boy's existence. Herod knew whose face it was that lit up like a bulb in his psyche.

It was the face of his son. A son he had refused to acknowledge. The product of one night of incredible lust.

And love.

The offspring of a promise he was forced to break.

Herod took his time, allowing his breathing to slow down. Soon he felt his claws retract, his jowls disappear. His heart returned to its normal size. Small growls continued to emit from his chest. He clenched his jaw as he opened his eyes, anticipating the tail end of the pain he experienced. He took a deep breath and expelled it noisily before he stood unsteadily to his feet. He looked around. No one must see how vulnerable he had become at that moment. It wouldn't do him any good. Any sign of weakness and Dac would take the sword to his neck. He had no illusions that Dac would keep him forever. As it was, his liege lord had become irrationally jealous of him. Herod had no ambitions of leading the Scatha Cruor. No, he wanted to be the backroom boy. That was where the real power lay. Anyone seated on the throne could easily be manipulated. If Dac only knew what Herod had been doing for all these centuries, he would have every reason to doubt him. Even Herod was beginning to doubt himself, and why he did all those things. His harsh laugh echoed through the stone corridor. His actions were those of a Cynn Cruor, not a Scatha Cruor. And every time he caught himself doing a good deed, it rankled.

Herod started to walk, sighing in relief when his feet obeyed. He jogged toward the exit. He had wasted too much time. Correction. His mind took away the time he could have used to get to the orphanage. He had no intention of acknowledging his spawn. He hadn't acknowledged his son's existence when he was born. Neither did he acknowledge his existence when he bumped into him during the Cynn Cruor's raid of Dac's now defunct club *Dare You!*. The moment he saw the Cynn Cruor warrior, he knew. And so did the warrior. At that moment an invisible line connected them to one another. And no amount of denial or refusal on their part would break that bond now. He didn't know his name. He had no intention of ever making his acquaintance. But with the clashes of the Cruor becoming more frequent, it was inevitable that their paths would cross. And when they did, Herod would kill him. He didn't need that particular unnecessary complication in his life.

As if the gods had conspired against him, the lights in the passageway blinked off.

"Fuck!"

****

Five teams of Cynn Cruor surrounded Dac's Fortress. They zoomed toward the fort. To an ordinary mortal they would have looked like shadows in the wind. The kind of shadows that looked like transparent curtains in the pouring rain. And it was pouring, a deluge that seemed to want to thwart the warriors in their mission.

Colin and his team stopped by the trapdoor Deanna had identified. Water cascaded down his body armour from his face, the wind whipping around him and his team, but they were unfazed. He bent down to get a grip on the iron handle and pulled, flinging the iron door aside as though it were cardboard. A member of his team approached with a grenade. Pulling the pin, the Cynn warrior let it go. They zoomed a few feet away and waited. The flare was visible before they heard the explosion.

Colin approached the warrior. "Well done, mate," he shouted, nodding at the man. "I don't recall seeing you before."

He chuckled, showing white teeth against the darkness and the sheets of rain. He spat out the water that entered his mouth. "It's the first time I've been sent by my Faesten."

"Where is that?"

"Harlech."

"Hhmmm...Wales isn't too far from here," Colin muttered as he looked down the tunnel that would lead them to Herod's room.

"I'll be point man," the warrior roared back.

Colin nodded before looking up at the sky. The raindrops fell like shards of black glass. They looked sharp, only to fall on their bodies with a plop. The Team's heads and faces were soaked, but their armour kept them dry, warm, and ready to do battle. Colin narrowed his eyes at the new man before he jumped into the hole.

Craig. Colin called telepathically to his second-in-command. He couldn't risk being heard in the din of the downpour. *I've not seen him before.*

He's always been with us, Colin, Craig said, his face puzzled. *Even during the first recon mission here.*

Why the hell didn't I notice him? Colin scowled. Something wasn't right. The warrior was too smooth.

Craig shrugged. *He pretty much keeps to himself. Said he was assigned to us by Temple.*

Colin shook his head. *Graeme wouldn't do that without letting me know beforehand.*

Craig suddenly straightened. The rest of Colin's team closed in. Colin set his concentration on the minds of his men, opening the telepathic line only his men could hear.

Keep an eye on him. But don't let him know you suspect him. Act normally. I'm sure you can all do that.

Understood.

"All clear!" All of them heard him say.

You have your orders, men.

They all nodded. When everyone except Colin and Craig had left, Colin halted him. *What's his name?*

Craig didn't bother to use telepathy. "Luke Griffiths."

****

Along the passageway which led toward Herod's chambers, Luke heard Craig Shaw say his name. Thereafter, there was silence before the rest of Colin's team jumped down the hole. His mouth thinned. He knew they were communicating telepathically and he had been excluded. He continued walking like nothing had happened. He looked back and gave Colin's team the thumbs up. Soon Colin and Craig joined the team.

Luke knew he was running out of time. He had to finish what he'd been asked to do before the Cynn Cruor found out.

If he didn't, he wouldn't have anywhere else to go.

****

Assault teams took out the strong points surrounding Dac's fortress. Screeches and howls of the Scatha Cruor fought for dominance over the roars and bellows of the Cynn Cruor. Rain continued pouring in torrents, but that didn't deter the warriors from continuing the battle. Cynn mates fought side by side with their warriors. The Scatha jumped from the fortress' battlements like huge winged beasts, only to clash in mid-flight with the Cynn Cruor, guns blazing and swords slashing. Some got through the aerial shield wall and found their marks, slashing through Cynn warriors. The banshee screams of their mates filled the air before they charged to the side of their partners. Several of the warriors had already fallen in the first assault.

Grimly, Roarke said a prayer for those who had been wounded. There might still be time to save the lives of the fallen if their mates worked quickly. If a Cynn warrior saw a fallen comrade, they would fight their way to their brethren's side and pull the warrior to safety. Zac wasn't the only medic who had joined the battle. There would be others of their kind who would take care of the wounded. But Roarke knew he couldn't waste more time and let the warriors continue to fight Dac's fiends. He was driven all the more to battle his way into the fortress.

No one noticed the rain had abated to a drizzle. They continued to wipe their faces, mud, blood, and water tainting their skin.

Despite the confusion of the battle, Roarke immediately improvised a new axis of attack. A flanking assault would support those who had been part of the first attacking force. Soon the fortress' bailey filled with fighting men, women, and monsters. Roarke, Finn, Graeme, and Zac hacked and shot their way through the melee. Their silver bladed swords stained green, Scatha blood and gore all around as silver bullets wrought their carnage. They were all in their element. They all revelled at the sound of their swords slashing flesh and sinew, of bullets smashing and splintering bone to cut down the Scatha Cruors. All had one goal in mind.

The capture of Dac Valerian.

"Dux, over here!" Zac shouted over the din of battle. There was a break in the bailey which allowed them to run toward their goal.

"Roarke, the control centre will be at the back of the fortress." Deanna's voice came in clearly through his earpiece.

"We found it." Roarke's voice was much louder against the clamour around them.

"Be careful, my love."

"I will," he said. Intense emotion filled his chest. "I love you, Deanna."

Suddenly half a dozen Scatha came screaming at them from all sides, their glowing eyes filled with rage. Their jowls filled with teeth emitting a stench so great Roarke had to suck in enough air into his lungs in order to kill the Scatha who came close to him. He knew the others had to do the same.

Roarke and Finn stood side by side. For each enemy Finn shot, Roarke sliced his sword through its neck. But one Scatha saw a gap in their defence and charged at him. Roarke parried a fatal blow with his arm. The steel like claws cut through his armour and slashed through tendons. He roared at the burning pain before he decapitated him with a looping swing.

Graeme and Zac disposed of the Scatha who attacked them. Zac strode toward Roarke whose left arm hung limply by his side. Blood oozed from the limb, dripping down to the ground. Zac lifted his arm. Roarke winced before growling. Finn and Graeme walked to his side.

"Watch it, McBain. It hurts."

But instead of being careful, Zac firmly gripped Roarke's wrist and slowly turned it from side to side. Then Zac chuckled.

"What's so funny?" Roarke demanded.

"It's healing already. You'll survive."

True enough, Roarke noticed the blood almost tricking to nothing. New skin had started to interlock over the wound. The only evidence of any damage was to his tattered sleeve. He grunted in appreciation.

Deanna's blood had healed him.

Roarke made a fist and flexed his arm. His new skin stretched tautly and was a little stiff, but he had the use of his arm again. He exhaled in relief. "Let's go."

They zoomed toward the back door of Dac's fortress. Graeme, Zac, and Finn continuously covered two, six, and ten. Just as they halted by the door, two other Cynn warriors met them. Roarke's face broke into a grin. Connor Boyd and Ewan Blair. When Hamel Dun Creag had been overrun by Dac and the Scatha, they were the two warriors who lit the trail of gunpowder underneath the Faesten to give their survivors time to escape.

"Dux," they greeted Roarke.

"Connor, Ewan." He grinned. "Thank you for coming. I didn't realize you were here."

"We wouldna hae missed the party," Ewan said, grinning too. His ginger hair almost glowed in the dark. He opened his satchel to take out a cylinder not so different from a scuba diver's oxygen tank.

"Yer mam and da want ye to come home for a wee bit to meet yer lass, Deanna," Connor said, helping Ewan set up the charges.

"News travels fast," Roarke muttered as he wondered. "How did The Hamilton and my mother find out?"

"The Ancient Cynn sent word to your parents to let them know Deanna was alive," Ewan said, continuing to prepare the charge. "No wonder you couldn't die, Roarke."

Roarke stilled. "How could the Ancient Eald have known that?" Finn pondered.

Roarke remained silent. He had delayed telling the Ancient Eald and the Deoré about Deanna's existence. He was sure of his men's loyalty. While they swore fealty to the Ancient Eald, their allegiance belonged to Roarke. The warriors never interfered in the lives of their brethren. It was part of their code of ethics. It was each man's own prerogative to inform the Ancient Eald what happened in his life, if he wished so. Roarke knew that. His men knew that. His eyes narrowed, staring unseeingly at what Connor and Ewan were doing. He shook his head imperceptibly. No. He refused to entertain the thought. He briefly closed his eyes. Disappointment and a feeling of betrayal threatened to cloud his judgement as he thought of Colin.

Colin was one of Roarke's most trusted comrades. Roarke wouldn't have thought Colin capable of doing such a thing had it not been for his friend's scepticism about where Deanna's loyalties lay.

"Wait until you talk with him, Roarke," Finn's voice broke into his reverie. "I doubt Colin would talk to the Ancient Eald about Deanna. Besides, hardly anyone has been able to gain an audience with the Ancients except for you and your parents."

Roarke exhaled, almost growling. "You know me so well, Qualtrough," he said, looking at the man who grew up with him.

"Yes, too well. Sometimes being in your head is not a pleasant place to be," Finn muttered, trying at some humour amidst the gravity of their situation.

They were interrupted by Connor and Ewan's diatribe.

"Too much is too little for ye, isn't it Ewan?" Connor stated, shaking his head. Ewan had taken two cylinders out of the bag. Breaking each into two, he set one on each corner of the door. Connor pulled out a shorter, fatter cylinder and placed it in the centre of the door.

"We dinnae ken if there's another door behind it." Ewan defended. "This beauty will kick both doors in. Any blast will be bigger than the fireworks during Hogmany."

"Clear." Connor turned to the rest of the warriors as they zoomed away.

"In four." Zac started the countdown.

Roarke took in the battle still being fought.

"Three."

His eyes quickly scanned the area.

"Two."

Roarke grunted. At least he didn't see as many Scatha as there were earlier.

"One."

Before Roarke could speak, the charges detonated. The white light from the explosion temporarily blinded them. The battle came to a halt for only a millisecond before the remaining Cynn Cruor warriors bellowed their war cries, drowning the furious and indignant howls of the Scatha.

Roarke could feel it. Victory was within their grasp. His chest swelled with pride. The blood in his veins ran strong, enriched with Deanna's essence. He looked at his men. They were men chosen from different times. Yet all were his brothers in arms with a common cause.

The capture of their nemesis.

He grinned. The bloodlust was in all their eyes. The red-orange colour of battle.

He bellowed. His Cynn Cruor brethren followed his lead.

After tonight, Dac would be no more.

Chapter Twenty

Frustration made Herod want to trash everything in his path, but that wouldn't do him any good. The bikes were not working. Their electronic circuits seemed to have been fried. How in the hell the Cynn Cruor managed to do that he didn't know.

But if he were honest with himself, the Cynn Cruor were at par, if not better, than the Scatha in using new technology. And when the lights had gone out in the passageway, his initial guess was that their enemy had tripped the electric switches. And now that the bikes were not working, he was definitely sure a form of electro-magnetic pulse had been used. His sensitive hearing had picked up the commotion and ensuing assault on the Fortress. He wanted to return and engage the Cynn Cruor, but he had to start moving the children and it was a long way to the dug-outs. He could opt to transform and travel faster to reach his destination. It was, after all, the night of the full moon. But it had been over two days since he'd had sex. Just like a Cynn warrior, he needed reserves of strength which only came from slaking his lust. Sex was the fuel that kept any Cruor warrior strong. If he had to fight them later on, a transformation would sap a lot of his much needed strength.

Growling, he moved from one bike to the other, throwing them out of his path until he saw the black Kawasaki. He noticed the battery wasn't connected. He looked at the bikes he had trashed. Their batteries had been connected. Sensing his chance, he took the battery and connected the leads. He pressed the power switch and twisted the ignition. The bike roared to life. He grunted in approval, swinging his leg over the seat. He took one last look at the dark recesses of the passageway, and gunning the motor, sped out of the cave.

****

Deanna and Eirene watched the carnage from the confines of the command centre. They had argued with their warriors, who refused to let them join the battle. Finn argued that Eirene needed to track the warriors in the field. Roarke didn't want Deanna to be captured again. In the end, both warriors gave their women kisses which melted their stubborn hearts to comply with their wishes. Deanna had screamed the moment she felt Roarke get hurt. Her left arm suddenly became useless. Eirene had helped her to sit as the pain went through her.

"It will be fine." Eirene had assured her.

"How do you know?" Deanna had asked, wincing. There were no gashes on her arms, but when she pulled back her armour's sleeve, there were red welts like second degree burns on her skin.

"When your Cynn Cruor warrior hurts, so do you," Eirene replied. "But once your blood inside Roarke starts to heal him, your pain will subside too."

True enough, in a few minutes, the scorching pain dulled before it disappeared completely.

Now, as they watched the carnage from the command centre and worried about their mates, they noticed a heat signature coming from a different part of the fortress.

"Eirene," Deanna began.

"I know," Eirene said. Her eyes narrowed before she typed on the keyboard. "The heat signature is green. Cynn Cruor heat signatures are red."

"That might be Dac," Deanna said, her voice so soft it was almost undecipherable. Fear trickled down her spine like ice. Her heart pulsed inside her chest in a deadly slow beat, making her almost stop breathing. She opened her mouth. No air passed through her air passages. Panic assailed her. Had she forgotten to breathe? She could feel her skin tighten. She slowly doubled over.

"Deanna!" Eirene held her up as she almost crumpled to the floor.

Deanna heard Eirene, but her mind was too immobilized with fear.

All those children.

It felt so surreal. Flashbacks filled her mind like bubbles floating toward the surface of a stormy sea. Every time Dac used her she had felt degraded; the memory of those horrible days clung to her like grease stuck to every pore of her body. She remembered the sleepless nights of counting the days until she could finally escape. Then the feeling of dwindling hope like the sands in an hourglass falling to add to the quagmire below. Could she allow what happened to her, to happen to the children as well? The Scatha Cruor would break them easily.

She closed her eyes, her jaw clenching. Her fear warred with her need to do what was right. She thought of Roarke and of all the memories he shared with her when they'd given each other their blood. He, too, had been in situations where he had to make difficult decisions, decisions which pitted his morals with the need to do what was right for the Cynn Cruor.

But what was right for her may not be right for the children. Deanna shuddered to think of their broken bodies and the feeling of worthlessness that would eventually encircle them in its death grip. They would never know any other way of living.

They would never know any other way of loving.

Deanna's eyes clouded before a tear slipped down her cheek. She sniffed. She didn't even know the pain she felt inside had shown itself outside. She was too engrossed grappling with what she had to do and she didn't know whether Roarke could forgive her this time.

But to save the children, she had to go.

The right choice was clear, but very hard to make. The wealth left to her by Emeline was nothing compared to the burden of her conscience if she didn't do something to save the lives of those who'd yet begun to live. And she had lived. Oh, she had lived. She sighed as she closed her eyes to bring Roarke's face to her mind. The past few days were the best she'd ever experienced in her immortal life. There was no doubt in her mind that Roarke still loved her and she was counting on his love to understand why she had to sacrifice herself. It was the right thing to do.

For everyone.

For the Cynn Cruor.

She wasn't quite sure if Roarke could sense her sadness or read her thoughts in the midst of everything happening around them.

She didn't want him finding out so she continuously threw a barrier around her thoughts of leaving him by thinking of something as mundane as going shopping with Eirene.

Deanna pressed her lips together in sadness. She would always be a part of Roarke as he would be a part of her. Their bond could never be broken. She would remain a Cynn Cruor mate even if she was pushed out. She called on the new memories, putting them around her shoulders like a beautiful warm blanket. These had to be enough to put whatever was left of her heart back together again. After tonight, there was no way she would be able to return to Roarke. Everyone would think she was the Scatha Cruor's spy even if it was the furthest thing from the truth. By leaving, she sealed her fate.

Deanna heard one of the Cynn Cruor mortals call to Eirene. Eirene hesitated a moment before she moved away. Deanna stood to see what had happened. It might just be the last time she would be able to know what was happening to Roarke. She brushed away her heart's pain at the thought.

"They've breached the door," Eirene said, trepidation and excitement in her voice.

"It won't be long now," Deanna agreed. She walked toward the back of the command centre to the small aid station. There was a door there where the injured could access the field clinic and the blood bank. She looked back. Eirene was busy talking to the Cynn mortals. She carefully opened the door and left.

Outside, she saw Colin's blue Subaru and the Range Rover. They had also brought several bikes with them. Deanna walked toward the Ducati. She checked the instruments. The command centre had been parked outside of the thousand metre radius and the pulse which fried the Scatha's electronics didn't disable their own vehicles and instrumentation. She twisted the key in the ignition, lighting up the instrument panel before the engine roared to life. Deanna programmed the bike to "wet" so the tires didn't skid on the road.

"What the bloody hell are you doing?"

Deanna whirled around at Eirene's enraged voice. Her shoulders slumped, but she continued to prepare.

"I'm going after that Scatha. It might be Dac."

"Why would you do that?" Eirene asked her in disbelief. "After what he did to you, you'd go back? What's this? Stockholm Syndrome?"

"Oh, God, you couldn't be further from the truth!" Deanna laughed almost hysterically as hurt pierced her at Eirene's accusation. "I would have expected a lot of people to doubt me, Eirene. But I didn't expect it from you."

Eirene stepped back with a gasp. She looked at Deanna for what seemed like a long time before she let her shoulders drop. "I'm sorry, Deanna. That was uncalled for."

"You're bloody right it was."

"But what did you expect me to think when you slipped away?" Eirene defended.

"Would you have allowed me to go if I told you?" she countered.

Eirene exhaled loudly. "No, I wouldn't."

Deanna nodded. She and Eirene would make amends later, but right now the children were her priority. She needed to follow the Scatha who had left the fortress. She straddled the bike before fitting the helmet over her head.

With an unladylike oath, Eirene strode toward the other Ducati bike and climbed on before she started the engine.

"What are you doing?" Deanna asked. Her hand was raised, holding her hair while the other held her helmet.

Eirene raised a brow, her voice dripping with sarcasm. "What does it look like I'm doing? There's no way on God's green earth you're leaving without me. You need my kick-ass skills to protect your sorry bum. Besides, if push comes to shove, I'm your only witness against any accusation the others might heap on you."

"Eirene, I—"

"Save it for later, Deanna," Eirene said, her voice brusque. Deanna sensed her friend was hurt, but she didn't have time to give a complete explanation.

They both resumed putting their helmets over their heads. Fitted with Bluetooth intercoms, it would allow them to talk with each other and the command centre. They both adjusted the volumes before easing their bikes away from the centre. Deanna heard Eirene test her intercom as she spoke to the mortals on board the converted camper.

"Finn is so going to kill me for this," Eirene muttered.

"Shit, Eirene, if you're going to be such a pain in the arse, you don't have to go," Deanna snapped, immediately regretting what she said.

"Point taken," Eirene said, her huge sigh coming over the headset like a gust of wind. "This war is getting on my nerves."

"It's getting to all of us," Deanna replied. "But we have to focus. I doubt the children will still be in the fortress. I have a feeling that creep we saw is going to the orphanage."

"Oh, Dee, I feel like a bitch."

"Don't sweat it, Eirene. We all become bitches at least once in our lives," Deanna said. She turned to Eirene, who revved the motor beside her. Both their visors were still open. "So what will it be? Be all maudlin or kick some Scatha Cruor balls?"

Grins tugged on their lips. They reached up for their visors and locked them in place.

That kind of question didn't need an answer.

****

The roar of the blast had hurled the entire slab of the door into the Scatha's control room. It mowed down people and equipment in its path. The flash and fireball which followed immediately behind the door blinded everyone inside the command centre. The few Scatha warriors in the path of the fireball were flash-burned. The concussion wave that came a few milliseconds later threw others like rag dolls against the walls, and sent others skidding across the floor. Roarke, Finn, Graeme, and Zac were in the control room seconds after the wave did its lethal work. Connor and Ewan decided to join the battle in the bailey. With disciplined and accurate fire, Finn and Zac quickly engaged and dispatched several Scatha still dazed by the ferocity of the attack. Roarke and Graeme were terrifying figures with their long blades, slipping in with superhuman speed, only the sparks of the blade tips striking metal giving away their position.

Screeches of the Scatha who entered the control room to help their fallen comrades rent the air. The stench coming from their mouths filled the vast enclosure. The Cynn team moved as one, guns trained at their enemies, spit after spit of silver bullets smashing through the jowls and bodies. Roarke and Graeme lunged at any Scatha Cruor hit by bullets to decapitate them. Dust and gore surrounded them. Breathing proved to be most difficult. As one, the Cynn Cruor jumped as high as the fortress' ceiling would allow them, expanded their lungs to suck in air before bearing back down on the jowl-gaped Scatha.

"Dux! Dac!" Graeme shouted in warning.

Roarke whirled around at Graeme's voice, but it was too late. Dac moved away from the Scatha Cruor warriors surrounding him and fired his weapon, his face breaking into a maniacal smile, his teeth long and sharp.

"You are mine now, Hamilton." His voice was guttural.

An involuntary shiver trickled down Roarke's spine. Dac's voice sounded inhuman, as though it came from the coldest depths of hell. Quickly assessing the situation, Roarke knew there was no way he would come out unscathed. His last thought was of Deanna, but as he waited for the bullets to hit him, a body slammed into his. Graeme's body jerked as the rounds meant for Roarke bit into his friend's back.

"No!" Zac roared.

Colin and his team appeared in the gallery above the control room. They trained their weapons on Dac's personal guards. Dac was livid, his eyes blazed as he gave an ear piercing scream which sounded like nails on a blackboard. He swung his weapon at Colin, who flinched only for a millisecond before putting a bullet in the middle of Dac's head. The Scatha leader gave a grunt of surprise as he staggered back. Black blood oozed from the hole.

Then he laughed, the laugh of the unhinged.

Two of his personal guards dragged him away while the three others opened fire at the advancing Cynn Cruor.

"Stay with Graeme, Roarke. I'll go after Dac," Colin shouted before he and his team left in hot pursuit.

Roarke lay Graeme on his stomach. Blood spurted and fell in ribbons to the floor.

"Stay with me Temple, dammit!" Zac shouted as he took a dagger from his boot. Graeme's armour held off the rounds that blossomed like mushrooms. Zac made an incision on the armour. The bullets slid off, but the silver cores had buried themselves deep into Graeme's back.

"Fuck!" Zac swore. Blood continued oozing from Graeme's wounds without let up. "Dux, I need something to stop the bleeding."

"I'll get it." Finn volunteered. In a flash he catapulted himself on to the gallery.

"Find any alcohol." Zac turned to Roarke. "I need to wash the wounds, but I can't do that if it keeps pooling on his back."

Roarke walked away to look for what Zac asked for. His jaw hardened. Graeme had placed his own life on the line to save him. Had Dac been successful, Deanna's blood could have healed him. But Graeme? He didn't have a mate who could fortify his blood.

Roarke ran his hand through his hair. He closed his eyes, overcome with emotion. He owed Graeme. Big time.

Then he felt it. A pull in the centre of his chest travelling down to twist his gut. Deanna. He frowned as he sensed her moving away.

"God damn it, Eirene!" Finn exploded.

Their red orange eyes narrowed as they looked at each other.

"Your mate?" Roarke asked.

"You think?" Finn countered, raising a mocking brow. He contacted the command centre to check on Eirene and Deanna as he moved away from Roarke.

"Shit!" Roarke muttered. His narrowed gaze looked at the carnage around him.

At one time, he would have gloried at the sight of the ashes of the enemy. The elimination of a Scatha Cruor warrior meant they were nearing a form of peace. Of détente.

An old word in a new time.

A word that described the best they could all hope for. If they reached even that far, maybe he would be able to hand over the reins of the Faesten's leadership and start a family with Deanna.

Roarke closed his eyes and Deanna's face filled his mind. He once thought he would remain adrift forever, but she was his anchor, his safe haven. She was his strength and the love his eternal soul had searched for.

"Roarke! Eirene and Deanna are gone," Finn said, his voice filled with anger and worry.

Roarke swore, feeling a terrible sense of loss. He had been right when he felt the distance between Deanna and himself increasing. "Where the bloody hell did they go?"

"Command centre says they were on their way to the orphanage, but they got cut off a few minutes ago. They rode off on the bikes."

"Hamilton, you and Qualtrough go." Colin interjected. "I'll help Zac get Graeme back to Manchester as soon as possible."

Roarke nodded, fear gripping his heart like a vice, but there were more important things to be done. Fear had no place in his mind or heart right now.

"We can track the bikes. Take the van. If the children are there, we need to get them out right away. I'll take the SUV."

Then he felt Colin grip his arm. "After you get Deanna, we need to talk."

In the aftermath of Graeme being injured, he'd forgotten he needed to speak with Colin. He nodded. "Yes, we must."

Chapter Twenty-One

"Where the bloody hell is he going?" Eirene shouted through her headset against the din of the bike's engine.

"This is the road to Dalby," Deanna shouted back. "The orphanage is there, but I'm not quite sure where."

"Did you ever see it?"

"No." Deanna shook her head underneath her helmet. "They spoke of it all the time. I was never allowed to venture far away from the Fortress."

Deanna and Eirene sped through the A27 Port Erin to Peel Road toward Dalby. They didn't switch their headlights on, depending on their now enhanced eyesight to tail the Scatha warrior. They were worried they might have lost sight of the Scatha Cruor ahead of them, but they saw his tail light in the distance once they passed Glen Rushen. The copse of trees to their right rose like shadowy giants standing guard against the dark sky. They both eased up on the accelerator to keep a comfortable distance. They followed as he left the main road which narrowed the nearer they got to the Irish Sea. Halting their bikes, they switched off the engines. Then taking their helmets off, they looked up at the sky with one thought in mind.

"Dawn will be coming soon," Eirene commented, running her hand across her nape to allow her hair to tumble over her shoulders. The air was fresh with the scent of rain as a misty downpour caressed their faces.

"I know," Deanna replied. "That's why we need to hurry."

They got off their bikes, parking them where they stood before walking slowly, avoiding anything that would crunch underneath their boots.

"I'm sure the Scatha Cruor already know we're here," Eirene muttered.

Deanna didn't reply. Instead, she concentrated on where they were going.

The path opened to a wide field coated with thick grass. The waves sounded muffled, yet peaceful as they slapped idly against the rocks. Deanna and Eirene walked softly, trying to blend in with the shadows thrown by the bushes and scrub. The Scatha Cruor's figure was silhouetted against a lightening horizon. Then he disappeared.

"Where did he go?" Eirene hissed.

Deanna's eyes widened. "That isn't the orphanage," she whispered. "He's gone inside the bunker."

"Bunker?"

Deanna nodded. "Those bunkers formed part of the country's radar system during the Cold War, but they abandoned them a few decades ago." She narrowed her eyes, looking at the horizon.

"There's a boat," Eirene said, following her gaze.

The boat they both saw bobbed in the dark waters several hundred yards away. Deanna was sure the Scatha Cruor would have a small motor boat by the shore to ferry the children off the Isle of Man.

"I see it. C'mon," she said, moving toward the bunker. "We have to get to him. We don't have much time."

"Dee, he'll see us!"

Deanna whirled around. "Eirene, he's a Cruor. He's already seen us." She bit her lip before letting out her breath. "I've seen the Scatha do this before with the older children and women. They will give them something which will make them docile. I can't allow that to happen."

Eirene sucked in her breath. "Bastards."

Deanna nodded. "Yes, they are."

They started sprinting.

"I hope Finn and Roarke come with back up soon. We lost contact with the command centre half way back." Eirene puffed.

Deanna almost tripped at Roarke's name. She had hoped to ignore her heartache until all of this was over. Unfortunately, her strategy didn't appear to be working.

As they neared the mouth of the bunker, they heard voices of men and children. Cold dread trickled down Deanna's spine. She and Eirene lay flat on the ground, the grass bitterly cold against their hands. It was a good thing the armour insulated their bodies. She couldn't do anything about her red hair, but knowing how transfuges could be, she prayed they didn't come over to investigate.

Soon, they heard the whimpers of children. Cautiously, Deanna raised her head to look. She counted a dozen Scatha walking out of the bunker followed by ten children who looked as though they had been drugged. Their age range appeared to be from five to ten years old.

"Dammit, Dee, we've got to help them!" Eirene whispered fiercely.

"We will."

This was it. Her only wish was that Roarke would find it in his heart to forgive her.

Deanna inhaled deeply before letting the air out slowly. She glanced at Eirene, who still had her eagle eyes on the children.

"Dee, they're moving away," Eirene said in panic.

Deanna took a glance. The Scatha in front had grabbed hold of the arm of the first child and proceeded to move toward the sandy shore.

"Eirene, look at me."

When Eirene turned to her, she continued.

"No matter what happens, know that I will never betray Roarke or the Cynn Cruor."

"Dee—"

"No, listen! There isn't much time!"

"No, Dee!"

"Yes, Eirene. Keep the children safe and wait for Finn and the rest. They will come."

"God damn it, Deanna!" Eirene hissed as her hand shot out to grip Deanna's wrist. "What are you going to do?"

"Please, Eirene! I have to save the children!"

Before Eirene could retort, Deanna stood up. The Scatha warriors guarding the children started in surprise when they saw her walking toward them. They glowered at her, their eyes turning a glowing dark green. Deanna had to stop herself from retching at their horrible smell. She'd never got used to their scent then, and she completely abhorred their smell now. Their faces were morphing, their jaws widening into jowls when she saw someone she hadn't expected to see. Her skin crawled when she heard his chuckle. Her heart thudded in earnest. She wasn't so sure now if her plan was going to work. But the memories of her time with the Scatha Cruor strengthened her resolve.

His stance was relaxed as he crossed his arms over his massive chest.

"Deanna," he drawled. "I never thought I'd see the day."

"Herod," she greeted him. Taking a deep breath and letting it out slowly, she said, "I've decided to come back."

Chapter Twenty-Two

Luke cursed under his breath. Had he been wrong about Deanna?

After leading Colin and his Team through the secret passageway that led to Herod's quarters, they had spread out. Colin had assigned his second-in-command, Craig, with Luke. As soon as they opened the door of Herod's room, they saw several Scatha Cruor running along the corridor. The Cynn Cruor had engaged them in close quarter combat. The Scatha came at them with assault weapons and claws, their jaws snapping and trying to take a bite off them. The Cynn had taken hits as their armour absorbed the bullets' velocity, deflecting the silver core. Only their skin was singed, a superficial wound, nothing Zac's adrenaline-like serum wouldn't heal. The Scatha scattered when they saw many of their own fall. Colin gave chase. As they ran, Luke turned back toward the passageway and out to the bailey. He had just passed the mobile command post when he saw Deanna and Eirene leave.

"Shit!"

Luke had no choice. He would have to sprint and follow them on foot.

Now, as he watched Deanna face Dac's second-in-command, he wondered whether the person who hired him was also wrong about Roarke Hamilton's mate.

****

Deanna warily watched Herod as he approached. Her knees knocked so hard it took all of her willpower to tamp down her fear and keep upright. 'Think of the children' became a mantra she clung to.

"Dee, please!"

Eirene's pleading didn't slow her down. She walked toward Herod.

"No!" Eirene gripped Deanna's arm, but was curtailed when two Scatha grabbed hold of her. She winced when their claws punched through her armour.

"Don't touch her!"

All of Deanna's fear turned into anger when she saw Eirene was bleeding. She raised her foot and kicked the crotch of the nearest Scatha. The warrior screamed in agony, letting go of Eirene's arm to cup the pain between his thighs. As he doubled over Deanna kneed his face, breaking his jaw. She cringed at what she was about to do. She held his head with both hands and twisted hard. She heard the neck snap, taking the warrior out of the fight. Eirene swung her free arm toward the other Scatha's face. The sound of another jaw breaking cracked in the pre-dawn air. In one swift move, Eirene took out her butterfly knife, stabbing the warrior in the heart before making several quick slashes through his throat. She managed to get two criss-crossing slashes before another claw grabbed her wrist and twisted her arm behind her. She screamed in agony. A third Scatha warrior had zoomed toward her when he saw his fellow Scatha on his knees.

"No!" Deanna screamed. With strength she didn't know she possessed, she bolted across the distance, planting a kick at the Scatha warrior's head, the spike of her stiletto cracking through the skull. The warrior roared.

"Enough!" Herod thundered.

Everyone stilled. Deanna was breathing hard and fast, adrenalin still spiking through her system. She stood up from her crouched position and lifted her heel away from the warriors head. The warrior roared in pain.

She bent down, collaring the Scatha. "When I say no, *dumbass*, I mean no."

The warrior growled, but didn't retaliate.

She looked at Herod. Straightening up, she walked toward him.

"Deanna, no!" Eirene pleaded, also breathing heavily from the fight and the pain caused by the Scatha's claws.

"Impressive, Deanna. Your time with the Cynn Cruor has toughened you." Herod's teeth gleamed as he smiled, his voice carrying a tinge of admiration. He looked at Eirene, chuckling. "Did you think I wouldn't know there was another Cynn Cruor mate with you?"

"You hurt her and I swear to God I will kill you."

Herod roared with laughter. The other Scatha warriors by his side cackled.

"Brave words from someone who used to beg me to end her life. How many times, Deanna?" When she didn't answer, he continued. "Every time Dac used you, you would plead with me to kill you." The sound of hoots and catcalls encircled them and with it came the stench from the Scatha warriors' breath.

"They're not just brave words, Herod. I will kill you if you hurt my friend or the children."

In a split second, Herod had his hand around Deanna's neck.

"If I had any scruples, I'd say you were out of your mind," he said softly, his nose pressed against Deanna's cheek. He licked at her ear and chortled when she shuddered. Then his fingers morphed into claws. Deanna hissed in pain when Herod's razor-edge claws sliced through her suit, nipping the skin of her throat.

"Dac will kill you if you return," he continued.

"It doesn't matter," she said flatly. "I will go with you in exchange for the lives of my friend and the children. I will tell you everything you need to know about the Cynn Cruors' operations."

Deanna had no intention of telling Herod Eirene's name. If he knew who she was, her precarious position of negotiating their release would plummet.

"Deanna! God damn you!"

Eirene's furious voice made her jerk. Deanna saw a blur coming from behind Herod.

"Don't hurt her." Herod barked at the warrior. He looked down at his captive. "Her life and that of the children's hang in the balance, whore."

Deanna closed her eyes. Her heart shrivelled at the rage in Eirene's voice. It didn't matter if Herod had called her a whore. She had been that at one time, but she had to continue with her plan.

When she opened her eyes, Herod's own dark green neon ones bored into hers. She held his gaze evenly. She wasn't afraid any more. Soon, she felt Herod's grip on her neck ease. She swallowed. "Let them go, Herod."

"What if I just kill all of you?"

"You know I'm more valuable alive," she replied. "Let them go."

Herod's eyes bored into hers. After a slight hesitation, Herod's claws became fingers once again. It didn't stop the little wince from Deanna as the claw slid against her neck, deepening the cut, blood oozing from the wound. Herod stepped back, scrutinizing her.

"Let the woman go. The children as well," he ordered the Scatha warrior holding Eirene. She bowed her head, slowly exhaling a sigh of relief.

One down. One to go.

The warriors in charge of the children pushed them toward Eirene. A child fell and whimpered. Eirene pushed away from the warrior holding her. He didn't let go, attempting to steal a kiss. She gave him a hard slap, kneeing him in the groin. He growled in outrage even as the other warriors snickered.

"Enough!" Herod bellowed. "Control that bitch, Deanna."

But there was nothing to control. As Eirene strode toward the children, she bumped her shoulder against Deanna. Righting herself slightly, she followed Eirene.

"Stay here," Herod commanded.

She whirled around, blasting Herod with all the fury and vitriol in her gaze.

"I am going to make sure she and the children are safe," she said, stressing every word. "The Scatha are not exactly known for keeping their word."

"I can take care of them, Deanna," Eirene said, her feeling of betrayal colouring her words.

"Stop being so high and mighty, Eirene." Deanna shot back, suddenly tired of all the bickering. She heaved a sigh, before bending at the waist, pretending to check on the child that fell. "Please don't judge me. I would never do anything to hurt Roarke."

Eirene's head whipped to her. "But—"

Deanna swore softly. "For someone so tech savvy, you can be pretty dense."

"You're about to betray the Cynn Cruor and yet you hurl insults."

Deanna straightened, shaking her head. There was no point talking to Eirene in her current frame of mind. She took the hands of several of the children. "I will accompany you until you reach the edge of the field, then I have to go back."

Even though Eirene didn't say a word, Deanna heard the continuous sniffs that turned into ill-concealed sobs. Her chest tightened. Her teeth clenched. Oh, God! She didn't know if she could go through with it.

They reached the edge of the field.

"Take care of the children, Eirene." Deanna repeated as a sudden gust of wind whipped her hair, giving her a fiery halo against the lightening sky.

"Don't do this, Deanna," Eirene sobbed, tears spilling down her cheeks.

Deanna cupped her cheek tenderly as her mouth lifted in the barest of smiles. "I have no choice."

"What about Roarke?"

The back of Deanna's own eyes suddenly pricked with tears, at the same time the living muscle inside her chest squeezed in anguish. "I will always love him, Eirene. I hope he knows that."

"Dee—"

"Go," Deanna said softly, relieved to hear Eirene call her by her pet name. It was going to be all right. "Wait for the Cynn Cruor."

Eirene hesitated before her shoulders slumped. Talking to the children in a happy voice which belied her true feelings, she held on to several hands as she herded the rest toward the bikes.

As soon as they were far from the field, Deanna pivoted, but stopped short when she saw a warrior had followed her. The closer she walked toward Herod, the nearer the warrior was to her until his fetid smell enveloped her. She couldn't help the heaving of her stomach even though she had hardly eaten. She fell on all fours before raising one knee. Her hand quickly clung to her right boot, then her left, gripping the daggers concealed there.

The Scatha laughed with glee. He bent to grab her hair to pull her up. But his cackle turned to a gurgle of surprise. He looked down as a silver dagger sliced across his mid-section. Deanna removed the dagger before crisscrossing both daggers against the warrior's neck. In a second, he turned to dust, his head rolling away from its body. As the cloud of dirt settled, she faced Herod. Her fury at the Scatha touching her suffused her entirely. Screeches filled the air as the remaining warriors waited, not moving from where they stood until Herod told them to do so.

Herod remained still, his arms by his sides. Slowly, his fingers reverted to claws. His stance was nonchalant, but Deanna knew from the time she spent with the Scatha that Herod never relaxed.

"Again another impressive show," he commented, his voice carried by the wind.

Deanna didn't respond. Knees slightly bent, she turned her attention to the warriors.

"You never really intended to return, did you?" Herod asked before chuckling. "Were those children worth your life?"

"Those children are so much more than me or you, Herod." Deanna's voice was strong. "They belong to their families. Not with Scatha scum."

Growls of anger rent the air. Deanna chuckled. For the first time, she became amused at the whole situation.

"As Dac's second, Herod, you're pretty gullible," she said. "Are you not afraid Dac will flay you alive for what you've done? I honestly can't believe how you quickly agreed to let the children and my friend go."

This time, it was Herod who remained silent. Deanna goaded him further.

"Is it even remotely possible somewhere in that bleak Scatha heart of yours, there is still a seed of compassion? That you still have some sense of humanity that Dac's poison has not corrupted?"

"You forget yourself, slut," he snapped.

Deanna laughed. "You can call me whatever you want, Herod. It doesn't matter anymore. For whatever it's worth, thank you."

"What for?"

"For giving the children up," she said, before continuing in a softer tone, "And for trying to make excuses for me when I was with the Scatha to prevent Dac from torturing me."

Deanna's sharper sight saw Herod's face contort with fury.

"You will die, bitch!"

Deanna grinned, surprised that she looked forward to fighting Herod. "Do your worst, arsehole."

Herod roared in rage that even the warriors backed away. He launched himself at Deanna. Deanna's heart leaped to her throat but she stayed her ground. She planted her feet firmly to take the force of Herod's weight. As she raised her arms to parry his claws, another sword intercepted the fatal blow. The clang of steel echoed in the air.

"Your claws will not touch her," a familiar voice roared.

Deanna staggered back in shock. "Luke!"

Chapter Twenty-Three

Herod glowered at Luke. They separated before circling each other, trying to find a weak point.

"I'm going to find pleasure in killing you, Cynn Cruor."

Luke laughed in amusement even as he continued to gauge Herod's every move. "I'm not a Cynn Cruor."

Herod raised his brows in surprise.

"Neither am I Scatha."

Herod stopped circling and slowly straightened. His head inclined slightly to one side, his face curious.

"But you know of us," Herod murmured, almost to himself. "Why not join us? We will give you all the power, wealth, and prestige you could ever desire. You'll never want for anything."

Luke's shoulders shook in mirth. "Funny, that's exactly what the one who hired me said. But the difference is that you're such a crock of shit."

Herod growled. Luke threw himself against him, taking Herod by surprise with his agility. The Scatha grunted when Luke stabbed him in the gut. Herod hurled Luke so far away that he landed almost a hundred feet from where they stood. Luke jumped up and crouched, a growl coming from his throat. The bloodlust ran thickly through his veins. He felt his eyes cloud, but he couldn't see what colour they were.

He sprinted back. "Shit!"

Deanna was being attacked from all sides. Herod purposefully strode toward her. Luke saw Deana was holding her own, but the warriors' consistent taunting and slicing through her suit to nick her made her weaken.

Then, from his peripheral vision to his right, a lone figure came running toward them. Luke turned to his left. Headlights bounced off the darkness. Cold dread worked its way down his spine when he saw Deanna fall with Herod almost on top of her.

"No!"

Luke didn't know whose roar was the loudest. Roarke's, his, or the stranger who suddenly launched himself at Herod, knocking him away from Deanna's unmoving form. Herod and the stranger rolled away. Luke caught the nearest Scatha warrior unaware as he plunged one sword to the heart before taking off his head with the other sword he held in his hand. He saw Finn and Roarke do the same with the remaining Scatha. The dust hadn't settled before Luke and Roarke approached Deanna's body.

Luke ran toward Deanna.

"Stay away from her," Roarke said, his voice harsh. "She belongs to me."

"I've no intention of taking her away from you." Luke bit out as he sheathed his weapons "She's hurt."

Roarke knelt down. When Deanna stirred, the relief that washed through them was palpable.

Roarke scooped Deanna in his arms before turning to Finn who'd arrived with Eirene. "I need to get her to Zac quickly. You take the Range Rover. I'll ride with Eirene. We'll divide the children between the cars."

Eirene came running toward them. At that moment, Herod stood up and so did the stranger.

"Blake!" Eirene's shocked voice carried through the wind.

But Blake didn't seem to hear her as he and Herod continued to size each other up. Then Herod straightened. So did Blake. Everyone turned to see the sun peeking through the horizon, turning the sky a pale pink. Except for the Cynn Cruor mates, there was no way they would be able to keep their strength.

They heard Herod chuckle.

"I never thought I'd be grateful to see the sun." Herod's claws and jowls retracted. He took a longer look at his opponent, then nodded. "Perhaps some other time."

Then he was gone. Blake attempted to follow him.

"Blake. Don't," Finn said, his voice troubled. "Please. Come back."

Blake kept his back to them. His body tense. "I can't," he said, his head bowed. "I have to do something before I can be worthy."

"Worthy of what?" Eirene approached him. He turned to her. A ghost of a grin lit his face.

"Worthy of being a Cynn Cruor."

Luke did not need to hear this. There was some dynamics going on between the Manchester Cynn Cruor and this Blake guy. He had his own problems to deal. He had enough evidence to give to the person who hired him. That was enough.

Slowly, he eased back. In no time at all, he'd moved to the parallel world, and clouded the minds of the assembled. He turned and walked away. They wouldn't know he had gone and when they did, he would already be on a boat over the Irish Sea.

He was tired of travelling. He was tired of fighting without any backup. He had seen the camaraderie of the Cynn Cruor and it struck a chord deep within him. He wanted to belong.

But where did he come from?

And after he reported to his superiors, where would he go?

****

Deanna stirred. She moved her head from side to side and grimaced. Automatically, her hand touched the offending part. She hissed, the pain sending a burn around the wound that rippled outward. Then memories of Herod flooded her mind. The next thing she noticed was that she wasn't lying on the cold ground. Neither could she feel the cold wind against her cheeks.

And she was naked.

Slowly, she opened her eyes. The familiar blues and greys of Roarke's bedroom greeted her. Torment ran through her like a derailed train. She was supposed to die in Dalby. Eirene had heard her offer herself to Herod. She was sure Eirene would have already told the Cynn Cruor what she had done. What Eirene didn't know was that Deanna had no intention of betraying the Cynn Cruor. Now that they'd brought her back, how could she convince them otherwise?

And there was the appearance of Luke. Deanna couldn't have been more surprised to see him on the Isle of Man since he'd tried his pick up line on her. Was he Cynn Cruor? She didn't recall seeing him anywhere in the Faesten. On the other hand, there were so many warriors in the Faesten she could have easily missed him. She vaguely remembered how he took on Herod, before she herself had to take on the Scatha who attacked her.

She raised herself on her elbows, the sheet falling to expose her naked breasts. Goosebumps skittered across her skin as she felt a waft of coolness in the air. A fire glowed in the hearth, the logs crackling, sending sparks against the grate guard. The scent of pine filled the air, its woodsy scent bringing back memories of a simpler time in the Highlands.

Of the time she and Roarke first made love.

Her gaze was drawn to the solid shape of her mate looking out the window. He was silhouetted by grey clouds and the rain splattered window, water running in transparent ribbons down the glass pane. Being disoriented, she didn't know what time it was.

"You've been asleep for over twenty four hours," Roarke answered her unvoiced question before turning around to look at her.

Roarke's voice was distant, but she expected that. She waited for pain to fill her chest, but none came. She was just numb and she wanted to get this over and done with. Good thing she didn't give up her flat. She'd be alone again. With Phil and Jenny gone, she'd need to find someone she could trust implicitly and she knew from experience that would take time.

A very long time.

She got out of bed. "Why am I here Roarke? You should have left me in Dalby." She walked to the closet, uncaring that she was naked. She grabbed a set of underwear and put it on before donning a pair of jeans and a grey sweater. Ballet flats were the first shoes she grabbed. They would do. She dug into the closet and got her suitcase out.

"What are you doing?"

Deanna flipped her suitcase open and started putting her clothes into it. "What does it look like I'm doing?" Her voice was more resigned than angry. She just didn't have any more fight left in her. "I'm going back to my flat."

"Why?"

Deanna expelled her breath. Arms akimbo she looked at Roarke. There. Pain slammed into her, knowing this could be the last time she would see him. "Roarke, I gave myself up to Herod."

"In exchange for the children's and Eirene's life."

Deanna sucked in her breath.

"Eirene told us," he said. "She begged you not to. But you did it anyway."

"Nevertheless." Deanna returned to what she was doing. "By this time every Cynn Cruor warrior and their partners would have heard about what I did. And the one thing I will not allow is for them to doubt you."

"And that's why you have to go."

"Yes."

"What if I won't allow you to?" Roarke moved toward her, as stealthy as a panther. And every inch of space he covered spiked Deanna's pulse rate. There was no denying the way he affected her. "You are my mate, Deanna. Forever entwined."

Then he pulled her into his arms and kissed her. It was a tender kiss filled with love. Deanna melted as she kissed him. With a groan, Roarke slanted his lips and plundered her mouth with his tongue. The kiss turned desperate, heated, and possessive. Deanna held him tight against her, desire running full blown through her body and down to the apex of her thighs. She wanted him so badly, but how could she? Roarke was right. She was his mate and she would love him for the rest of her life.

From the outside.

Finally, Roarke broke the kiss. His breath skimmed against her skin, his lips brushing her jaw. She shuddered as his tongue licked the sensitive skin behind her ears before trailing the tip over the shell of her ear.

"We will get through this, Deanna. I promise." His voice was firm and final. "I willna let anyone speak ill of you."

"That will take a lot of your time," she said, placing her head against his chest. She closed her eyes, sighing as Roarke smoothed her hair and kissed her forehead.

"I will give up the leadership of the Faesten."

"What?" She gasped. She raised her head, pushing against his chest. "You can't!"

Roarke smiled. The back of his fingers caressed her jaw. "Don't you see, Deanna? You are my life. Now that I've found you, do you think I would let you disappear again? I want to make up for lost time. I am nothing without you."

"But—"

"No buts," he interrupted. "Finn is more than capable of ruling the Faesten. I've wanted to let go of the leadership for a long while. This time is just as good as any."

She felt the sharpness at the back of her eyes that signalled the impending flood. In no time at all, tears tumbled down onto her cheeks. She couldn't trust herself to say anything. She soaked Roarke's shirt. He continued to hold her, absorbing her pain. She didn't know what to say to Roarke's generosity of heart. And she loved him all the more for it.

And I dinnae ken what to say to the generosity of yours, my lady.

She chuckled softly against his shirt. "I forgot you could read my mind."

"As you can read mine," he murmured against her hair. "And can you read what's in my mind right now?"

She hugged him tighter as his thoughts entered her head.

Same as my thoughts. You love me all the more for it.

And that is the truth, my lady.

"I can't help but think that my presence in your life led you to give up the Faesten."

Roarke sighed. He sat Deanna down on the bed as he knelt in front of her.

"The night you showed up, I had been looking for you," he began. "Deep in my gut, I knew it had to be you I saw in Dac's club. But I couldn't find you. I thought I was losing my mind and your ghost was there to haunt me."

"I didn't know how to find you," she said, her hand caressing his face.

He smiled. "I was summoned by the Cynn Eald to Wales. We spoke of you."

"Me?" Her eyes widened as she queried in surprise.

He nodded. "Everyone thought you were dead, but we couldn't understand how I could still be alive. And that's when the Deoré suggested you might still be alive. The talk about you was making me despair for you, so I ended the conversation by taking my leave. But before I could, the Deoré asked me what I would do if you were truly dead."

"And?"

"I told them I would come back and ask them both to end my life."

Deanna's breath stuck in her throat. She looked down at the silver blue orbs she wouldn't mind drowning in.

"So you see, Deanna, now that I've found you, I willna let you go. Nothing matters except you."

Roarke stood up, helping her to stand as well.

She nodded.

"C'mon, I need to see Graeme. Zac's serum isn't working as fast as it should."

"Are you sure you want me to come with you?"

"Deanna, you are mine. No matter what, my men will always respect that."

She hesitated a little, unsure of the reception she would get. But here, beside her, was the man who loved her. The man who'd give up everything for her. The man who wanted her by his side. For eternity.

Deanna straightened her shoulders, giving Roarke a tight smile. The side of his mouth lifted as he entwined his hand with hers and they left the room.

Chapter Twenty-Four

Roarke and Deanna made their way to the Faesten's hospital floor. Unlike the time when Colin was recuperating, the wing now looked more like the Accident & Emergency department of a local hospital. Cynn Cruor mortals walked past, bringing bags of blood for the wounded. There was a ward filled with unmated warriors with serum drips attached to the backs of their hands or the crook of their elbows. Deanna felt the stares of the warriors speaking in groups outside their fallen comrades' rooms. She didn't sense any hostility. Still, she kept her eyes straight until they reached Graeme's door.

Everyone turned toward them as they entered the room. Deanna didn't need to look further for Eirene. The other woman acknowledged her with a nod before turning her attention back to Graeme. Apart from Finn, Zac, and Colin, there was another man beside Graeme's bed. He wore denims, a shirt and a pea coat. His hair was windswept and unruly on his head. His face was serious as he stared at Graeme. His stubble emphasized his hollow cheeks and sunken eyes. Deanna sucked in her breath when he turned to her. Heart pounding at the truth she'd unearthed. She kept her thoughts to herself, immediately meriting herself a frown from her mate. She looked around the room. How could anyone not notice what she could clearly see? Graeme, that was the reason, her mind explained as though Deanna was an errant child.

The man walked toward her; a smile lit his wide mouth. He stretched out his hand.

"You must be Deanna, Roarke's woman. I'm Blake Strachan."

"Hello, Blake. I wish we could have met under better circumstances."

So this was Blake. A part of Roarke's inner sanctum. The Cynn Cruor warrior who had left. And Deanna knew why. Blake looked at her eyes. They widened, a sliver of panic showing in their depths. With the slightest of moves, Deanna shook her head. Surprise flashed for a moment in his gaze before Blake exhaled, acknowledging her with his own imperceptible nod. It wasn't for Deanna to tell the group. She was already knee deep into her own problems and she was never one to interfere in someone else's affairs.

"I'm truly glad that Roarke finally found you again," he said. "If it would have taken much longer, he would've been howling at the moon."

Deanna's mouth slowly curved to a half smile at the picture Blake evoked.

"Still the joker, eh Blake?" A voice croaked from the bed.

"Graeme." Blake pivoted back to his friend's side. "Good to see you, mate."

"You've come back. That's good." Graeme noted before he swallowed. "I'm glad."

"I heard what Dac did to you," Blake said instead. A low rumble emitted from his throat. "He'll pay for what he did."

"No way are you taking him out on your own," Graeme retorted in a stronger voice. "I want a piece of his arse as well."

Blake grunted before turning to Zac. "You should have given him more pain killers to keep him quiet. He's raring to fight again."

"Aren't we all," Zac muttered as he rubbed the nape of his neck. "Glad to see you awake, Graeme. You had me worried there. I just can't understand why it's taking longer for you to heal. Even without a mate, you should already be on the mend with the amount of serum I've pumped into you."

"Have you checked the silver used?" Roarke asked.

Zac nodded. "It's being analysed as we speak."

Suddenly Graeme convulsed. The machine monitoring his vital signs let out a shrill beep.

"Shit!"

Zac pushed Blake away. Graeme's body arched violently.

"No!" Eirene cried. Finn held her back, his face hardened with worry.

Roarke stood at the foot of the bed. Colin and Blake faced each other as they tried to stop Graeme from thrashing about and dislodging his IV line. Deanna stepped back, unsure of what to do.

"No," Zac said. "I need to see his wound. Turn him over. Blake, move to the other side and keep on talking to him."

Blake whizzed to face his friend.

"Stay with me, Temple. We're hunting Dac down, remember?" Blake growled.

Graeme tried to smile, but a snarl came out of his mouth instead. His lips were pulled back as his incisors started to descend.

The smell of burning flesh permeated the air.

"Fuck! Turn him over completely."

The silver seemed to have transformed into a living organism. It ate its way over and around the wound. Graeme roared like a wounded animal.

Just then, Luke entered the room.

"You!" Colin seethed. "If I wasn't holding Graeme down, I'd skin you alive."

"You can do that later," Luke replied, curtly nodding. "But first, there are people here who can heal Graeme."

"Who?" Zac asked, desperation in his voice.

"Us."

"My Liege!" the warriors exclaimed in unison.

The Cynn Eald and his Deoré entered the room.

As the men were trying to stop Graeme from hurting himself, Eirene and Deanna started to kneel.

"There's no need for kneeling," The Deoré spoke, her mouth lifting to a smile before it disappeared as she turned her gaze to the thrashing warrior.

"Cynn Cruor, if you will excuse us, we have a sick warrior to heal. Zac, stay with us. Luke, join them," the Cynn Eald said. Then, in front of everyone, the Cynn Eald and the Deoré held each other's hands and placed them right over the wound. Graeme let out a wounded roar, but he couldn't move. Gradually, his convulsions slackened and completely disappeared. A sigh escaped from his lips as he lay unconscious again. The Cynn Cruor were able to let go. Sighs of relief sounded like the whisper of waves before it reached the shore. The Cynn Eald let go of his wife's hand to remove his jacket, tossed it to the nearby chair, and roll up his sleeves. As they filed their way out of the room, the Cynn Eald spoke.

"Colin, Luke wasn't Dac's spy." He paused, pinning the Cynn Cruor warrior with his stare. "He was mine."

Chapter Twenty-Five

Deanna's eyes flew to Luke's. He returned his gaze apologetically, but didn't say anything. Her heart plummeted.

When the door closed behind them, Colin blazed at Luke. "You better tell us what the fuck is going on."

Luke's stance was defensive, but not threatening.

"Why don't you have a crest?" Eirene asked, her eyes zeroing on his bicep.

Only then did they notice he didn't have a Cynn Cruor crest embossed on his suit.

Finn's eyes narrowed. "Everyone should have a crest. And the only person we can ask is lying unconscious inside that room."

"Graeme sincerely believed I had a crest."

"But?" Roarke prodded as he raised a sceptical brow.

"I have a gift. Invisibility."

Eirene's eyes widened. "Seriously?"

"Go on," Colin said as his eyes narrowed.

Luke folded his arms across his chest. "I'm able to slip in and out of parallel planes. That's how my invisibility works. I decided to take a position with your team." He nudged his chin at Colin. "Craig and the rest could see me, but you couldn't. Not until we assaulted Dac's fortress."

"Awesome, mate!" Blake grinned.

Deanna saw the cloud of despair lift from his face. No wonder his brothers missed him. He had a joie de vivre which reminded her of a naughty schoolboy and it was infectious. She saw the affectionate grins of both Roarke and Finn and couldn't help the smile tugging at her own lips.

"So..." Finn clapped Blake on the shoulder. "When are you coming back?"

Blake's smile slowly fell and his eyes shuttered. "Not for a long while yet."

Colin paced the corridor. He linked both his hands behind his neck and looked up before he shook his head in bafflement and exasperation. "I don't get it," he ground out. "I've never fought Dac in such convoluted circumstances."

"You're not the only one," Roarke agreed. He turned to Deanna and took her hand, lacing his fingers through hers. Deanna saw all the love he had pour forth from his gaze. It touched her soul.

Roarke turned to Luke. "Were you sent to spy on Deanna?"

Luke turned to Deanna. "Yes."

****

Disappointment crept into every crevice of Roarke's being at what the Ancient Ones did. His mind warred with his emotions. He felt betrayed. But did the Ancient Ones truly betray him? Hadn't he also done the same thing? He had often asked Graeme to do background checks on warriors and mortals who could be working for the Scatha Cruor. He dry scrubbed his face before massaging his nape. The battle on the Isle of Man felt as though it happened eons ago when it had only been a few days. His perception of time had been distorted by everything that had happened. But he was now sure that every Cynn Cruor warrior in the corridor was loyal to the Ancients. Luke had been vetted by the Cynn Eald himself.

That left Deanna. He looked at her. Her face, impassive, resigned, and it hurt to see her that way. Even if he was one of the fortunate few who could gain an audience with the Cynn Eald and the Deoré immediately, he was still a warrior just like any Cynn Cruor who waited on their orders. He could not know what was in their minds. In the same way he wouldn't know what they had in store for his own beloved.

But there was no way he would leave her. She was his life. She was the air he breathed. She was his soul. There was no point in living if she wasn't by his side.

"Why were you asked to spy?" he asked Luke. "Which Faesten do you belong to?"

"To your first question, I think the Ancients should answer you. To the second, I don't belong to any Faesten."

There were snorts of scepticism from the warriors and puzzled glances from their mates.

"That's not possible," Finn stated. "Everyone chosen has a Faesten."

Luke shrugged. "I wasn't chosen and I don't have one."

Finn placed his hands on his hips, giving the unaffiliated warrior a speculative glance. "Then stay with us," he invited. "After how you fought, there is always room for another warrior in Manchester."

"In your dreams, Qualtrough." Colin snorted. "He chose my team. He stays with my team in Leeds." He shook his head, grinning. "Bloody hell, that gift of yours can come in handy during recon missions!"

Finn grunted, but didn't object.

Luke's mouth lifted in a lopsided grin. "Thanks for the offer, but I have to decline."

Colin's eyes widened.

"There's something I have to do first before I can accept your offer. I need to know where I came from."

"Surely the Cynn Eald can help you," Roarke interjected. "The Cynn archives are in Anglesey."

Luke nodded. "They have given me a possible lead. It's something I have to investigate on my own."

"And you?" Eirene turned to Blake, who had been silent the whole time. He had been leaning on the corridor wall, his hands inside the pockets of his pea coat. He pushed away from the wall.

"I only came back for Graeme," he said. "I'm not staying."

"Why?" Eirene asked, placing her hands on her hips. Her voice was strained. "This is my fault. If I hadn't found that stupid code..."

"Stop it, Spence, it's not your fault," Blake admonished. "If you hadn't found the code, we wouldn't have found Dac. And you wouldn't have found your mate. Everything happened for a reason."

Eirene's shoulders slumped. Finn pulled her to him, enclosing her in his arms. "He's right, you know?" He kissed her hair. "I wouldn't know you had been made for me."

"Then why are you all falling apart?" Eirene's voice was muffled against her mate's chest.

No one had an answer.

Blake turned to Roarke. A ghost of a smile slightly lifted his mouth.

Roarke could sense that Blake was indecisive about something. It was in the way he held himself—aloof and yet straining slightly forward as though wanting to tell him something. The youngest of the Manchester Cynn Cruor warriors, Blake had always been the first to approach him when he wanted to say something. That openness had disappeared. In its place was a man haunted by something he didn't want his Cynn brothers to know. Roarke was definite that it had something to do with Dac. But he wouldn't press Blake. Besides, now wasn't the time. The Cynn Cruor had to regroup. They had lost a lot of men and their spouses. It fell upon his shoulders to inform the Faestens about their casualties. It wasn't a duty he was comfortable with. He also had to report to the Council of Ieldran, although now that the Ancients were in the Faesten, this was now the Ancients' fortress. That meant he would have beef up security.

And they might lose Graeme.

"What is it you can't tell us Blake?" Roarke asked.

"I have to go," Blake said instead as he prepared to leave.

Eirene left Finn's embrace to give Blake a quick hug, unmindful of her mate's resigned sigh.

"How will we find you?" Finn asked as he pulled Eirene back to anchor her by his side.

Blake snorted before sobering. "I'll keep in touch."

He turned to Deanna.

"Deanna," he said, closing the gap to extend his hand. "I'm glad Roarke is now complete."

Deanna didn't take his proffered hand, but embraced him instead. "Thank you," she said.

"No, Deanna," Blake said as he pulled away to look deeply into her eyes. "Thank you."

Deanna released him and nodded, smiling at him. Roarke caught a glimpse of what Deanna was thinking before she shut it from him. He frowned. He sensed she was troubled, but blamed it on the possibility of the dire news the Ancients would tell them. When things had settled down at the end of the day, he would ask her.

With one last nod, Blake turned away from the group, taking the stairs instead of the lift.

"This can't be happening," Eirene whispered. "I can't believe you're all being destroyed. And that bastard, Dac, isn't even here."

Finn and Roarke looked at each other. Eirene was spot on. Despite the Cynn Cruor seizing the fortress, the disarray Dac had caused from the moment they had found him again was a pyrrhic victory for all.

Now Roarke had to brace himself for what the Ancients planned for Deanna.

Even without Dac knowing it, he had won.

****

Blake stepped out from the warm confines of the Faesten. He shivered, not because of the cold. He shivered at the sight of the Ancients. Surely they would have known his secret? They had informants everywhere. Someone must have already told them what had happened in Dac's club. But the whole time they were there, they acknowledged him as though he still belonged with Roarke's team.

That he was still one of them.

A wave of fear crested over him before he swallowed it down. Blake had never been afraid of anything. He was a Cynn Cruor. Finn had taught him well. And Eirene. Beautiful Eirene. One of the kindest souls with a kick-ass attitude he was proud to call a sister. He was happy for them both. Yet all of Finn's teachings paled in comparison to the albatross around his neck.

A wave of loneliness followed his fear, threatening to engulf him. He didn't stop it this time. Fear, he could control. Loneliness? He'd never realized how painful loneliness could be. More painful than being pierced by a sword or slashed by a Scatha's claws.

Blake looked up at the night sky. It was as dark as what was inside him. They seemed to have left the rain on the Isle of Man.

Outside the Manchester Faesten, it was cold. Frigidly so. For once he wished he knew what it felt like to freeze as an ordinary mortal would, but the Kinare kept him just cool. He had hoped if his mind was occupied with something as mundane as his body temperature, he'd be able to stop thinking about his problem which had no solution. The worry was filling his every waking moment.

It might just make him lose his mind.

He needed to find peace, yet how could he, knowing his secret was the very thing which could destroy him? He might as well have been damned to hell.

He hunched deeper into his jacket, pulling up the collar against his neck. Looking from left to right, he crossed the street and disappeared into the darkness.

Chapter Twenty-Six

They assembled in the Library. The windows were closed against the pouring rain and the fire in the hearth gave the room a cozy glow which contradicted the palpable tension in the room. The Cynn Eald and Zac talked in hushed tones in one end of the room. Graeme had gotten over the worst. Roarke saw Zac's eyes widen before nodding his head, his face filled with dark determination.

Finally, the progenitor of the entire Cynn Cruor turned to them and walked toward the Deoré, who sat on the couch facing the hearth. Zac sank tiredly on the couch to her right where Finn and Eirene sat. Roarke and Deanna sat to the Deoré's left while Colin and Luke flanked the fireplace, like black encased guardians.

The Cynn Eald spoke.

"Perhaps you're all wondering why Graeme didn't heal when he was hit by Dac's silver bullets and why the rest of the Cynn Cruor healed when they were hit by the Scatha warriors' assault weapons."

They all remained silent for a moment before Finn spoke.

"Graeme took the bullets for Roarke and his armour should have deflected them, but it just went right through."

"We have come across that kind of silver only once," the Deoré said. "But that was so long ago."

"How long ago, my lady?" Colin asked.

"Two thousand five hundred years ago."

Almost everyone sat up straighter, their faces incredulous.

"It was the first time I met Alaghom-Naom and fell in love with her," the Cynn Eald spoke, his voice deep as he turned to his spouse. "I was living with the people who became the Mayans' ancestors. They showed me their wealth, something that would later on be coveted by those who conquered them. But I wasn't interested in their wealth; I was interested in their knowledge. I knew how to read a mineral's composition and the minerals found in their part of the world fascinated me. Graeme was struck by bullets with the same composition as the silver I saw at that time."

"Holy shit," Eirene breathed, then reddened. "Sorry, my lady."

The Cynn Eald smiled and the Deoré chuckled. "You know, all of you should stop thinking of me like I was some fragile Dresden doll. I'm hardly that. It's not like I disappeared from the world and stopped learning."

Everyone looked at Deanna.

"My Lady..." Roarke started. He may be a Dux in the Cynn Cruor, but he wasn't going to let anyone denigrate Deanna. Not even the Deoré.

"It's all right, Roarke," Deanna said, placing a hand on his thigh. She faced the Deoré.

"I never disappeared. I was taken prisoner by the Scatha Cruor and when I escaped I tried everything I could think of to find Roarke." She paused, sighing. "Because of the length of time I stayed with Dac, I can understand there will always be a cloud of doubt as to where my loyalty lies. But my loyalty has never wavered, even then. It belongs to Roarke because I love him, and by extension, it belongs to the Cynn Cruor."

The Ancients remained silent and pensive.

"Eirene may have heard what I told Herod. That I would divulge the Cynn Cruors' secrets." She looked at Eirene. "But I would never do that. I had to think of a bargaining chip for Herod to let the children go in exchange for me giving him information."

"Herod could have taken both you and the children. You were outnumbered," Finn commented.

"Neither did I want him to take Eirene."

Finn nodded, his jaw hardening. "I thought of that. I owe you one."

She shook her head. "You don't owe me anything. Being in the company of the Scatha isn't something I'd wish on anyone."

"Oh, Dee. I'm so sorry I doubted you."

"Apologies aren't necessary, Eirene." Deanna's mouth lifted in a half-smile. "The moment you called me Dee when I helped you with the children on the Isle of Man, I knew things would be all right between us in the end."

Deanna turned back to the Ancients. "So you see, I never did anything wrong."

"No explanation was actually necessary, Deanna, although we appreciate that you have given us one," the Cynn Eald said. "You see, we never doubted your loyalty."

Bewilderment marred all of their faces, except for the Ancients' and Luke's.

"Roarke," the Deoré spoke. "When we summoned you to Anglesey, we wanted to tell you we had found her."

He let out a disbelieving snort and he couldn't suppress the anger which laced his words. "Forgive me, my lady. But you were not exactly forthright in saying so."

"If we told you at that moment, what would you have done?" the Cynn Cruor leader asked with an enquiring brow. "You are a Cynn Cruor warrior first, Roarke. A chosen mate second. You had just located Dac and the Cynn warriors from Faestens all over the world had just arrived. You are the Dux. You cannot deviate from the responsibility which comes along with being one."

Suddenly Roarke stood up, hands clenched at his sides. His face hard, the tick in his jaw more pronounced and beating furiously. His breathing was slow and deep. He heard the Deoré's growl so low in her throat that no ordinary human would have been able to hear it.

All the warriors went on alert. The silence was deafening as a mantle weighing everyone down. Time seemed suspended. The logs popped and sizzled in the fireplace, the only sound in a room where one move could mean the death of a Cynn warrior in the hands of the Ancients. Never had Roarke ever thought of going against the Ancients as much as he did now.

"Thoughts like what you have right now is understandable, Hamilton." The Cynn Eald broke the silence, his voice laced with steel. "But they can also get you killed."

The silence was ominous as Roarke trembled with his ire. But with another huge breath, Roarke slowly exhaled and backed down.

He looked at the Deoré. "Surely loving the Cynn Eald the way you do, you'd understand what I'm going through."

Their eyes clashed. The Deoré searched Roarke's face. He had nothing to hide. Her eyes had turned molten gold while Roarke's eyes remained as stormy coloured as the sea. What only lasted a few seconds felt like ages. Roarke allowed the Ancients to search his mind as well. To see that he didn't mean any harm. To see the pain caused by what they had done and his acceptance of the burden of responsibility that fell on a Faesten leader.

Eventually, the Deoré relaxed and gradually the tension dissipated, but her eyes never left Roarke. For one brief moment, Roarke saw the pain flash in her eyes and he knew she had remembered the day Dac had nearly killed the Cynn Eald.

The Deoré breathed out. "He speaks the truth."

"How long did you know I was alive?"

The Cynn Eald looked at Deanna. "As soon as Mrs. Dalton took you in."

"That long?" Deanna asked, stunned.

"We couldn't let you know. Would you have readily come with us if we told you you'd be taken to a Cynn Cruor Faesten?"

Deanna bit her lip. She shook her head.

"Where does Luke figure in all of this?" Colin interrupted.

"We needed someone to watch over Deanna," the Deoré replied. "Suffice to say I had my doubts. Luke was completely convinced of Deanna's loyalty."

She looked at Deanna, her eyes kind. "I almost lost the Cynn Eald. I couldn't be too careful."

"I understand, my lady. I would have done the same thing."

"Luke has a special gift, and all of you can attest to that," the Deoré continued. "We would help him find where he came from in exchange for watching over Deanna."

"Why did you finally decide to show yourself?" Roarke asked.

"Deanna was coming out in the open." Luke shrugged. "I didn't see the need to watch her anymore."

"And yet you did that when she confronted Herod," the Cynn Eald commented.

"Just to protect her until Roarke and Finn arrived," he replied. He turned to Deanna. "When you gave yourself up, I couldn't believe it. What you did was nothing short of courageous. You were willing to die for the Cynn Cruor."

"And that information was what we needed. Deanna is innocent. Anyone who says otherwise will be answerable to the Council of Ieldran," the Cynn Eald added and looked at Deanna before a slow smile lightened his face. "The onus of doubt isn't yours to bear anymore."

Collective sighs of relief filled the air. Roarke felt the heavy burden he'd carried on his shoulders all this time slowly lift. He turned to Deanna whose eyes were brimming with tears. Even in the informal atmosphere of the Library, both he and Deanna knew she had been tried and acquitted. He locked her in his embrace before crushing her lips with his. She opened up like a flower, her mouth fitting his perfectly. He didn't care if they had an audience. Deanna was his. His Cynn Cruor mate. A mate worthy of a Cynn Cruor Dux.

When he ended the kiss, her eyes were shining. He looked at Luke, who grinned. He stood up and walked to him. He extended his arm in friendship. "You have my eternal gratitude, Luke."

Luke gave him a smile as he clasped Roarke's arm in friendship.

"As you do mine," Deanna said with a grateful smile. She gave Luke a kiss on the cheek.

Roarke growled low in his throat.

"Now you understand how it feels when Eirene is surrounded by our brethren," Finn stated with mock brevity.

"It was a kiss of gratitude," Deanna protested. Her face filled with incredulity when she faced Roarke.

"My point exactly." Finn laughed.

Roarke immediately placed his arm around Deanna's waist, keeping her to his side. Luke and Colin's shoulders shook in quiet laughter. Roarke had to admit it might have looked unreasonable. But dammit, Deanna was his.

"Right!" Colin moved away from the wall. "I'm returning to Leeds, but I'll be back. Just need to make sure that everything's as I left it."

"You'd better stay there until we call you, mate," Roarke said. "We can do the debriefing remotely. We can't be too sure where Dac is at the moment. You better beef up security there too."

"Understood." Colin gave him a curt nod. He turned to Luke. "You belong to the Leeds Faesten. So anytime you're ready to join us, you're more than welcome."

Luke clasped Colin's arm. "Thanks. I'll keep that in mind."

The Ancients stood and bid everyone goodbye.

"Luke will join us to Anglesey," the Cynn Eald said as the Deoré helped him into his jacket. "When he finds what he's looking for, he'll make his way to Leeds."

"You sound pretty sure of me joining you lot." Luke stated as he raised a brow.

The Cynn Eald chuckled, his moss green eyes twinkling in the firelight. "Let's go, Griffiths," he said instead. "I may be immortal, but it doesn't mean I don't feel it in my bones."

Luke snorted. With nods to everyone and another arm clasp with Zac, he opened the Library's glass door for the Ancients. As soon as they left the Faesten, everyone relaxed.

Colin blew out another long breath. "The Ancients," his voice filled with awe. "Who would have thought I'd see them in my immortal life."

"No one did," Finn replied, chuckling, then looked at Roarke. "They must really hold you in high regard for them to keep Deanna safe. No matter how questionable their actions were."

Roarke nodded, tightening his hold on Deanna.

Finn was right. The Ancient's stamp of approval of Deanna would stop anyone cold from questioning her place as his mate. And for that he was grateful.

"Everyone get some shut eye," Roarke commanded. "God knows we need it."

Chapter Twenty-Seven

Deanna stared at the licking flames in the fireplace. She and Roarke had gone to their room. The warmth of the fire seeped through her bones, finally putting her fears she'd kept for so long to rest.

It was over. Deanna was weak with the realization that she was free. Finally and irrevocably free to live the life she was meant to live. Her nightmare was over. The retribution she had expected for what she had done didn't materialize. Now she could be with the only man she had ever loved.

Roarke Hamilton.

They would need to go to Scotland soon. Roarke's parents couldn't wait to welcome her back. A wistful smile tugged at her lips. Her whole family was gone. She hadn't been even able to say goodbye to them when Hamel Dun Creag fell and she had been captured. But in their stead would be Roarke's family. With Roarke at her side, she would find the strength and resolve to mourn those she had loved and lost.

Roarke sat down beside her on the floor. She sighed as she made herself more comfortable. Roarke kissed her hair.

"Aye, it's over." His deep voice brought tingles of awareness down to stoke that spot between her legs.

"Oh, Roarke, I still have to get used to that." She sighed even as she turned into his embrace. She looked at him, the flames casting shadows around the dark room and putting Roarke's features in harsh relief. God, how she loved this man! She would have died for him. She would have given all for him at that very moment when she confronted Herod. If she had died, she would've waited for Roarke in the afterlife where nothing could touch them or ever keep them apart.

"Deanna, don't think that way." Roarke leaned his forehead on hers, his voice tight with emotion. "Dinnae think that for one minute you'll die ahead of me."

Suddenly, the weight of everything that had transpired bore down on her. Her lashes became wet with even more tears. For a long time, she had forgotten how to cry. Now, it was as though the dam holding all the water inside her soul had cracked and there was no way to stem the tide. Roarke lay her down on the carpet, kissing her tears away. She clung to him like there was no tomorrow.

Then Roarke's mouth was on hers and she felt her passion bloom and flame.

Their frenzied breathing filled the room, but Roarke seemed to be taking his sweet time and it frustrated her to no end. He chuckled and raised his head. Slowly, he dragged the zipper of her sweater down, the metallic sound heightening her need to have him fill the ache which was growing inside her. When Roarke dipped his head to flick his tongue over her lace covered nipple, she was lost. With her own little growl, she fumbled for Roarke's belt and removed it before cupping his erection through his jeans. Roarke and Deanna couldn't get out of their clothes fast enough. They helped each other tear their clothes off, stealing kisses, nipping and licking each other's flesh in between. Finally, skin met skin. Their tongues mated and explored. Deanna moaned as Roarke's mouth blazed a trail from her jaw, sucking on her earlobe and licking the sensitive spot behind her ear before grazing his teeth against the column of her throat. Her head dipped further back and her body bowed as he hungrily devoured her breasts. His hands cupped and squeezed them together so he could alternately flick his tongue and suck on them almost at the same time.

"God, yes!"

Liquid heat leaked between her thighs. Deanna could feel it moisten her labia, readying her for Roarke's sweet invasion. Her hands delighted in the feel of Roarke's body, finding pleasure at the way his skin felt against her palms. How his silky smooth but granite hard shaft prodded her hip. She wanted him inside her desperately, so with one tilt, she raised her thigh and angled her wet channel toward his shaft.

"Roarke, please. I can't wait," she breathed softly as her hips seduced him.

Roarke lifted his head and Deanna smiled at the gold flecks in his eyes. It fuelled her own lust and desire to be one with him completely. She doubted if she'd ever get tired of this wondrous sight. His jaw clenched, Roarke teased her opening, causing her to whimper.

"I love you, Deanna."

"I love you, Roarke. Oohh!" She gasped. Roarke thrust deeply into her, burying himself as deep as he could reach. Pleasure spiralled through her like ripples from a pond, suffusing her entire being.

Claiming her very soul.

"Exquisite," Roarke whispered, slowly thrusting into her. With every deep thrust, Deanna felt molten heat flow through her. Her nipples puckered against his chest. She lifted her head to place licks and kisses against his shoulder and his throat. Her tongue blazed a trail down to his nipples and she sucked. Roarke growled and thrust deeper into her.

"Oh, God, yes! Faster! Harder, Roarke! Yes!" Deanna cried against his skin. She fell back against the carpet when Roarke did as she commanded. Her back arched and she moaned when his mouth latched onto her hardened peak. Her heart stuttered as she felt Roarke lengthen and thicken inside her. He growled, his hunger driving her to reach her own crest. Her incisors turned to fangs, her breathing erratic at the joyous knowledge of what was to happen. And when she felt the first tide of her orgasm about to overwhelm her, she raised Roarke's head and buried her teeth against the flesh covering his heart. Her mind exploded with her orgasm. Her channel throbbed and squeezed Roarke, the spiking pleasure electrifying her entire being. She drank in Roarke as much as she gave, and fully sated she lay back and smiled. It was Roarke's turn to take as much as he wanted.

Roarke had never felt bliss such as this. He saw Deanna's eyes and smiled. Her eyes had the same gold flecks his had now. The desire in those blue and golden orbs shone through. His balls throbbed with his seed. His cock soaked itself in Deanna's sheath. He upped the pace, growling his pleasure with his every thrust and Deanna's whimpers. Her femininity sucked and laved his manhood with its muscles, squeezing him tight and milking him. He wanted nothing more than to brand Deanna and claim her as his.

And his alone.

She screamed at the same time he felt his seed fountain into her.

"Deanna!"

His orgasm caught him unaware. He thrust faster before he plunged his incisors into her breast.

"Oh, God, Roarke! Yes!"

Roarke felt Deanna's orgasm shudder through her body, radiating into his cock. He savoured her sweet blood before he felt his own essence pour into her.

In the flickering firelight, they continued their lovemaking. The glow that signified them as Cynn Cruor mates enveloped them in an opalescent cloud. All was right with their world.

****

Several hours later, Roarke closed the door behind him, leaving Deanna to sleep. He would have stayed in the room for a week if he could and make love to her, just hold her. They had a lot of catching up to do, but his sense of responsibility nagged him and reluctantly he knew he had to check on how the Faesten was running.

He made his way to the command centre. The rain had stopped and the sun was making an attempt to cut through the clouds. Cynn Cruor mortals were in the centre, taking over the controls. They greeted Roarke, answering his questions about the Faesten's operations. Satisfied, Roarke left and met Finn in the lobby. Nodding to him, they both went to the elevator with one thing in mind. To visit Graeme.

Zac was in Graeme's room when they arrived. He was talking to one of the Cynn mortal doctors about Graeme's condition. When he saw them, he finished his discussion and approached them.

Roarke looked at Graeme, noting his relaxed and regular breathing. His face looked peaceful. Gone were the lines of pain which had etched his visage. Roarke breathed a sigh of relief.

"How's Graeme?"

"He's much better. If it weren't for the Ancients, I wouldn't have known what to do," Zac said, raking his hand through his hair. "Never had anyone die in my care."

Finn clamped him on the shoulder. "And no one will."

Zac gave him a grim smile. He nodded. "I have to go. Graeme is in good hands. The Cynn mortal doctors are some of the best in the world." He looked at Graeme's sleeping form. "He'll be good as new by tomorrow."

"You'll be here to see to that, Zac." Roarke frowned. "Why are you talking as though you won't?"

"Because I won't be here," Zac said. He rubbed his eyes tiredly. "What's happened to Graeme was a close call, Dux. Even the Ancients saw that. When the Cynn Eald realized what kind of silver it was, he became worried. He has asked me to help find the silver again."

"Shit!" Finn blew out, shaking his head. "Eirene isn't going to like people leaving the Faesten."

"It's not going to be for good, Finn."

"Well, you better get your sorry arse back here soon," Finn said gruffly, resignation almost in his voice.

Zac gave him a half grin. "Will do."

Roarke nudged his head. "Where are you going?"

"El Salvador and the Honduras."

Roarke raised his brow. "That's pretty far away. Never mind. Give us your coordinates so we can let the Faestens there know to lend a hand and protect you."

Zac placed his hands on his hips. "I'm afraid I won't be able to do that."

"Why the bloody hell not?" Finn bit out. "McBain, if you're going to tell me that you have to find your bloody self or where you come from I'll sock you in the eye. I will not have people leaving the Faesten."

"Easy Finn," Roarke said, putting a hand on his shoulder.

"I wish that were so, and I wouldn't mind you punching me if you like," Zac answered wearily.

"Then what is it?" Roarke asked. "You tell us everything that has to do with the Faesten. Why can't you tell us where you're going now?"

Zac looked at both at them before he spoke.

"I really wish I could, Dux, but I can't. The place I'm going to doesn't exist."

THE END

ABOUT THE AUTHOR

Isobelle Cate is a woman who wears different masks. Mother-writer, wife-professional, scholar-novelist. Currently living in Manchester, she has been drawn to the little known, the secret stories, about the people and the nations: the English, the Irish, the Scots, the Welsh, and those who are now part of these nations whatever their origins. Her vision and passion are fuelled by her interest and background in history and paradoxically, shaped by growing up in a clan steeped in lore, loyalty, and legend.

Isobelle is intrigued by forces that simmer beneath the surface of these cultures, the hidden passions, unsaid desires, and yearnings unfulfilled.

Visit me:

Facebook: https://www.facebook.com/AuthorIsobelleCate

Website: http://isobellecate.beaucoupllc.com

Amazon Author Page:
http://www.amazon.com/author/isobellecate

Books by Isobelle:

The Cynn Cruor Bloodline Series

Rapture at Midnight (The Cynn Cruor Bloodline Series: Book 1)
http://amzn.to/1aY5L72

Forever at Midnight (The Cynn Cruor Bloodline Series: Book 2)
http://amzn.to/1ekfqbh

Other Books by Isobelle

Love in Her Dreams http://amzn.to/17HPKBF